V AS IN VICTIM

LAWRENCE TREAT

Edited, with an introduction and
notes, by Leslie S. Klinger

Published by Poisoned Pen Press, an imprint of Sourcebooks,
in association with the Library of Congress
P.O. Box 4410, Naperville, Illinois 60567-4410
(630) 961-3900
sourcebooks.com

This edition of *V as in Victim* is based on the first edition in the Library of
Congress's collection, originally published in 1945 by Duell, Sloan and Pearce.

Cataloging-in-Publication Data is on file with the Library of Congress.

Printed and bound in the United States of America.
VP 10 9 8 7 6 5 4 3 2 1

In Memory of SAM SLOAN

CONTENTS

FOREWORD

Crime writing as we know it first appeared in 1841, with the publication of "The Murders in the Rue Morgue." Written by American author Edgar Allan Poe, the short story introduced C. Auguste Dupin, the world's first wholly fictional detective. Other American and British authors had begun working in the genre by the 1860s, and by the 1920s we had officially entered the golden age of detective fiction.

Throughout this short history, many authors who paved the way have been lost or forgotten. Library of Congress Crime Classics bring back into print some of the finest American crime writing from the 1860s to the 1960s, showcasing rare and lesser-known titles that represent a range of genres, from cozies to police procedurals. With cover designs inspired by images from the Library's collections, each book in this series includes the original text, reproduced faithfully from an early edition in the Library's collections and complete with strange spellings and unorthodox punctuation. Also included are a contextual introduction, a brief biography of the author, notes, recommendations for further reading, and suggested discussion questions. Our hope is for these books to start conversations, inspire further research, and bring obscure works to a new generation of readers.

Early American crime fiction is not only entertaining to read but it also sheds light on the culture of its time. While many of the titles in this series include outmoded language and stereotypes now considered offensive, these books give readers the opportunity to reflect on how our society's perceptions of race, gender, ethnicity, and social standing have evolved over more than a century.

More dark secrets and bloody deeds lurk in the massive collections of the Library of Congress. I encourage you to explore these works for yourself, here in Washington, DC, or online at www.loc.gov.

—Carla D. Hayden, Librarian of Congress

INTRODUCTION

Lawrence Treat's *V as in Victim* was the first work of crime fiction to take an honest look at the workings of police departments. It may be surprising that it took more than one hundred years for such an examination: The first modern American full-time police force was formed in 1838 by the city of Boston, followed by New York City in 1845. In the 1850s, official police forces were organized or formalized in cities including Albany, New York; Chicago; New Orleans; Cincinnati; Philadelphia; Newark, New Jersey; and Baltimore. European cities had police departments much earlier: The first modern police force came into existence in 1667 in Paris under King Louis XIV. In 1812, a French national police force was organized and formalized a year later. The first formal British police force was the Bow Street Runners, founded by magistrate Henry Fielding in 1753 in London, though the organization was quite small until Sir Robert Peel championed the Metropolitan Police Act of 1829.

Semifictional accounts of the police followed. *Richmond, or Scenes in the Life of a Bow Street Officer* was published in 1827,[*]

---

[*] "Richmond" (the character's first name is Tom) appears to be a fictitious character, and the stories themselves are likely fiction or at least fictionalized. The author was likely either Thomas Skinner Surr or Thomas Gaspey, but no scholar has been able to amass convincing evidence on the authorship.

and the *Memoirs of Vidocq* (head of the French *Sûreté*) appeared in English in 1828.[*] Over the next fifty years, countless volumes of purported "recollections" or "experiences" or "diaries" of police officers dominated crime writing around the globe. Frankly fictional police detectives began to appear as well. Inspector Bucket, of Charles Dickens's *Bleak House* (1852–53), and Sergeant Cuff, in Wilkie Collins's *The Moonstone* (1868), were early examples. Inspector Gryce, who featured in *The Leavenworth Case* (1877) and nine additional books by Anna Katharine Green, was the first great American police detective, though he was aided by the amateur Amelia Butterworth in three of the stories.[†]

As crime writing progressed, however, amateur detectives and private investigators began to dominate the books, and the police were more and more dismissed by the hero-sleuths as unimaginative, ineffectual, boring, or a combination of all three—especially in the stories of Sherlock Holmes and a host of imitators. By the late 1920s, however, American readers were turning away from English crime writing. Dashiell Hammett was the leading light of the so-called hard-boiled school of detectives (inventing characters such as Sam Spade, Nick Charles, and the Continental Op), and he and many other writers fed the public a diet of realism and stories of the streets.

In 1945, however, Treat brought crime writing full circle, by again focusing on stories of the adventures of the police, but this time without fictionalizing how police investigations actually occurred. While *V as in Victim* was not Treat's first

---

[*] The four-volume French edition appeared in 1828–29, undoubtedly written by a ghostwriter.

[†] See, for example, *That Affair Next Door* (Naperville, IL: Sourcebooks in association with the Library of Congress, 2020).

novel, it was his first to abandon the traditional, English-style amateur detective. Writing about ordinary police officers—no heroes here—he singlehandedly created the genre now known as the "police procedural." These were stories about regular police detectives, usually working in tandem with other officers or technicians, using ordinary police work to solve crimes.

Treat believed that for a writer to succeed in this new field, knowledge of police work was essential. In *Mystery Writer's Handbook*, edited by Treat and published by the Mystery Writers of America (of which he was a founder), he urged the writer to acquire "up-to-date editions of texts on criminal investigation...on forensic medicine...and on police science... There is a vast amount of useful literature covering different aspects of the crime field—law, forensic medicine, ballistics, fingerprint and voice identification, and so on—and new scientific methods are developed every year."[*]

Scientific detection was not the innovation here: Sherlock Holmes used new and developing forensic techniques, and Craig Kennedy, the "American Sherlock Holmes" created by Arthur B. Reeve in the 1910s, was constantly introducing newfangled inventions and devices for the investigation of crimes.[†] The innovation was the *ordinariness* of the techniques. Treat's books featured tools that police actually used, applied by normal (and occasionally fallible) government employees.

---

[*] *Mystery Writer's Handbook* (Cincinnati: Writer's Digest, 1976), 3. This is a far cry from the philosophy of the earlier generation of writers, who viewed their mission as creating *fiction*. Arthur Conan Doyle, in his autobiographical *Memories and Adventures*, wrote, "I have never been nervous about details, and one must be masterful sometimes. When an alarmed Editor wrote to me once: 'There is no second line of rails at that point,' I answered, 'I make one'" (Boston: Little, Brown, 1924, 103).

[†] See *The Silent Bullet* (Naperville, IL: Sourcebooks in association with the Library of Congress, 2021).

George N. Dove, in his groundbreaking study *The Police Procedural*, laid out three elements introduced by Treat that differentiate the subgenre from earlier forms of crime writing:

> *First, he showed his policemen employing those procedures and following the routines that we normally expect: questioning witnesses and suspects, using the police lab for the analysis of evidence, setting up tailings and stakeouts... Second, he introduced the reader to the police mind, a constellation of attitudes and prejudices that characterize [the detective]. Third, Treat established...a tension between the old-fashioned, largely disorganized approach to police work and the emerging development of police technology.*

The eminent historian of crime fiction LeRoy Lad Panek went further, identifying fifteen conventions created by Treat that would permeate the police procedural subgenre:

1. Being a cop is a job, not a calling

2. The characters verbalize in "copspeak," the patois of police

3. Policing is generational; uncles, fathers, siblings, children become police officers

4. The police bond among themselves, creating a family

5. It's cops vs. civilians

---

* Bowling Green, OH: Bowling Green University Popular Press, 1982, 10–11.

6.   Cop knowledge is handed down

7.   Cops have partners

8.   Policing truisms are expressed

9.   There is a lore of the police, what Panek calls "cop tales"

10.   Politics abound within the police department

11.   Paperwork is a burden

12.   The police are subject to temptations

13.   Old policing conflicts with new policing

14.   The working conditions are shabby

15.   Weather is a nuisance or an impediment

"For the first time," noted Panek, "[Treat] presented readers with characters built on issues and attitudes of real police officers."[*]

V as in Victim was a far cry, however, from the episodic stories of a hundred years before. Treat blended a sense of realism with a traditional narrative method, producing a volume that is prosaic but suspenseful. Yet his conventions did nothing to the basic structure of the mystery. Treat was not an innovator with regard to the overall outline of a classic mystery. The crime occurs, the cast of suspects is introduced, and the

[*] LeRoy Lad Panek, *The American Police Novel: A History* (Jefferson, NC and London: McFarland, 2003), 37–40.

detectives slowly but surely solve the case. He skillfully handled the introduction of clues and embraced the "fair play" conventions espoused by a generation of earlier writers, building to an honest solution to the mystery and an explanation in the grand manner of a Holmes or Hercule Poirot.

The public's appetite for a realistic treatment of crime solving extended beyond an appreciation of Treat's novels (he eventually wrote eight more featuring these police officers). In 1949, America was glued to its radios (and later, in 1952, to television sets) to follow the tales of Sergeant Joe Friday of the Los Angeles Police Department (famously wearing Badge No. 714), the star of *Dragnet*. Producer/director/star Jack Webb became known throughout the world, and his tight-lipped "just the facts, ma'am" became a catchphrase for pundits as well as comedians. The show ran for seven seasons on television, between 1951 and 1959, with Webb as Friday and Ben Alexander as his partner Frank Smith, and was later revived in 1967 for another three seasons (again starring Webb but with Harry Morgan, as Bill Gannon, replacing Smith as Friday's partner). After Webb's death in 1982, additional television shows attempted to recreate the *Dragnet* magic (by using the name) in 1989–90 and again in the early 2000s.*

The *Dragnet* effect was widespread in crime writing. Police procedurals by writers like Hillary Waugh (whose *Last Seen Wearing*,† published in 1952, probably set the high-water mark for critical acclaim for procedurals), John Creasy, and Evan Hunter, writing as Ed McBain, dominated the crime fiction

---

* There were also three feature film versions, in 1954 and 1969 (the latter was the pilot for *Dragnet 1966*, the relaunch of the television series, but didn't air for several years), and a comic version in 1987 starring Dan Aykroyd as the nephew of Joe Friday (also named Joe Friday) and Tom Hanks as his partner.

† Republished by Sourcebooks in association with the Library of Congress in 2021.

bestseller lists. By 1957, Chester Himes was producing socially insightful tales of the Harlem police team of Grave Digger Jones and Coffin Ed Johnson (the first was *For Love of Imabelle*, later republished as *A Rage in Harlem*). Elizabeth Linington wrote three series of police procedurals, the earliest featuring Lt. Luis Mendoza, a Spanish-American detective in Los Angeles, whose first appearance was in *Case Pending* (1960).* Nor were procedurals limited to the United States: unlike the "hard-boiled" detective series that flourished here, popular procedural series appeared in England, Sweden, Denmark, the Netherlands, and South Africa.

The introduction of the police procedural naturally created a vehicle for the indirect examination of crucial socioeconomic issues and contemporary problems of the justice system. As Hillary Waugh pointed out in his thoughtful essay titled "The Police Procedural," "The police procedural, by showing policemen as they are, shows, by definition, the social ills they contend against as *they* are... The very nature of the procedural provokes a type of story totally beyond the aim of the other forms [of crime fiction]."† Real-world police must deal with the realities of street violence, drugs and drug cartels, mass incarcerations, the discriminatory treatment of persons of color, wrongful convictions, corrupt or incompetent law enforcement officers, and the changed and changing attitudes of the public toward the police. These are now the common concerns of modern tellers of "cop stories" in the thought-provoking books of Joseph Wambaugh, Michael Connelly, and many others and in the daily output of "cop shows" on television and film. Although Treat's novel treads

---

* Republished by Sourcebooks in association with the Library of Congress in 2020.

† Hillary Waugh, "The Police Procedural," in *The Mystery Story*, ed. John Ball (San Diego: University Extension, University of California, San Diego, 1976), 186.

lightly in this regard, his pioneering work laid the ground-work for the mystery genre to achieve a new importance as social commentary.

—Leslie S. Klinger

ONE

I

Around ten o'clock that evening Mitch Taylor, detective third grade,[*] sat hunched over a desk in the detectives' room in the Twenty-First Precinct[†] and drew circles on a sheet of paper. He was a short, chesty man with dark dry hair brushed back over his forehead. His lips, overthick, were firmed up in an aggressive pout. There were no planes or angles to his features and no shading to his complexion. It resembled a reddish gouache spread over the solid layer of his flesh so that he had a double insulation, first the gouache and then the pad of flesh. It gave the

---

[*] Detective third grade was the lowest rank of patrolman detailed to the detective squad. In 1960, there were 1,762 such detectives, and the annual pay rate was $6,324. This was better than the pay of a patrolman first grade (which required three years of service), who received $6,076 annually. A promotion to detective second grade might have brought a raise of as much as $600 per year. For some perspective, the average annual wage of a service employee in New York was about $2,500–$3,000 per year.

[†] Historically, the 21st Precinct was located near Gramercy Park in Manhattan, the precinct house at 100 E. Thirty Fifth St. In 1929 the Manhattan precincts were remapped, and the 21st disappeared. From 1953 to 1956, *21st Precinct* was a radio crime drama broadcast on CBS, taking place in a fictional precinct that roughly coincided with the actual 23rd Precinct on the Upper East Side of Manhattan.

impression that you might jolt him, but you could never slice through.

Although he had spent many hours at that desk, he had a vague sense of not belonging. Had you asked him about it, he'd have said simply, "I don't like paper work," and let it go at that. For he had no need to analyze his feelings. He knew that he liked movement. Once he started he kept going, and as soon as he stopped he went sound asleep. The area between the two states was something he had never explored. It was the drawing of circles on a desk pad.

He felt the pinch of his jacket and he tried to roll the tightness out of his shoulders. Somehow, a suit never did fit him. Amy always told him he ought to buy the next bigger size, but when he tried it on he found it was cut too long and hung halfway down to his knees. He'd a damn sight sooner have it tight on the shoulders than look as if he were wearing his grandfather's suit made over. He guessed Amy just didn't understand.

He put the pencil down and wondered what Butch Keenan was doing. Butch was on the night shift with him, from four in the afternoon until eight the next morning, every fourth day. Butch had gone out to check a complaint about some violation of the sanitary code down at a bar on Amsterdam Avenue. He should have been back long ago, but when Butch had business in a bar he usually stuck around for a few beers on the house. The chances were he wouldn't be in before midnight.

Mitch stared at the ceiling and wondered whether the paint chips would start flaking off tonight or wait until next week. He tried to remember when the place had been painted, but his memory didn't go that far back. The point was that the whole building was falling apart. He remembered how some smart rookie with a law degree used to beef about the age of the precinct houses. He had some cockeyed theory about their psychological effect. Nobody had liked the guy much and he'd gone in the army and Mitch had heard he'd got his in France. But now that he was dead, Mitch could admit that maybe he'd had something.

Only a jackass ever got himself into the department. You worked every day in the week and you didn't get overtime; and you never went anywhere except in bad weather and if anything happened you were supposed to take over, no matter what. You could be going to a show with the wife and you had to carry your gun with you. You got used to that. But if something happened outside the box office you could kiss the show good-bye and start working.

And that was the least of it. You were wide open to every crank civilian who didn't like the angle of your hat. All he had to do was write a letter to the commissioner and then you were considered guilty until proved innocent. So you even lost your constitutional rights.

Mitch curled that one around his tongue. He felt as if he'd accomplished something important, bringing it down to constitutional rights. He went back over his line of reasoning to try and reconstruct it, so he could shoot off his mouth later on. But he'd forgotten where he'd started, and it didn't matter, anyhow.

He picked up the pad again and tore off the top sheet. What made a guy draw circles, anyhow? What was the sense to it? He considered the question, not thinking and not trying to solve it, but letting it float around his mind because it was one more complaint against the universe. Then the phone rang.

He picked it up and said briskly, in his high, tenor voice, "Taylor."

The sergeant at the switchboard growled at him. "There's been a hit-and-run over on West End near Ninetieth.* Patrolman

---

* This intersection is in the Upper West Side of Manhattan, in the contemporary 24th Precinct, far from the location of the original 21st Precinct.

Levy phoned it in. Better take Murphy and a squad car and get over there."

"Okay, Sarge," said Mitch. He got up, rolled his shoulders to bring his jacket higher on his neck, picked up his hat and started downstairs.

He began to feel sore before he even reached the bottom step. He was sore at the hit-and-run driver and sore at the sergeant for telling him about it and sore at the world in general for pulling him out of doing nothing and finally he was sore at himself for being sore.

He climbed into the squad car and sat down next to Murphy. "Come on," he said in a tone of annoyance. "Let's get going."

Murphy muttered something about keeping his shirt on and started the car with a jerk. Mitch stared through the windshield and didn't speak. He supposed he'd been drawing too many circles on a piece of paper. He'd been alone too long. You go nuts from solitary confinement.

When he saw the crowd and the sedan with the wrecked door and the injured man lying on the pavement, he knew he didn't have to worry about being alone any more. He got out of the squad car, slammed the door and elbowed his way through the crowd. Patrolman Dan Levy greeted him with a sigh of relief. Mitch was here. Mitch would take charge.

Mitch said hello and then stared morosely at the injured man, lying near the curb. He had blood on his face and one leg was bent sharply outward, as if it were broken. He was elderly and his eyes were closed and his head was resting on a woman's lap. She was probably his wife, decided Mitch. She was crying and her hat was falling off her face.

She looked up at Mitch and said, "Get the ambulance. For God's sake, get the ambulance. What's the matter with it? He's hurt—can't you see?"

"It's on the way now," said Mitch. "Going to be right here." He edged away and looked at Levy. "What happened, Dan?"

Dan Levy took out his memo pad and read from it. "Ten forty-seven. Around then. This guy"—he pointed to the injured man—"Simon Treeberg, had just parked and was getting out of his car when the other car came along. Smashed into the side and kept right on going. I got here at—" He had to study his writing. "I got here at ten-fifty. Around then. Called the MVHS."

Mitch nodded. The Motor Vehicle Homicide Squad. When they got here, they'd take charge. All he'd have to do would be to work with them. His report would consist of an "aided" card, to show he'd helped the MVHS.

"There was a witness who saw the whole thing," continued Dan. "Barbara Evans. She's here."

He pointed to a meek, faded blonde and Mitch marched over as if he were going to run her down. He said accusingly, "You're Barbara Evans. You saw it all happen."

She shook her head timidly. "No. I mean yes. That is, I saw it, but my name isn't Evans. It's Devens, with a D."

Mitch took out his memo pad and wrote the name. "Tell me about it."

"I was going to cross the street," she said nervously. "In the middle. That's why I looked so carefully. I saw the car opposite. The man was just getting out. He had the door open and then his wife said something to him and he changed his mind and waited."

"And the other car?" prompted Mitch.

"It was about a block away. It was going slowly and I was wondering whether I ought to cross or not. There was nothing else in sight. It was near the side of the street and I don't think it was going more than ten miles an hour. Maybe even five."

Mitch jerked his head at the damaged sedan. "Five miles an hour, and it made a dent like that?"

The Devens girl drew in her breath. "Oh, no. I mean before it hit. It was going slow and then suddenly it picked up speed and smashed into the other car. The man was still holding the door open. It was simply horrible."

"What made the car pick up speed like that?" asked Mitch.

"It must have been the scream."

"Who? Mrs. Treeberg, in the car?"

"Oh, no. Somebody up there. I saw a woman lean out and scream."

The girl pointed and Mitch looked up at a small rooming house wedged between two mammoth apartments. There was a light on in a third-floor window.

Mitch frowned and turned back to the girl. "See the license numbers?" he asked.

She shook her head in the negative. "No. It happened so fast—"

Mitch turned away and asked the crowd in general, drilling at them in his sharp, biting tenor, "Anybody else? Anyone see the plates on the car that did it?"

Nobody answered and Mitch swung back in annoyance. The one thing he wanted, and none of these dummies had noticed it.

"What else?" he asked the blonde girl. "The car hit and then this woman screamed and then the car beat it."

"No," she said in an unexpected burst of temper. "Not after—before. She screamed at least ten seconds before it happened."

"That don't make sense," said Mitch with finality. He'd put it down his way in the report. Or maybe he'd forget about it. Yeah. That would be better.

But the big doorman from the apartment house stuck his

nose in. "Before," he snarled over the heads of the crowd "Before. Like she said. Maybe ten seconds. Maybe more."

"Did you see the license numbers?" asked Mitch.

The doorman grunted, "No."

"I'm trying to find out what the car was like. Make model, color. Who drove it. What he looked like and what kind of clothes he wore and how many people in the car."

"It happened so fast," said the doorman. "I was just coming out with a package, when—"

Mitch interrupted. "You're a hell of a witness. Didn't see the license, don't know what color the car was, don't know what make it was, but you heard a scream. Sure. The one time when there couldn't have been one. All I want to know is what the car looked like."

Gradually, from a half a dozen sources, he managed to piece together a general description. The car was a late model sedan, dark in color, and it had damaged a fender and then sped away with one headlight out. Mitch scribbled the description, such as it was, and marched over to one of the radio cars.

"Want to get that on the teletype?" he asked.

It wasn't much, but the boys from the MVHS ought to be here soon and they'd take over.

Still angry, Mitch turned his back on the crowd that was watching him. What did they expect of him anyhow? Repair the guy with the broken leg and dream up the hit-and-run license numbers? Sure. And probably chase the guy from the running board of a commandeered car, at fifty miles an hour up West End Avenue. With his gun blazing, too.

Civilians—nuts! Not one of them had had the sense to do the obvious, easy, simple thing that would take care of the whole business. License numbers. Instead, they handed them fairy tales about a car going five miles an hour and a woman screaming out of a window before anyone could even guess there was going to be an accident. Next thing he knew, somebody'd tell him it was done on purpose, too. Nuts!

He was all snarled up and it made him doubly mad. First of all there was the whole idea of a hit-and-run accident. Ever since a nephew of his had been killed that way up in the Bronx, Mitch had an unreasoning, murderous hate for anyone who left the scene of an accident without stopping. On occasions Mitch could stomach a crook. There were good and bad, and with them it was just business. But some snotty driver who sent a guy to the hospital and then ducked out—that got Mitch sore.

And besides, a hit-and-run meant two trials. A criminal case for leaving the scene of an accident and a civil suit by the injured party. Consequently Mitch would have to testify twice and hang around court for hours, waiting to be called to the stand. And for reasons which Mitch had never been able to figure out, court cases always came up on his day off. It was a kind of conspiracy against him. He glanced at Simon Treeberg, lying there flat on the sidewalk. His wife was bent low and crooning words at him, but he couldn't possibly hear. The sight made Mitch madder than ever.

"Anyone got a blanket?" he snapped. "There ought to be one in some of these cars. Go ahead and borrow it."

There was a murmur of approval and Mitch saw he was beginning to make a better impression. His huff at the girl and the doorman had been all wrong. Some crank might drop a letter about it and he'd be hauled up on the carpet and the promotion he'd set his mind on would be a year further away.

He went back to the girl and got the rest of her account. It was screwy, of course. Everybody began putting in his two bits and getting the story all balled up, and then the girl finished it off with a corker, just as he'd expected.

"In fact," she blazed, "he did it on purpose! I know."

Mitch smiled slyly and his high, thin voice dripped with sarcasm. "Did he tell you?" he asked. "Or just write a letter about it?"

She turned crimson and a couple of people muttered angrily at him. Immediately he regretted his remark and made up his mind to control himself. But he had to recreate his good impression. The ambulance was taking a hell of a time to get here and the crowd seemed to blame him.

Then, out of the blue, Mitch had his bright idea. He crunched a fragment of glass, and the inspiration hit him. He was almost cheerful as he turned to big Dan Levy towering in his blue uniform above everyone except the doorman.

"Hey, Dan," he said. "Will you call the laboratory for me?"

Patrolman Dan Levy stared as if he'd suddenly found himself in the middle of a Hollywood movie with a phone line that no self-respecting cop would ever use.

"Laboratory?" he asked vacantly. Then his big face beamed with understanding. "Oh," he added. "Sure."

Dan muttered and walked off. Mrs. Treeberg looked up with approval. Mitch stepped on another shard of glass. The technical research laboratory was supposed to be good at things like this. They identified headlights from fragments, and they matched up pieces of paint that you could hardly distinguish with your naked eye. Mitch could see it all there in the report. "Detective Taylor notified the laboratory at once." It would look good. Besides, he was about due for a promotion. Detective second-grade meant two hundred a year extra, and make believe he couldn't use it!

Feeling as if he'd gotten things started, anyhow, Mitch pushed his way through the crowd, yanked open the undamaged door of the sedan and peered inside. There was nothing, of course. Just gray upholstery, and a handbag in the seat. He picked up the bag. He'd keep it for the woman until she got into the ambulance with her husband. She was all upset and otherwise she'd forget it.

He kept on staring at the upholstery, chiefly to collect his thoughts and dope out how people could think a woman had screamed before the accident instead of after. Well, maybe a second or two before, when someone had realized there was going to be a smashup. But five or ten seconds before? That was crazy. And why would the car pick up speed just *before* hitting? That was cockeyed, too.

Now the way it should have been, and probably was, was like this: A car comes down the avenue going too fast. A man starts to step onto the street, the driver of the moving car jams on his brakes, skids and smacks into the parked car. Then he's scared stiff and keeps going. Maybe Mitch could get hold of a real witness, instead of that mixed-up blonde and the half-wit doorman.

Mitch heard the distant clang of an ambulance bell and saw red headlights coming up the avenue. He slammed the door shut and walked back to the injured man. He knew what to do now, anyhow. And by the time Treeberg left in the ambulance, the MVHS boys would be here. And maybe the laboratory truck, too.

Mitch began wondering why he'd sent for it. After all, what could they see that he couldn't?

II

The ambulance had come and gone.

A pair of men from the Motor Vehicle Homicide Squad had arrived, made their examination and remarked that the guy wasn't dead and so this shouldn't have been their headache.

Then they'd gotten another call and they turned the work over to the laboratory man and had left. Consequently Mitch was still on the scene and practically carrying the whole business.

A couple of uniformed cops were holding back the crowd and the laboratory man was doing his stuff under the glare of a powerful light. From the corner of his eye, Mitch watched him collect bits of broken glass and scraps of paint from the dented door and runningboard. Vaguely Mitch asked himself what good could come of it.

But he was too busy to give it much time. The brass hats were here. He had to satisfy the captain and a deputy chief inspector who had showed up in the course of the private war on hit-and-run drivers.

For Mitch, it was just a nuisance. They asked a hundred questions and had a couple dozen theories, and he'd have to do all the leg work and run them down.

He read from his notes, repeating the facts patiently and ending with his description that had already gone out to the teletype. Wanted—a dark sedan, '39, '40 or '41, make and plates unknown, with a smashed right headlight and damaged fenders, probably front and rear.

Barbara Devens, the dizzy blonde, hovered in the background and wanted to tell her story all over again. Mitch held her off as long as he could. When she finally got the captain's attention and dived into her act, Mitch stood up and interrupted whenever he thought she was going to tell about the scream. He managed to sidetrack her, but just when he thought the crisis was over she came out with a beauty. "And what's more," she said, "he did it on purpose!"

The captain gave Mitch a withering look, as if he realized Mitch had held out on him, and Mitch shook his head slightly to indicate the girl was nuts. The captain got the point. After all, he was as uninterested as Mitch in buggering up an ordinary street accident. Like Mitch, he had his record to think of.

"How do you know about this?" he asked the girl.

"You could tell. He had the whole street to himself and could have gone anywhere, but instead he banged right into that car."

"Maybe he skidded," said the captain gently. "Maybe he just wasn't looking. We don't know why he did it—we just know that he did."

"Well," she said, in an injured tone, "it seems to me—"

The captain stared at her and she spluttered out. Mitch heaved a sigh of relief. She was through at last and she hadn't mixed things up.

"A cop stepped from a patrol car and told the deputy chief inspector that he was wanted downtown. In a flurry of importance, he left. The captain went over to the laboratory man and spoke to him. Mitch glanced at the rooming house. A woman had screamed, huh? The third-floor light was still on and the window was wide open. Scream or no scream, maybe somebody had noticed the license plates. It was worth a trip up there, just on the chance.

"The captain got into his car and drove off. Detective Freeman, attached to the technical research laboratory at 400 Broome Street, came over. He was a quiet, pleasant guy, not much taller than Mitch, with alert features and dreamy blue eyes. He was on the blond side and he had plenty of weight. Mitch, liking him and deciding he was a good guy to know, wondered how he liked spending his life in a laboratory.

"Well," said Freeman, "that's the works. I have a collection of paint scrapings and a half-pound of glass fragments. I would run into a mess like this just when my partner was called out. Same thing happened two months ago. They thought they found a bomb out in a Queens factory, and Callender, my side-kick, was out. So I had to go up there all alone and ask somebody to help with the X-ray equipment."

"Did you get the bomb?"

Freeman grinned. The light caught his cheek and shone as if it were metal. "Bomb?" he said. "It was three Mexican jumping beans in a tin can. Somebody'd tried to play a practical joke, but I bet it was the first time anybody ever used portable equipment to X-ray a bean. On this hit-and-run car—get any leads?"

Mitch made a face. "Naah. I was hoping you'd have something."

"All by myself? We don't work that way. You find the car, and then we can tell you whether you're wrong or not."

"How about the headlight?" asked Mitch. "I thought you could trace the car from that."

Freeman shrugged. "There isn't a decent piece of glass in the whole collection. Too many people were walking around. And even if I had a larger sample—you don't know the year of the car, do you?"

"No. Everybody seems to think it was a late model, but the year? I'm not even sure of the make."

"That's too bad," said Freeman. "Ever since 1939 when they put in the sealed-beam unit, headlights don't help much. Now with the older cars, you could match up headlight and sometimes even find the serial numbers, and then you'd know something." He smiled apologetically and a dimple played along one cheek. "Anything else?"

Mitch hesitated, sizing up Freeman. So far Freeman had kept his nose in his own business. Mitch had a feel for things like that. He could spot the guys who never thought about anything except how to grab off the credit and impress the lieutenant.

Freeman didn't look like one of those. The chances were he'd

give Mitch a break on the written report, so he was worth playing along with. Besides, Mitch had a feeling that Freeman could
short-circuit a lot of work.

"There's something about a scream," remarked Mitch, in his
high voice.

"This Devens girl said a woman leaned out of the third-floor
window of this building and yelled. I'm going up now and see
what it's all about. Want to come?"

"Sure," said Freeman. "Glad to." Side by side they marched up
the steps and rang the janitor's bell.

A small glum man opened the door and they stepped into a
paneled anteroom with blue carpeting.

"We're police," said Mitch. "We been investigating that accident and we want to find out if anybody in here saw it. There's a
woman lives up on the third floor, isn't there?"

"Minx," said the glum little man, as if he disliked the name.
"Miss Andrea Minx. Everybody wants her tonight."

"Who else?" asked Mitch automatically.

"He didn't tell me his name. He didn't tell me what he wanted.
He didn't tell me anything. But he come here twice, looking for
her, and he was sore."

"What about?"

"He didn't tell. He didn't tell me anything. He wore a brown
suit and he was a big tall guy." The glum man surveyed the two
policeman as if he didn't think much of them. "Bigger than either
of you. You can take the elevator up, if it works." He turned on
his heel and walked away.

Mitch Taylor and Jub Freeman squeezed into the miniature
elevator and pressed the button marked 3. There was click and
a groan and a shiver. The cage bumped upwards and slowly
ground its way to the third floor. Neither of the two cops spoke.
They were still unsure of each other, measuring each other up.

A lab man and a precinct detective. They represented different points of view, and the two didn't mix.

On the third floor the cage shuddered and stopped. Mitch pushed open the door and walked towards the front. A ten-watt bulb barely illuminated the name on the door. Andrea Minx.

Mitch knocked.

There was a gasp inside and a woman's clear voice called out in relief. "Peter! At last!"

Quick footsteps pattered and the door was flung open. Andrea Minx exclaimed, "Oh! I thought it was—" Then she put her hand to mouth.

Mitch stared. She was one for the book all right. It reminded him of a picture he'd seen in the Metropolitan* once, when he'd had to go there to watch for a dip† who worked the Sunday museum crowds.

Amy had gone with him, over his protest, and he could still remember the picture. Amy had said it was a madonna, but no madonna ought to do what that picture had done to him. A dark girl with black hair and eyes and with an impish expression under a quiet sort of innocence. Amy had explained something about curves. She'd gone to a class on art, once, before they'd been married, and she knew all about it. But even so, it had taken Mitch quite a while to realize Amy was talking about a different set of curves than the ones he was looking at. She'd meant the background and the composition, whatever that was. And somehow, this dame had the same thing.

So he stared. Then gradually his training went to work and told him that the Minx woman was scared and she'd been

---

* The Metropolitan Museum of Art, that is.

† A pickpocket.

expecting a guy and that whether or not she'd seen the accident, he ought to stay here and find out what this was all about.

"Sorry to barge in like this," said Mitch politely. "We're the police. Maybe we can help."

Her black eyes got bigger than ever and she shook her head. "Oh, no. Unless you can find Peter. I don't know what's happened to him."

"Who's Peter?" asked Mitch wanting to put his arm around her and tell her he'd take care of her.

"Peter Jarvis," she said. "A friend of mine. He was supposed to be here long ago and he isn't. And I can't get him at his hotel, either."

"What's he done?" asked Mitch. "What's the trouble?"

"I'm so upset," said Andrea Minx. "But not about him. I'm just curious. What I've been crying about is Stanley." She dabbed at her eyes and Mitch stepped past her. Two guys in one breath. That explained most of it. She had a date with Peter here and with Stanley somewhere else, and she couldn't make up her mind which date to keep.

"Who's Stanley?" asked Mitch.

"Here." She turned and walked over to the couch and picked up a small, cream-colored cat. "He's dead." She squeezed the furry little thing against her chest and drew another breath. "When I came home, I found him like this." Mitch looked around the room. It was nicely furnished. Underneath the window was a studio couch with a lot of pillows, and at the opposite end of the room was a corridor with a kitchenette. The door off the corridor would be a bathroom. The place was decorated with a lot of knick-knacks and you could sleep for a week in any of the chairs. He wondered what the empty carton with the clawed edges was doing there in the center of the room.

Then he figured it out. Every cat has a box, and this one was

Stanley's. Still, Mitch would have expected a wicker basket and a pillow. A dame who fussed over her cat wouldn't give it an ordinary grocer's carton.

He snapped his mind back to the thing for which he'd come. "Look," he said. "There was an accident downstairs. Somebody said you screamed just before it happened, so you saw it, didn't you?"

"No. I screamed on account of Stanley."

"You claim you didn't see the accident? You were right by the window, weren't you?"

"Yes."

"Then you must have seen something. All I want is the number on the license plates."

"I'm sorry. I didn't even know there'd been an accident until I saw the crowd. You'll have to forgive me for being so scatter-brained. I'm not usually this way, but it was all so queer."

"What was queer?" asked Freeman.

She turned towards him and for the first time she spoke in a level, friendly voice.

"Let me tell you," she said. "My mind's in such a whirl. I came home—I don't know exactly when. I suppose it was a little after ten-thirty. I opened the door and turned on the light. I expected Stanley to rush over and rub up against me. He always does." She was still holding the body of the cat. She glanced at it in bewilderment and then placed it gently on the studio couch. She sat down in one of the deep, high-backed chairs. "He talks to me," she said in a shaky tone. "He always does."

"He's Siamese, isn't he?" asked Freeman.

She nodded, holding her head high and stiff on her long slender neck. She avoided looking at either of the two men.

"Yes," she said. "He has blue eyes and I'm awfully fond of him. He always says hello when I come home. When I didn't see him, I looked around and then I noticed the bathroom door was closed. I'd locked him in there once before, by mistake, and I thought I'd done it again. Am I being silly, telling so many details?"

"No," said Mitch. "Just go ahead."

"I opened the bathroom door and I had such a peculiar sensation. It seemed cold, like a dungeon, and I remember thinking I'd better get out of there or else I'd suffocate. And then I noticed Stanley, lying in a corner behind that carton. I picked him up and ran into the main room before I realized he was dead. He was so cold, so very cold. That's why I screamed. I went panicky."

Mitch stared at the pathetic little body on the couch. "It don't look as if anything happened to the cat," he said. "Maybe he just went and died, of old age or something."

Andrea Minx flushed. "No. He was only two years old. He was killed. He must have been."

"Who'd kill him?" asked Mitch.

"I don't know. Please. You ask so many questions."

"Who'd be liable to kill your cat?" asked Mitch imperturbably. "You got any enemies?"

"No, but—" She hesitated and shook her head.

"Go ahead," said Mitch. "But what?"

"Well, I was just thinking of Peter Jarvis. He hates cats."

"Is he a big tall guy?" asked Mitch suddenly.

"No. He's medium height and sort of elderly. He was to meet me here and go to the studio. I sing."

"There was a big tall guy trying to see you," continued Mitch. "Janitor says he was here twice, asking for you."

"I don't know who it could have been," she said, "unless it was Jack. He might have come unexpectedly, on furlough." She licked her finger. "It hurts," she added irrelevantly.

"Maybe you caught it in something," said Mitch.

"No. It feels as if it were burnt." She tapped her finger on the arm of her chair. "It hurts," she said again.

There was a long silence and Mitch looked from Freeman to the girl. They were staring at each other in a kind of a trance. Mitch had the feeling that the two of them had seen something that he'd overlooked. He studied the room, but it didn't tell him anything.

"About this accident," said Mitch. They both started forward as if they didn't know what he was talking about. "It happened around quarter of eleven and you say you came home a little after ten-thirty."

"Yes, to meet Peter. I think maybe something happened to him." Her dark brown eyes fastened on Mitch with an expression of terror. She knew something and she was scared to tell it. She was in a jam and she couldn't talk about it and yet she couldn't keep it to herself, "Something terrible," she added in a low, hushed tone.

"Such as what?" squeaked Mitch. "You think he got hurt?"

She gazed at Mitch. The movement of her head was so slight that he wasn't even sure she meant yes.

Then she seemed to pull out of it. "What time is it?" she asked suddenly.

Mitch glanced at his watch. "A little after twelve."

With that, she uttered a gasp and burst into activity. She scooped up her pocketbook from a table, dashed across the room to a closet and grabbed her hat. "I have to go," she said excitedly. "I'll be late for my broadcast. I have some things to look over. Please—I have to hurry." She wriggled into her coat, slipped the bag under one arm and grabbed Stanley.

"Please," she said. "I don't know how I'll get there on time. It'll be awful if I'm late. And Peter—couldn't you find out what happened to him? Peter Jarvis. He lives at the Hotel Quaker.* It's

---

* A fictional hotel.

near here. Oh *please*—come!" Her voice rose to a shrill, excited pitch. "I'm going to be *late!*"

"What are you going to do with the cat?" asked Mitch. "Put it on the air?"

She stared at the body as if she were noticing it for the first time. "It's cold," she said uncertainly. Then, without reason, she dropped it on the floor and began screaming hysterically.

"Stop it!" snapped Jub Freeman in a quick, angry burst.

She obeyed at once. "Yes. But I'm going to be late. What will I do?"

"Come on," said Jub. "We'll get you a taxi and you'll be down-town in no time at all."

He held the door open. Mitch, aware that Freeman was maneuvering to be the last to leave the room, watched closely. He saw Freeman's hand slide across the latch and heard a low, metallic click.

As soon as they'd seen Andrea safely in her cab, Mitch turned on the lab man.

"What was the idea of slipping the latch, Freeman? See anything?"

Freeman shook his head and grinned, with the dimple slicing across his cheek. "No. She seems okay."

"You got a reason for wanting to go back there, haven't you?"

"Sort of."

"Well, what?"

Jub Freeman smiled again, apologetically. "Only one thing I can think of. I'm going to swipe the cat."

III

Mitch didn't take the squad car back to the precinct. Instead, he hung around and watched Jub Freeman go upstairs and return with the body of the cat. While Freeman attached an identification tag to it, Mitch examined the truck. It was a big green thing with the driver's seat built high, over the engine. A pair of doors at the rear took you into a narrow space lined with shelves and compartments. It didn't mean much to Mitch. He identified a big generator and the portable X-ray equipment and let it go at that. Forward of the corridor was another door.

"What's in there?" he asked.

"That's the dark room. Develop films right on the spot."

"Yeah, good idea," said Mitch thoughtfully, as if he understood why you put a dark room on wheels. He led the way out and Jub followed and slammed the doors shut.

"Going over to the precinct?" asked Jub. "I'll give you a lift."

"I ought to stop off," said Mitch. "I got some business over at the Quaker."

"Jarvis?" asked Jub. "I figured you'd want to look into that." He hoisted himself into the cab and Mitch climbed in next to him. He had no intention of bothering with Jarvis, but there was no point in explaining.

Jub turned on the ignition and checked his lights. "You don't know whether Treeberg was actually struck by the hit-and-run car or just jammed against the door, do you?" he asked.

"I wouldn't know," said Mitch. "Why?"

"If he was hit directly, I might find something on his clothes. Certain substances might cling to the cloth where they'd leave no trace on the metal of the car."

"I didn't have a chance to look," said Mitch. He twisted up one side of his mouth and made a clucking sound. "It's too soon to call the hospital. He had a busted leg and some minor cuts, but I guess he'll pull through."

"Hope so," said Jub.

He started the truck, rolled slowly up West End Avenue and

turned into a side street. He drew up in front of the Quaker and Mitch climbed out.

"Well, be seeing you," he said.

Freeman frowned. "Wish I could come along," he said. "This whole thing has me guessing."

Mitch stopped short. Why would Freeman want to go up when he didn't have to? Mitch had never yet heard of a cop who made work for himself. You did what you had to, but you didn't stick your neck out.

"If I run into anything," he piped genially, "I'll call you. You'll be over at the precinct for a while, anyhow."

"Sure," said Jub. "You can get me there."

He slipped the truck into gear and Mitch watched the red lights swing down the street and slow up as they reached Broadway. Mitch slid his hat back on his head and scratched one ear. Jub was a new kind of cop. Asking for work and then making funny with the body of a cat. Why did a guy like that join the force, anyhow?

The question stumped Mitch and he stood there on the empty street and fussed over it. Then he wondered why *he'd* joined the force.

He'd never thought of it much, although for most of his boyhood he had more or less assumed that eventually he'd be a cop. There were plenty of reasons for it. He had the tradition, he had stamina, he had sense. He liked people, and he disliked buying and selling. His uncle who was a cop used to say, "Well, Mitch, some day you'll be wearing the uniform." And Mitch had accepted the fact much as another boy would have accepted the prospect of going into his father's business.

Besides all that, there was Hogan. Mitch's uncle had often pointed out that there was no sense in being a cop unless you had a rabbi. A rabbi was a guy with influence, who took care of you. He couldn't pass the civil service for you, but once you were in he saw to it that you got the breaks that were coming to you. Without a rabbi, you could be a patrolman all your life. With a rabbi, you stood a chance of getting places.

Mitch's rabbi was a guy named Hogan. He lived a few blocks away from Mitch, out in Queens. Mitch did him an occasional favor and dropped in regularly at Hogan's saloon for a glass of beer. Hogan was related to Mitch's mother, and when she was alive Hogan used to drop in two or three times a year. "She's the only pretty girl in the family," he'd say, as if that meant a lot to him.

There had been a time, of course, when Mitch had sat down and asked himself whether he really wanted to be a cop for the rest of his life. He hadn't had much of an argument. On the one hand there was security and a decent income. He'd be with people like himself, who thought his thoughts and spoke his language. He'd belong.

Reasons to the contrary? There really hadn't been any. Danger comes once or twice in a career, and anyhow, Mitch had few fears. He'd never dreamt of making a million, and consequently he was giving up nothing. So when the time came he went to the institute, took his physical and then passed his civil service. He was a cop.

Only one new element came into his life. He discovered that he had an alter ego, his record; like the book Saint Peter keeps at the gate of Heaven, it told his accomplishments and his failures. He learnt to fear above all else the crank civilian who wrote letters and got him up on charges, for that marred the record. He learnt to be aggressive before the other guy could be, and then to avoid the issue he'd made. He learnt stoicism and morale and the trick of passing the buck, so that there were as few marks on his record as possible.

He rarely entered anything as a crime, since it might remain unsolved. Instead, he listed the bulk of his work as investigations, for an investigation didn't have to carry through to an arrest. This afternoon, for instance, a woman had phoned in that she'd had a barrel of china stolen from her storeroom in the cellar of a large apartment house. Mitch had gone there and found a fussy old lady who was suspicious of everything. For her benefit he'd made a lot of notes, which he'd later thrown into the waste-paper basket, and had examined the storeroom and pretended to look for fingerprints. He'd stated that it was an inside job. In a week or two he'd stop in and tell her that one of the apartment employees was the thief, but had disappeared.

He intended to speak to the superintendent and ask him if he knew who had done it. If the super knew, Mitch would go after the guy. Otherwise he'd have nothing to start from and he'd forget about it. The woman was insured and in due time she'd collect, and Mitch had merely entered it as an investigation. The result would be satisfactory to everyone concerned.

He wasn't shirking on the job and would have bitterly resented any such accusation. Rather, he was using common sense, which was fifty percent of police work. The other fifty percent was pure luck.

So Mitch knew in general why he was a cop, and everyone he came across fitted more or less into the same pattern. But Jub Freeman was different, and the difference bothered Mitch. It made him stand on a sidewalk at one in the morning and think, until he concluded that Freeman probably belonged in the catch-all category. Security. He'd joined because he thereby acquired civil service status, and because he hadn't been able to get a job elsewhere.

With that settled, Mitch noted that the lights were still on in the Quaker Delicatessen and he walked in.

Earlier in the evening Harrison, the delicatessen proprietor, had visited the precinct house to report that he'd lost twenty dollars out of his register and suspected his clerk. Mitch, who had been on duty, had told Harrison to mark his money and then borrow a few dollars from his clerk just before the clerk went off for the day. If the bills were the marked ones and if the register was short again, he was to call Mitch to make the arrest.

Harrison looked up now with a pleased expression, which Mitch interpreted with neat accuracy. Harrison was a taxpayer, he'd made a complaint and he was getting service.

"Just thought I'd drop over and see the layout," remarked Mitch, looking around. "Like I figured, when you're on the other side of the store taking something off the shelves, a guy could go through the register easy." He glanced at the glass counter. "That's a nice looking ham you got."

Harrison beamed. "The best. Like me to make up a sandwich?"

Mitch condescended. "I could eat," he said. He watched Harrison cut a couple of slices on the machine and spread mayonnaise liberally.

"Looks like you got a pretty good business here," observed Mitch. "Hotel people ought to make you some steady customers."

Harrison slid the sandwich onto the counter. "Some do and some don't," he said. "The trouble is they all want credit. You can't make money that way."

Mitch tasted the sandwich, chewed it critically and gave his verdict. "Not bad," he said. He took another bite and remarked off-handedly, "A guy by the name of Jarvis. He wouldn't be a customer, would he?"

"One of my best," answered Harrison. "Lives in Ten-B. He's

a bachelor and when he orders, he wants everything just right. Willing to pay for it, too."

Mitch finished the sandwich and looked around for something else. He decided against a beer and then noticed the soft drink container.

"The cokes cold?" he asked.

Harrison obliged and Mitch drank a bottle and then wiped his hands on his handkerchief. "Glad I saw the layout," he said. "You just do what I tell you and we'll get the guy. There's no sense going off half-cocked. I could pull him in now, but I wouldn't have any evidence. I'd question him all night and he'd sue you for false arrest in the morning. Then where would you be, huh?"

Harrison nodded. Mitch said, "I'll be seeing you," and went out. Jarvis. 10-B.

Mitch had gotten the information without any trouble, but he didn't see the sense in following it up just because this lab guy was interested.

Mitch walked down to the corner. If he went back to the precinct, he'd have to sit at a typewriter and make out his report, whereas if he hung around here, Freeman and Dan Levy would turn in the information and somebody might even get it down on paper. And nothing was quite as bad as paper work.

Mitch thought of Andrea and then he remembered how he'd given the impression that he intended to check on Jarvis. In a way, Mitch had more or less promised Freeman to have a look, and it was that which decided Mitch. He turned and headed back to the hotel.

Unlike most hotels in the region, the Quaker had been built and designed as a hotel. It had a two-story lobby and a ballroom on the mezzanine. A placard told what had gone on in the ballroom this evening.

"Monday, September 11th,"* it read. "How Astrology can Predict the Election. T. Digby Outhouse and Others. Admission 50¢. 8:30 p.m."

At fifty cents a throw, reflected Mitch, astrology ought to be a nice racket. He walked briskly past the sign and entered an elevator. "Tenth," he said in his high-pitched voice.[†]

On the way up, he wondered what point there was in barging in here at this hour in the morning. Just because some dame asked him to find out why a guy stood her up on a date. Mitch should have known better. Still, here he was.

The elevator let him out on the tenth and he strode to the right. His chest protruded like a pouter pigeon's and his jacket was tight across the shoulders.

He rang the buzzer bell of 10-B and waited. As he had expected, there was no answer. The corridor was deserted and the heavy carpeting absorbed the sound of his shuffling. Anybody could walk in here and give a floor number. A competent crook with a pass key could get a nice haul out of the place. There had been a couple of complaints from the Quaker in the last year. Mitch wondered why there hadn't been more.

He tried the buzzer again, with no effect. He shrugged and put his hand on the knob. To his surprise it turned. He opened the door and walked in. The light from the corridor showed him

---

* This places the events in 1944, the year before publication, when September 11 was a Monday. The presidential election, set for November, was between Franklin D. Roosevelt, seeking a fourth term, and Thomas Dewey. There was little doubt about the outcome, and FDR won the popular vote by a 9 percent margin and with a wide Electoral College margin as well. An election for US Senate was also on the New York ballot, handily won by Robert F. Wagner, the candidate of the Democratic/Liberal/American Labor coalition.

† Indicating that there was an elevator operator. Automatic elevators were invented around the turn of the twentieth century, but human operators persisted for decades, in part because of public fears. The Hotel Quaker evidently didn't wish to incur the expense of upgrading to an automatic elevator.

the electric switch and he snapped it on. Then he let out a low whistle and pursed his lips.

He thought of going back to the precinct and not mentioning it. He could say he'd stopped in at the delicatessen for a few minutes. His time would be accounted for. No elevator boy would think of identifying a precinct detective as the man who'd come up to the tenth floor around one o'clock that morning. He could slide out of it nicely. By the time it was discovered, he'd be off duty. Or at worst, it would be Keenan's job. Since Mitch had handled the hit-and-run, the next case would be Butch Keenan's.

Mitch turned slowly and closed the door. He was too good a cop to take a powder.* If he walked in on this, he was tagged. He'd go through with it.

He stepped into the living room and turned on another light. A heavy-set man with a thin nose and pouchy skin over thin, predatory features was leaning back in a comfortable, high-backed chair. The light, blue-gray eyes were glassy and stared straight at Mitch. He took a couple of paces to the side and the eyes seemed to follow him.

"Nuts," said Mitch aloud. "Nuts to you, Fish-Eye. With your skull caved in like that, you ain't really looking."

Superficially, he examined the wound. It was broad and shallow, with a fair amount of blood. Quite a whack, too.

He walked around the body to the telephone. He picked it up gingerly and tipped it at varying angles. He didn't see any prints. You never got prints from an obvious place like that, anyhow. Nobody was that dumb.

He gripped the phone in his fist and lifted it. He gave the

---

* "To take a powder" means to leave, to escape. Eric Partridge's *A Dictionary of the Underworld: British and American* (New York: Bonanza Books, 1961), 527, reports the first usage ca. 1920 and in print in R. J. Tasker's *Grimhaven* (1928).

precinct number and asked for Freeman. After a few seconds, Freeman answered.

"Hello," said Mitch. "This is Taylor. I'm up at the joint and you better get here. Bring your equipment along, too. You'll need it." He hung up.

He had five or ten minutes. He thought of going down to the delicatessen for another coke, but he didn't want to make any extra trips on the elevator. They'd look bad.

He wondered whether he was giving Freeman a break or a headache. There were going to be a lot of embarrassing questions asked about this. A cop doesn't do an errand for an hysterical woman and walk in on a homicide. Somehow, if Freeman were here with him, the whole thing would look a lot better and explanations would be easier.

On the other hand he'd have to divide the credit, and the whole thing yelled right out at him. That girl sending them here, to the scene of a crime. Why? What was she so upset about and why had she sent them? There was only one answer.

Mitch strolled leisurely around the room, looking for the weapon. It would be smeared with blood, of course. So it wasn't the standing ash tray and it wasn't the lamp and it wasn't the bronze bookend.

Mitch stopped in front of the secretary-desk. A small ash tray was powdered with the heavy gray ashes of a cigar, and the chewed butt reposed on the edge. It smelt stale. He picked it up and stared glumly. Then he replaced it.

A scratch pad and a blank application form for life insurance lay next to the ash tray. They didn't tell him a thing. He stepped over to the body and slipped his hand into the inside pocket of the coat. He came out with a wad of papers and a leather card case.

He went through the papers quickly because he wasn't

supposed to touch anything until the medical examiner had finished. He found a few addresses, a lot of notations and some business cards. So—an insurance guy, huh? The leather case contained an identification card signed Peter Jarvis.

Mitch put them back in the pocket. The man was Peter Jarvis. No doubt about that.

Mitch went through a doorway opposite the entrance. On one side of the short corridor was a kitchenette. On the other was a bathroom with a couple of dirty towels on the floor. The bedroom showed no signs of recent use, beyond a pair of men's shoes on the rug and a suit hung over a chair. Jarvis must have changed before dinner. So what?

The pictures on the bureau were interesting. A large, framed portrait of Andrea Minx. Mitch wondered why Hollywood hadn't gotten on to her yet. With her face and figure, she'd pack 'em in. And with it all, she had that naive look, that honest, homey quality of the girl who lived next door. Well, you couldn't tell.

The next picture was of an older woman. She was flashy and well dressed and she'd signed the thing, "With all my love, Christie Mae."

The third woman was represented by three snap shots. In one of them a man's arm was holding her, but the guy had been cut out. She was a saucy-looking piece, too, built solid and staring right out at you.

Mitch returned to the living room. Three dames. But Andrea was the one who'd known something was happening.

He walked over to the radio, switched it on and tuned it to WLT.* He was just in time to hear the end of a recorded com-

---

* How did Taylor know to tune in to WLT? Earlier, he and Freeman had put Andrea Minx into a cab—she undoubtedly told them (or the cabbie in their presence) where to take her. The station is fictional.

mercial telling you that you had a headache and what to do about it. Then Andrea's voice tinkled.

"I've had so many requests to sing, that I'm going to oblige you. As a matter of fact, I love to. Usually I sit here and listen to recorded music, and all I can do is talk about it. So this is my chance and I'm going to sing, 'My eyes are wet and my heart is warm.'"*

Mitch listened to her. She was good.

The only comfortable chair faced the body and Mitch sat down and leaned back. When he moved, the image of the electric light shifted across the dead retina and gave the effect of blinking. Mitch didn't like it. The whole thing was ghoulish.

He thought of moving the chair, but he was too tired to bother. And, although Fish-Eye Jarvis wasn't pretty, he was in no condition to do anything and so Mitch might as well lean back and think.

Not that he had to do much of it. Andrea had been worried, she'd sent him here, she'd had an appointment with Jarvis, she'd hurt her finger. To Mitch's mind, it all added up. He'd get Andrea at the end of her program. He had plenty of time.

Mitch stared at Fish-Eye and Fish-Eye stared back. Mitch might get his promotion next month. As for Freeman, he'd get a break, too. Mitch was a big-hearted guy and didn't grudge him that much.

He moved his head and Fish-Eye blinked again. Somewhere in the building Mitch heard the rumble of the elevator. Then the whole room seemed to vibrate mysteriously and the radio began buzzing. A subway, of course, a half block away. Mitch reached out and turned the radio lower. The humming stopped, but so did the vibration. He ought to move his chair so that he

---

* If this is a real song, its author is unidentifiable.

didn't have to keep staring at the damned thing. Except that it wasn't worth the effort.

He wondered what Amy would think if she could see him now, sitting a yard away from a dead body. She was finicky, like all women. If she knew, she probably wouldn't touch him for a week.

Fish-Eye must have been killed some time this evening. The blood had clotted but it hadn't dried out, except where it had dripped down on one shoulder.

Well, Harrison was losing a good customer. Mitch wondered what kind of a guy Jarvis had been. Harrison had said he was a bachelor, and he had pictures of three women in his bedroom. But he looked hard, and his lips were smiling the way the lieutenant's did when he had somebody cold for a violation of rules. Mitch was glad Fish-Eye was dead.

He remembered the first corpse he'd ever seen. A guy had hung himself in the back of a tailor shop and Mitch had cut the body down. As it dropped, it let out a *whoosh* of air and Mitch had yelled and thought the guy was alive. Charlie Corrigan, who had taught Mitch all he knew about detective work, had laughed like hell. They all do that, he'd said. It was the air rushing out of the lungs.

Mitch squirmed. The lips had moved, definitely. He sat up suddenly and then he told himself he was a jackass. The muscles were contracting, that was all. The beginning of *rigor mortis,* maybe. He got up angrily, wanting to punch the stiff in the nose.

He didn't do it, of course. He merely went into the kitchenette. There was a box of crackers on the top shelf and he helped himself to a couple. Then he returned to the comfortable chair. Squirming, munching slowly, he stared into the dead, glassy eyes of Peter Jarvis.

IV

When the doorbell rang, Mitch got up. It was Freeman, lugging a heavy black bag. Mitch jerked his head towards the living room and said, "Jarvis. He got conked."

The lab man halted at the entrance to the room and let out a long, low whistle. His blue eyes danced with excitement and began jitterbugging around the walls and the furniture. After they'd completed the tour, they came back to rest on the corpse.

Mitch, watching closely, felt something of Freeman's bubbling, alert eagerness. For a moment Mitch felt himself pulled along and he listened expectantly while Freeman boiled over and popped the lid off his reactions.

"Head smashed in," he exclaimed. "I don't see what did it. He was sitting there relaxed. Must have been somebody who knew him and got him from behind. Wow! What's that?" He took two steps towards the secretary-desk and glanced at the printed form. "Somebody trying to sell him insurance? The cigar—say—notice it? Those tooth marks ought to tell us something. And how'd you get in? Door open? And when did you notify the desk? How soon will the homicide men be here?"

Mitch pulled himself together. Leisurely, as if it were an essential ceremony, he scratched his ear. Then he rubbed his hands together and looked up.

"I haven't notified anybody," said Mitch. "Not yet. So don't go off half-cocked. He's Peter Jarvis and he's an insurance man, and he has a picture of the Minx dame in his bedroom. The door was unlocked and I just walked in."

"Sure. But how come you didn't report this?"

"Waited for you," said Mitch placidly. "You saw the Minx with me. How would it look if I sneaked off without even calling in at the precinct, and then turned up a homicide? Think of how *that* would look to the lieutenant."

"I don't get it."

"Look," said Mitch. "Here's how it was. She asked us to look up Jarvis. I had an errand to do. The delicatessen guy downstairs wanted to see me, so I said I'd meet you here and we'd go up together. So we did. We just got here. Now we start moving."

He marched towards the phone, but Jub yelled at him. "Hey—prints!"

Mitch gave the lab man a look of disgust. "Naah—nothing. I looked." He picked up the phone and gave the precinct number. "Hello, Sergeant? Taylor reporting. There's a homicide at the Hotel Quaker. A guy named Peter Jarvis, in apartment Ten-B. Me and Detective Freeman, from the laboratory downtown, found him." He listened a moment and hung up.

"They'll be right over," he said. He lifted the phone again and said in his high voice, "This is Ten-B. Send the manager up.... Yeah, I said the manager, the big shot. This is the police and you got trouble and you better call him quick." Mitch slammed down the receiver, went over to the chair and sat down again.

Freeman, with his lips pursed tight and the dimple cut deep into his cheek, was examining the head wound. When he stepped away from it, his complexion was pale.

"This is a break," he remarked. "Usually we arrive after the best evidence is destroyed. This time I'm going to get some scrapings from that wound, and I'm going over the place with a vacuum cleaner before it's all messed up." He grunted hopefully. "This makes the second time you called me in," he added. "Thanks."

Mitch shrugged. "I believe in science," he said dryly. "Most cops don't use the lab half enough."

"You're telling me!" exclaimed Jub. He hiccuped, looked

at Mitch and grinned. Then, he opened his bag and took out a small, fine brush and two bottles of fingerprint powder, one white and one black. He dusted the black carefully on the insurance form.

Mitch got up to look. There were a couple of blurs, a few useless smudges and, down in one corner, a dream print that was perfect in every line and whorl.

"Probably Jarvis's," remarked Mitch. "It wouldn't be hers."

Freeman spun around. "Whose?"

"The Minx. It can't be that easy."

"Andrea? You don't think *she* did it, do you? A girl like that?"

"I wouldn't know," said Mitch dryly.

Freeman gave him a sharp look and walked into the bedroom. Mitch sat down again and waited for the manager. Mitch figured he'd be busy enough later on. He might as well rest up while he could.

Presently Freeman called from the bathroom. "Hey, Taylor—come here!"

Mitch got up and sauntered into the bathroom. Freeman was on the floor examining one of the dirty towels.

"Look at this," he said. "Somebody came in here and washed up. There's stuff on the towel that looks like blood, and there are fibers, too." He took a magnifying glass from his kit and studied the towel intently.

Mitch spat into the sink. He felt a little ashamed of this guy. They'd kid the life out of him, back at the precinct. Him and Sherlock. He could see the locker-room scene next time he reported. "Hello there, Dr. Watson. How's your friend Sherlock? I hear you're going into the movies together."

Mitch glowered in disgust. "Listen," he said. "How the hell can you—"

Freeman turned around and grinned. "Can't now, but I will

down at the laboratory." He picked up the towel and went back to the living room.

After that, Mitch didn't bother. He understood finger-prints. Sure. They didn't work miracles, but they made sense and he thought in terms of them. But cigar ashes and fibers on a towel—they were book stuff. Why Jarvis had pictures of three women and who they were and what they'd all done this evening—the answers to that were real. You asked questions and people answered, and if you asked enough questions they made mistakes and then you had them.

That's what Charlie Corrigan had taught him, six years ago, and Charlie had had twenty years' experience as a detective when Mitch had first run across him in another precinct.

Charlie always knew what he was talking about and Mitch quoted him like a Bible. The first thing a detective needs, Charlie used to say, is a few good stool pigeons. Get something on them and they'll play ball with you. And if they don't, you sock down so hard they don't even know what happened. Then the others step right into line.

But stool pigeons weren't any good in a case like this. Even Charlie would have admitted that much. He'd merely have pointed out that the average cop could go through a lifetime without having a case that wasn't either obvious or depended on a stool pigeon.

It was good advice and Mitch knew it. Andrea was obvious. He hoped he wouldn't have to go any further.

Not that he'd leave it there, of course. He'd question relatives and friends and get Jarvis's background. He'd give Christie Mae and the other dame a thorough going-over, but he didn't expect to get anywhere with them. It would be just routine, to fill in the gaps and round out the reports. Andrea was his candidate. Love or jealousy—he didn't know yet. And he wasn't going to let her get away with the story that she'd been upset just on account of a cat.

The doorbell rang and Mitch marched over and opened it. A sleepy guy with a trim black mustache burst out nervously.

"You're the police? You wanted me? What for? What happened?"

Mitch blocked the doorway by leaning against the wall. "You the manager? What's your name?"

"Mortimer Peyser. Tell me what happened."

"Just keep your shirt on, Mr. Peyser. Whatever happened is our business. Suppose you tell me what you know about Jarvis. The kind of guy he was and who his friends were and so on."

"He's always been a model tenant," said Peyser. "He's been here three years and we never had any trouble with him."

"Well, you got trouble now. He's dead."

"You mean—" Peyser came fully awake. His mouth dropped open and showed the crookedness of his teeth. He made an attempt to slip past Mitch, but Mitch didn't move.

"You wouldn't want to go in there," he said. "He isn't pretty. Now you were telling me about his friends, weren't you?"

The elevator door at the other end of the corridor snapped open and the lieutenant in charge of the squad stepped out. Behind him came a group of cops.

Mitch maneuvered Peyser out of the way. The lieutenant approached briskly and said, "Hello, Taylor. Homicide, huh? Who is he?"

"Peter Jarvis, insurance man," answered Mitch promptly. He followed the lieutenant into the apartment and clicked out his information. "One of the witnesses in that hit-and-run business asked us to look him up, and me and Freeman walked in and found this. He's got pictures of three dames in his bedroom and I'm going to check on them as soon as I can find out who

they are. That's the hotel manager outside now. He may know
something, but I didn't have time to question him, yet. All I got
figured out so far is that Jarvis was trying to sell somebody an
insurance policy, and whoever it was slugged Jarvis from behind
and then went in the bathroom and washed up. It must have
happened some time this evening."

The lieutenant approached Fish-Eye and stared. Fish-Eye
stared back with the same poker-faced expression he'd given
Mitch, but he didn't have a chance with the lieutenant. Mitch
heaved a long sigh and marched over to Keenan.

"Look, Butch," he whispered. "The lieutenant say anything
on the way over about me walking into a homicide?"

Keenan, tall and meaty, looked down at Mitch and made a
face. "Nothing much. He was wondering why you didn't report
in first, and how come you were here with this lab man."

"Oh, just one of those things," said Mitch.

Then the lieutenant called him. "What have you done so far,
Taylor?"

"What I told you, Lieutenant. I been waiting for you."

"Well, I'm here now. Find out whether Jarvis had any visitors tonight and who they were and what they looked like. Then
check on who came up to the tenth floor tonight and where
Jarvis had dinner and with whom and when. And send that
hotel manager in. I'll speak to him now."

"Yes, Lieutenant," said Mitch. When the lieutenant was like
that, Mitch was glad to get away. He'd spend a half hour or so
with the elevator boys. Maybe longer. By that time the lieutenant would forget half the things he'd asked about.

Mitch turned and watched Freeman slip something invisible
into an envelope and write on the outside of it. The lieutenant
was watching with a queer, surprised expression. Mitch strode
resolutely down the corridor.

He ought to see Harrison again. Harrison might have some valuable dope. And even if he didn't, he had food.

It was nearly three o'clock when Mitch returned to 10-B. He'd figured his time carefully. He'd phoned the precinct and asked what had come in from the hospital on Simon Treeberg. He'd learnt that Treeberg had a badly fractured leg and internal injuries, significance unknown. He'd called WLT and been informed that Andrea Minx was on until six A.M., with a couple of breaks. So long as he got down to the studio by then, he didn't care particularly what happened. In the end, he'd stand them all on their ear by bringing in the one red-hot suspect. He had no worries.

He found the Jarvis apartment in pandemonium. The captain of the Detective District, a captain from the Homicide Bureau, the borough commander and the precinct lieutenant were all there, and each had his staff. In addition, the medical examiner and a representative from the district attorney's office had showed up. Throw in a couple of men from the photograph gallery and a liberal representation of the uniformed men in the precinct, and you have some idea of what Mitch walked into. Maybe fifty people were crowded into the two-room apartment.

He watched for a while. The photographers were about through and the fingerprint men were beginning to give the room the once-over. They knew where to look, but Mitch would have been willing to bet they wouldn't turn up a thing. Fingerprints would make this case too easy and nothing ever broke right for Mitch. Even the Minx—he wasn't sure how much he could pin on her.

Presently Mitch almost collided with the lieutenant. The lieutenant said, "So you're back. What did you find?"

"Nobody was seen coming up here," answered Mitch. "There was some sort of an astrology lecture down on the ballroom floor and a lot of the people there went up to the roof, to look at the stars. That kept the elevators pretty busy and the men say they don't even remember the steady customers. They all knew Jarvis, of course. He got home around eight. He had plenty of women and he used to entertain quite a bit. He had dough and he spent it. He was a bachelor and I guess he made the most of it."

The lieutenant got that look in his eye and Mitch shut up. After a moment the lieutenant said, "I don't know where you get all that accurate dope. Jarvis was married but his wife was dead. That makes him a widower. He had a married daughter named Fern Kent and she lives at One-Ninety West Sixty-Eighth Street. I don't know about the other women—yet. The hotel manager couldn't tell me. But you'd better go down and see this Kent woman and find out what she knows."

"Sure, Lieutenant."

"The doctor says he was killed around ten or eleven. Maybe a little earlier. He was hit over the head with a lead pipe, or something like that, but we haven't found it yet."

Mitch coughed. Freeman squeezed past, walked over to the corner of the room and picked up his bag. The lieutenant shook his head and made a face to indicate he didn't understand guys like Freeman. Mitch nodded to show that he agreed. Then he left. He waited for Freeman at the end of the corridor and they went down in the elevator together. Neither of them spoke until they were in the lobby and out of hearing of the elevator man.

"Glad to be out of that mob," said Mitch.

"Going downtown?"

Freeman nodded. "Yes. I've been out since eleven o'clock." He frowned slightly and shook his head. "You know, you'd think a man who got to be a lieutenant would realize you can get evidence with a vacuum cleaner, wouldn't you?"

"Him?" said Mitch. "The lieutenant? Frankie Waters put him there years ago, before you had to take an exam, and Jim Blansom keeps him there. Don't ask me why. You going past Sixty-Eighth Street?"

"Sure."

"You can drop me off at One-Ninety West. Jarvis's daughter lives there."

Then, for the second time that evening, Jub Freeman made a strange request. "I'd like to stop in with you. Okay?"

"Sure," said Mitch. "Come along."

190 West was a six-story brick apartment with a sign reading "Apartments, 1-2-3 rooms." A line had been drawn through each of the numerals.

The two cops woke up an elevator man, flashed their badges and learned that Fern Kent lived on the third floor, apartment E. They rode up, walked the length of a dull-red tile corridor, rang the E-bell and waited. From inside they heard vague sounds. The creak of a bed, the thud of a shoe. Voices murmured and dropped to a whisper. There was a sudden, sharp titter which was immediately choked off. They rang again.

A woman's voice answered them. "Who's there?"

Mitch glanced at Jub and signaled to let him, Mitch, handle it. Aloud he said, "Police. Open up."

The sounds inside were confused. The woman's voice called out, "Oh. Just a minute."

That wasn't the way the ordinary citizen reacted. When the police ring doorbells at three in the morning, the first question people ask is what for. When they don't, you wonder why.

Suddenly Mitch whispered, "There may be a back door. You stick here—I'm going around."

He wheeled and strode a half dozen paces to the fire door, swung it open and found himself on a darkened stair landing. If there'd been a bulb here, it had gone out. The door behind him slammed shut.

Mitch sensed someone was here in the darkness, but his eyes hadn't adjusted. He yelled, "Hey, you!" At the same instant he charged forward.

He banged straight into a fist that jolted him back against the wall. He hit the wall with his shoulder, but his head cracked against a projecting fixture. He went dizzy and he must have been out on his feet for a few seconds.

In a vague, black world that spun around him like an unseen merry-go-round, he seemed to hear somebody running. When his head cleared, he moved forward towards the stairs. But he was cautious now and he had one hand on his gun.

He saw the top step and saw the yellow flood of light from the floor below. With a snort, he began racing down. He went two steps at a time, with one hand on the banister, the way he used to do when he was a kid in public school. He erupted into the lobby and found merely a startled elevator man.

"Anybody come through here?" snapped Mitch.

The man blinked, opened his mouth and shut it.

"Well," barked Mitch. "You gone dumb?"

"N-no. N-nobody."

"If anyone comes down them stairs, you yell," said Mitch. "And if the elevator bell rings, stop on the third on your way up." Angrily, Mitch turned and climbed the stairs. On the third floor he stopped and lit a match. A window was open. He stepped to it and looked out. It gave on to a fire escape which descended to a courtyard. Whoever had socked him must have climbed out of here and gotten away long ago. Mitch grunted and returned via the fire door to the E-apartment.

The girl of the three snapshots was sitting in a chair. A big bed looked as if it had been slept in for a couple of weeks without having been made up. If Amy ever saw a thing like that, she'd have blown up.

The girl had light brown hair, small, pale green eyes and a regular profile. Her blue flannel robe was pulled tight around her, but Mitch could see she had nothing on underneath. Her ankles were thick. They'd have made two of Amy's.

"You're Fern Kent?" asked Mitch.

She indicated Jub. "I just told him so."

"Who was here with you?" demanded Mitch.

"I don't see that I have to explain," she retorted.

Mitch looked at her. So—she was one of them. She'd been sleeping with a guy and she didn't want the police to know who he was. It didn't matter much, but Mitch would get around to it later.

He shifted his attack. "Freeman tell you what happened?"

"Yes. My father's dead. He was killed."

"You don't look too sorry."

"Do you want me to faint?" she asked. "I might, if you insist, but really—the floor's too damn dirty."

"Any idea who did it?"

"I haven't the least idea. He had his own life, and I had mine."

Mitch kept on looking at her. There was brown in her eyes, too. Green and brown. And she was a tramp.

He couldn't make her out. She had a frank, trusting look and she said things like that about her old man. And she slept around and talked right back at a cop.

He had to pigeonhole her in his mind, and she didn't fit. Maybe because he'd spent a half hour staring at Fish-Eye. Mitch had a feeling that whatever Fern was, Fish-Eye was responsible. And the war, too. Maybe her husband was away and she had nobody else around—yeah. Mitch had read all about that kind of thing. It must be the war.*

---

* The war in Europe did not officially end until May 8, 1945 (the war in the Pacific would not end until September), and millions of US soldiers did not return home from overseas until late in 1945 and 1946.

Then he came back to the business in hand. His high-pitched voice rasped out with an impersonal, metallic quality.

"Did your father usually leave his door unlocked?"

"Almost always," she answered.

"Did he have any enemies?"

"Yes."

"Who were they?"

"Everybody who ever met him."

"Does that include you?"

"I'm his daughter."

That one stopped Mitch. He stared at her. If a girl didn't even love her own father, what good was she anyhow? He wondered what Amy would think.

"Let's have a drink," said Fern. She rose unsteadily and marched to a messy kitchenette. She returned with a bottle and three glasses. She poured two little ones for the cops and a big one for herself.

"Here's mud in your eye," she said.* She downed half of her drink without even blinking. Neither Mitch nor Jub joined her.

"Who's Christie Mae?" asked Mitch.

"That's my aunt. Don't tell me *she's* mixed up in this. That would be just too wonderful!"

"Where does she live?"

Fern gave the address. Jub got up, signaled to Mitch and started moving aimlessly around the room. Mitch remembered the way Jub had slipped the latch at the Minx place.

---

* This toast is said to have a long history, dating back to the nineteenth century and probably having its origins in fox-hunting and racing. Many suggest that it's a wish to have the winning horse, which would undoubtedly kick up mud into the eyes of the horses and riders following. Others have pointed out that in the Bible, Jesus cures a supplicant's blindness by spitting into some dirt and rubbing the mud into the afflicted man's eyes—hence, they say, this is a wish for good health. Like so many catchphrases, the exact origin will likely remain obscure.

Mitch liked working with him. He gave you the feeling that he was on his toes and that eventually he'd come up with something. All those samples he'd taken at Jarvis's, for instance— Freeman knew what he was doing. Even the cigar and the bathroom towel might make sense.

"Why do you say it would be wonderful if your aunt was mixed up in this?" asked Mitch.

"Wait till you meet her and you'll know what I mean," said Fern. "It's funny. She kept her virtue all these years, and now Peter gets murdered and it's too late." Fern studied the rest of her liquor. "Or maybe she didn't keep her virtue. If you find out, Officer, will you tell me? I'm dying to know."

"Was she sweet on your father?"

"She dripped," replied Fern. "It oozes out of her. But don't let her fool you. And wait till you start digging up the Jarvis background. It's priceless."

"Did he have any women?" asked Mitch.

Fern downed the rest of her drink. "Why ask me?"

"Did he?" repeated Mitch.

"Lord knows he tried. I couldn't tell you how successful he was. He was too smug to admit his failures and too conceited to deny them."

"Tell me some names."

Fern looked past Mitch and called to Jub. "What are you doing with those forceps?"

"Hairs," said Jub, without turning around.

Fern giggled. Mitch stood up in order to block her view. Then he repeated his question.

"Tell me some names."

Fern thought it over. "Well," she said, "there was Andrea Minx, the radio girl. He certainly tried with her."

"Did she have any reason to kill him?"

"I told you—everybody had reasons. I don't know whether she had particular ones or not. Ask her."

"Who was here when we came?" snapped Mitch suddenly.

Fern's pale green eyes wavered. "Really," she said, "you're awfully inquisitive."

Jub slid past Mitch and dropped a picture in his hand. It was a snapshot of a tall, thin man with curly hair. The photograph had been cut down the middle and one arm was off. Mitch identified it as the other half of the picture he'd found on Peter Jarvis's dresser.

He held up the picture. "Who's this?" he asked.

"That's Lee. My husband. It belongs on my bureau."

"Where is he?"

"I don't know."

"We're not going to tell him about the guy that was here," said Mitch. "Don't worry about that."

"I'm not worrying. He knows all about it." She giggled again. "In fact, he was here when you knocked, but he left. Surreptitiously." She had trouble with the word.

"Don't pull that," said Mitch. "No husband sneaks out at four A.M. with his pants down."

"Mine did," said Fern.

Mitch rubbed his cheek. "Look," he said. "Who was here?"

"I told you. Lee. My husband. And when you said you were the police, you should have seen him!" She began rocking with laughter.

"Why is he scared of the police?" demanded Mitch.

"We both were. We thought it was a trick. You see, we're getting divorced and he's not supposed to be here.* We thought it

---

* New York law, like that of many states at that time, set forth specific grounds for divorce. That is, more than the mere consent of the parties was required in order to obtain a divorce. If the parties were still having sexual congress, they would have been unable to prove various grounds set forth in the statutes such as an irretrievable breakdown in the relationship or abandonment.

was either a friend of mine or else a trick to show we'd been together and prevent the divorce."

"Who'd want to do that?"

"I don't know, but it seemed that way at the time. To both of us. I was tired. I still am."

"It sounds like a dumb idea."

She nodded. "It does now. It's four in the morning and I'm tired. I'll tell you all about it and then you can put me to bed and let me sleep. You see, I met Lee this evening and we thought it would be fun to go places together. It was and we—well, we ended up here."

"If he was your husband, he wouldn't run out when we knocked."

"But I'm telling you—he did. Can't you understand? It might have ruined the divorce."

"You're talking in circles."

"No, I'm not. We simply didn't want anybody to know we were seeing each other. We have to be careful about things like that. I—"

Her head wavered and she struggled to stand up, as if it were a complicated process. When she'd made it, she grinned sheepishly, took two steps forward and flopped on her face.

Instantly, Jub dropped to his knees and examined her.

"What's the matter?" asked Mitch anxiously.

Jub looked up. "She's drunk," he said. "She passed out. That's all."

Mitch shrugged. "You can't get answers from a drunk. Come on—let's go."

"And leave her here, on the floor?"

"Sure—why not?" said Mitch. "I hate drunks." He shoved Lee Kent's picture in his pocket and went out.

As soon as the door had closed, Fern got up and went to the telephone.

V

The cop who took Jub up to the seventh floor of the building at 400 Broome Street said conversationally, "Busy night."

"I'm the one-armed paperhanger," said Jub. "I go out on a hit-and-run, and there's a homicide right around the corner. Insurance man, in one of those uptown residential hotels."

"How'd he get it?"

"Somebody smashed his skull."

The cop shrugged. "There are lots of ways of going. I guess that's as good as any."

He'd mouthed those words before, under many circumstances, and he'd mouth them again, until the day of his death. Then in his last hours the phrase would recur. Suddenly, dramatically, it would apply to him, and with all his fading energy he'd reject it.

At the seventh floor he opened the cage door and Jub stepped out, past the glass show cases that housed the exhibits of the police museum and on through the double glass doors that opened into the research laboratory.

"Hello," he called out. "Cal?"

The answering voice was slow, and heavy with sleep. "That you, Jub? What time is it?"

"Around four."

There was the creak of a chair as Callender got up and stepped into the light. He was an oldish man, almost bald, with a large pink skull. His face was channeled with broad, wide grooves, as if life had marked him simply, without complications but in depth.

"I found your note when I got back," he said. "Been on that hit-and-run all this time?"

"That and a couple of other things," answered Jub. "Had

quite a time, without you." Curiously, he found himself reluctant to talk about the homicide. He thought briefly of Andrea, dark and lovely, shadowy, with one frightened hand raised to her mouth.

Jub led the way into the main laboratory room. It was large and lined with long, green-topped work benches that were as bare as a butcher shop during the meat crisis.* A network of pipes and conduits scarred the walls and ceiling. Jub dropped his bag on a table and approached a machinist's vise in which a gun was clamped.

"Been working on that?" he asked.

Callender nodded. "Yeah. When you stayed out so long, I thought I'd have a try at it."

Jub bent down. The serial numbers had been filed off and the police wanted them in order to trace the gun. Callender had smeared etching fluid on the metal and the vague, shaky outline of a few digits was beginning to emerge. On a pad next to the vise Callender had scrawled a few trial figures. As the acid bit in, the impressions of the original stamping changed so that some of the figures grew clearer and others faded out. You had to watch every few minutes, and Jub and Callender had formed the habit of jotting down whatever they saw.

"Looks like it begins with four-two," said Jub, "but I'm not sure."

"Four-eight, I make it," said Callender.

---

* As a result of the liberation of various countries as the war was ending, demand for meat skyrocketed, and the US began shipping meat products abroad. This led to rationing at home; by December 31, 1944, beef, veal, lamb, mutton, and pork were rationed. Children under six could consume only three-quarters of a pound per week; those between six and twelve were limited to one and a half pounds per week; older children and adults were urged to eat only two and a half pounds per week. Liver, sweetbreads, brains, fish, and poultry were not subject to rationing, though all meats, chicken, and eggs became scarce in 1945.

"Could be," said Jub, squinting. "Get any of the others?"

"It ends in seven-three. You could see it a while back, but it's gone now. The middle part's tough."

Jub stepped away. "Suppose we leave it while I change my clothes. We got a job to do, Cal, and it looks big."

Callender shifted his glasses high up on his nose and straightened his shoulders. He'd been a cop most of his life and had been hurt in an accident a few years ago. Somebody had had the bright idea of assigning him to the laboratory instead of pensioning him off, which would have cost the city money.

It had been a happy choice. Callender, who was as thorough as he was slow and as careful as he was orthodox, had always devoted his spare time to photography. Now he not only could indulge his hobby, but he found out that he was a scientist at heart.

"Job?" he said, following Jub into the locker room. "Job? What do we do? Compare some headlights for a change?"

"That's the least of it," said Jub. "This time we got a homicide. A nice fresh one, hot off the griddle. You should have been along."

"Well," said Callender, rubbing his hands together. "Isn't that nice? Tell me about it, Jub."

While Jub changed into an old pair of pants and a laboratory gown, he recounted the facts briefly.

"I swiped a little evidence when no one was looking," he finished complacently. "I want to show these bastards what the laboratory can do. I want the two of us to solve a homicide complete, here in this room."

Callender snorted. "They wouldn't believe it. They'd find other reasons. They'd say the lab helped, but the real work was done in the old way."

"There ain't going to be any other work," said Jub.

"Then they'll say it's a fluke. And if you do it twice, they'll say it's two flukes." Callender, who knew the police mind as well as he knew his multiplication table, sighed and started cleaning his glasses. "What did you swipe?" he asked suddenly.

"Junk. Dirt and scrapings. And a cigar butt." He hitched up his belt and grinned at Callender. "Too bad you don't smoke."

"How'd the boys across the street let you get away with it?" said Callender, referring to the Homicide Squad housed in the Centre Street building. "What with the tobacco shortage,* they fight for every ounce."

"Oh, they didn't see me. I got most of the stuff before they arrived." He walked back to the table and opened his bag. "Here's the cigar," he said.

Callender sniffed. "That thing smells."

"Sure, but take a look at the tooth marks."

"All I can see is the smell."

Jub placed the butt on one of the work benches. "The maid cleaned Jarvis's room at three o'clock this afternoon," he said, "and Jarvis didn't smoke. Maybe the killer did. We'll get him by his tooth marks." Jub laughed and rubbed his hands together. "All the Homicide Squad has to do is get the bite of every suspect and then we tell 'em who killed Jarvis. How does that strike you?"

Callender picked up the cigar. "Call those things tooth marks?" he said. "You're crazy. The stuff is too soft to take a decent impression."

Jub smiled and his round, shiny cheeks dimpled. Callender, looking at him and then looking at the cigar, wondered what he'd missed.

"What you get," said Jub, "is the alignment of the teeth. The

---

* Tobacco on the home front was another casualty of the extended war in December 1944, as cigarettes were shipped to US armed forces abroad.

impressions aren't sharp, but they show the relationships. Notice that deep dent well forward of the chewed part? A crooked tooth did that. A tooth that slanted forward and punctured the cigar about a quarter inch from the main bite."

Callender studied the cigar. "What do you want?" he finally said. "A cast? We'll need a couple of other cigars to make trial impressions with. I think I know where I can find some."

He tramped into the next room, opened a desk drawer and uttered a grunt of satisfaction. He came back, biting a cigar and studying his own tooth marks.

"The stuff's pretty soft," he observed. "I'll shellac it first and then use plaster of Paris, huh?"

"Right. Then we can photograph it and have it ready for comparisons. That's the number-one fast one we're putting over, and then—say, I almost forgot. There was another murder."

Impassively, Callender pried open a can of shellac. He wasn't sure whether Jub was kidding and he wasn't going to commit himself either way.

"Sure," he said laconically. "Homicides always come in pairs. Otherwise we don't bother with 'em."

"At least," said Jub, "it might have been homicide. I stole the body and brought it back in the truck. It's still downstairs."

Callender picked up a brush and spread a light film of shellac over the marks on the cigar. "Call the morgue," he said. "It'll only smell up the truck."

"You call 'em, Cal. You have a friend over there and he can get us a post mortem on the body."

"What do you need me for?"

"This case is a little unusual," said Jub. "The victim was a Siamese cat. Name of Stanley."

Callender swung around sharply. "Cut the fooling," he said. "What the hell kind of a screwball reputation will you get kidding around with a cat? Our job is to protect citizens, and a cat is not a citizen."

"I'm not kidding, Cal. We need that autopsy."

"How does the cat fit in? You said the cat was up at this singer's place, but the homicide was in a hotel a half dozen blocks away. Where's the connection?"

"I don't know. That's what I want to find out. Taylor thinks there's a connection and he's liable to crack down on the girl. I'm just collecting all the facts I can." Jub had his envelopes sorted. "Come on, Cal," he urged. "We've got a hell of a lot to do."

Callender shrugged and shuffled to the outer room. Presently his slow, measured voice spoke into the phone.

"Hello, Nick?…This is Cal, over at the lab. I want you to do a favor for a friend of mine. It's kind of a joke, see? Only he's a big shot and we had a few beers and I promised I'd get it done. He's got a cat that died and he wants a P.M. on it….Holy Moses, Nick—I'm telling you! It's a favor I got to do. He thinks this cat was killed on purpose. Maybe poison—I don't know….Yeah…. Oh…You won't get in any trouble, Nick I'll tell you what I'll do. I'll send it over now, labeled like it was part of a real case."

The phone clicked. Over his shoulder Jub yelled, "It is."

Callender's deliberate tread echoed the length of the laboratory. "Is what?" he asked.

"Is labeled and is a real case. Cal, if you'd seen that girl—"

Callender fumbled with the lid of a jar. "Women," he said. "The root of all evil."

Jub picked up his specimens and went to the other end of the room. He had the fibers on the towel to examine. He had the dust he'd collected in filters in his vacuum cleaner. He had hairs from Fern's bureau and he had hairs from Jarvis's room. He had glass splinters and paint chips from the accident and he had the scrapings from Jarvis's head wound.

That was a lot of stuff. When the day shift came on at nine o'clock, he'd talk it over with the acting captain in charge of the laboratory. There was too much work for Jub alone. Much too much.

He put the towel aside. He'd *give* it a microscopic examination later on. Right now he wanted to see what foreign matter was present in the sample from Jarvis's wound. If any.

He walked over to the spectroscope. Two upright electrodes, resembling a pair of black lead pencils, were rigged point to point near the short arm of an L-shaped tunnel. In the tiny cup of the lower electrode you placed your sample. Then you turned on the current, which blazed in a brilliant white light between the two points. A system of prisms broke up the light rays from the sample and sent them down the ten-foot tunnel, where they were recorded automatically in a photographic negative. The negative showed a long band with hundreds of vertical lines. The width and spacing of the lines told you, after laborious comparisons with known substances, the exact components of the original sample.

Jub placed a few grains of his first specimen in the electrode, checked his instruments and his photographic plate and turned on the current. He averted his eyes from the glaring white light between the electrodes. Then he switched off the current and repeated the process, at intervals, with his other specimens. Paint chips taken from the point of impact of the two cars, paint chips scraped from Simon Treeberg's car. The sample from Jarvis's skull.

It was a tedious job. Working with the complete unknown taken from the wound, it might be days before he could identify what he was after—if it was there.

Jub wasn't sure precisely what to expect. He figured he'd do a routine comparison of the samples taken from the accident. For the rest, he had a vague, wishful hope that the instrument with which Jarvis had been killed might have left some tiny deposit by which it could be identified.

He didn't know what sort of deposit he would find or how it would show up. Rust flakes, if the instrument had been rusty. Some foreign substance which might prove a clue to the weapon. Soft metal, even, which had chipped or rubbed off in minute quantities where it had struck bone.

Jub didn't know. He was playing a hunch that might lead nowhere and might bring rich results. He held himself in check. All he could do now was accumulate his facts. Spectrographs, meaningless to a layman, fascinated Jub.

He had always been drawn to the scientific, and as early as he could remember, he had sneaked out to perform rudimentary experiments on a tenement fire escape. He had been brought up by a streetcar conductor and an invalid mother. His father had counted nickels in his sleep and his mother worried over her aches and treated Jub as an errand boy whom God had brought forth from her loins for the express purpose of carrying packages from the corner grocery.

A tenement fire had made Jub an orphan at the age of twelve, and his Aunt Ella had come to New York to take charge of him. But instead of bringing him back to her upstate town, she had fallen in love with the city and stayed. For Jub, it was the beginning of life.

He had had ambitions of becoming a scientist, and Aunt Ella had planned to give him the best of educations. But her long illness had put an end to that. Jub, obsessed with the need of a steady salary to take care of his aunt, had looked around for a steady job with civil service status. Clerk's work he abhorred. Somebody mentioned the police department and it struck Jub that it would be as good as anything else, and less boring.

He spent his last dollars on a course in the institute and was amongst the fifty thousand who took the exam. He passed high. After three years of pounding a beat, he had asked for a transfer to the laboratory under special order 57.* The appointment, while retaining the civil service rank of patrolman, meant a designation as detective.

There happened to be a vacancy, and a lieutenant who didn't particularly like him mentioned his name to a politician who didn't want to do anybody a favor, but who was anxious to block the appointment of someone else. Jub was the pawn by which the maneuver was accomplished. He found a life's career in police science and he applied himself to it with enthusiasm. Outside of the occasional necessity of riot duty, holding back crowds at a parade and watching the polls on election day, he looked forward to a quiet life in a well-equipped laboratory. He did research in his spare time and performed routine projects for the rest. The combination satisfied him, and there were few men happier than Jub.

He worked steadily, not quickly, but with little waste motion. He forgot to be tired. The clock in the far room ticked on. Light poured in through the big windows. Callender had finished his cast and taken pictures of it. He returned from the dark room to find Jub poring over his negatives on the glass viewer. Callender bent forward and peered at them.

"Working on the paint chips, huh?" said Callender. "I thought they didn't get the hit-and-run car."

"They didn't," said Jub.

His mind didn't follow the remark. Ordinarily he might make a spectroscopic comparison of paint from a suspected car with paint chips deposited at the time of the accident. But the

---

*What special order 57 provided is unknown at this date.

procedure could be used only for comparison purposes, when you had the car you thought was responsible for the collision.

"If they didn't get the hit-and-run car," continued Callender, "what are you trying to match up?"

"I'm not," replied Jub, still engrossed in his problem of identification.

"But they do match," said Callender. His thick, stubby finger pointed out a series of lines on one of the spectrographs and then pushed another spectrograph below it and indicated a similar group of lines.

"Huh?" said Jub. He glanced up and looked at Callender's strained, rheumy eyes. "Huh?" said Jub.

"Those two things—they match."

"They can't," said Jub slowly. "You know what they are? One is a paint chip from the accident. The other is a specimen scraping from Jarvis's wound."

Callender grunted. "Then it looks as if Jarvis was hit by that car."

"And taken up to his room? Bunk!"

"What then?"

"I don't know," said Jub uncertainly, "but it looks as if we've got something. If I knew what all those lines meant, what substances they indicate, there'd be some sense to it. But this way— you know what we've done? We've hooked up the homicide and the hit-and-run!"

"An accident—a woman with a cat—a homicide. They can't all be part of the same thing."

"Why not?" snapped Jub. "Why can't they be?"

"Simply because of a spectrograph?"

"Best evidence I can think of," said Jub.

"Tell that to the next police captain you see," said Callender sourly. "Show him the lines and tell him that makes a hit-and-run part of a murder six blocks away. You'll be relieved of duty and transferred to a hospital. Psychopathic ward,* at city expense."

"I guess so," said Jub. He knew Callender was right. He knew, too, that he was on thin ice. Suppose those lines indicated ordinary rust. A rusty fender and a rusty piece of pipe. Was that his entire connection? No. The comparison was too complete.

He stood up wearily. Callender trudged away on big, flat feet. "I sent down for some coffee, Jub. I'll bring it over."

He poured it into a couple of tin cups and Jub took short, quick sips while he set up a microscope. Then, with a forceps, Jub removed the dark fibers he had seen on the bathroom towel. He placed them under his microscope and studied them intently. Presently, with infinite care, he mounted the fibers in the microtone† and cut cross sections. He placed them under his microscope. What he saw resembled assorted slices of salami and sausage.

After a long time he stood up and yawned. It was almost nine o'clock. The day shift would be here any minute. He'd be free until nine tomorrow morning, when he'd have to report on his regular day shift.

"Take a look, Cal," he said, "and see what you think."

Callender sat down fussily and peered into the microscope.

"Tan threads," he announced finally. "Dye hasn't penetrated so good. They're mostly wool, with one rayon. But whether they came from a suit and how they got there and when—who knows? The trouble with you, Jub, is that you expect too much."

Jub laughed. He heard the door open and a couple of patrolmen marched in boisterously. They were full of the latest news.

---

* In more modern parlance, the "psychiatric ward" (of a general hospital).

† The microtome (note the misspelling here) is a precision cutting instrument used to produce cross-sections of tissue. The inventor is likely John Hill, M.D., who appears to have used it to further his microscopic studies of wood, first published in 1774.

They'd picked it up at the desk downstairs, which in turn had it from the Homicide Bureau across the street.

"Hey," they called out. "You guys better go home and get to bed. And don't let anybody see you sneak out; I hear you got in on the Jarvis case."

"Ground floor," said Jub. "We're working at it now."

"Well, put it away and forget about it. Some precinct guy cracked the case. Put one over on the whole Homicide Squad."

"Taylor?" asked Jub. "Was it Taylor?"

"Yeah, that's the boy. He got some kind of a tip and they arrested a girl. Radio singer by the name of Minx. They're still questioning her."

Jub blinked once and walked stiffly into the locker room. Arrested? Had she been charged, too? He didn't believe it. They didn't have the evidence and they wouldn't charge her until they had it. They weren't that dumb.

But they were. They were even worse than that, for they were disagreeing with a spectroscope.

TWO

I

Early the following afternoon Mitch Taylor put down his second cup of coffee and wiped his mouth. He felt good, here at home. He'd slept like a log and waked feeling fresh, despite being up all night on a homicide case.

He took things like that for granted. When he was hungry, he ate; when he was tired, he slept. There were words like insomnia and indigestion, of course, but he'd never considered them in relation to himself.

Amy was chattering about a coat she'd seen and he said "Sure—sure," without listening. Anything Amy wanted, she could have. He watched the play of her lips and the exuberance of her clear, pointed face. He tried to find a word to describe her, but he didn't have that kind of a knack and after a moment or two he gave up. She was just Amy. She was just a feeling he had and an image in his mind.

While she went on about the coat, he looked around the kitchen. It was clean and neat and had blue-and-tan wallpaper. Her friends had told her she was crazy, putting wallpaper in here. A kitchen got painted, they'd said. But Amy had laughed at them and gone ahead, and now everybody admitted she'd been right.

Well, that was Amy. He hoped the kid would be like her, kind of wild and different. Six months yet. Six months to wait. He wondered whether she was scared.

She finished about the coat and said suddenly, "There's something I wanted to tell you, Mitch, only I forgot."

He smiled at her. She was a funny kid. She'd probably wake him up in the middle of the night to tell him she remembered what it was—that the handle had come off her meat chopper and could he fix it.

He wouldn't mind. That was part of Amy, being a little screwy. But when there was real work to do, boy, could she knuckle down to it!

He shoved back his chair. "You'll remember," he said. "Next time you're in the bathtub, you'll remember and you'll jump up and drip water all over the place."

She laughed at him. Then, as he got up, strapped on his gun and put on his coat, she said anxiously, "Mitch, you're not going to Hogan's, are you?"

"Me?" he said. "Hell, no. I got work to do."

Her blue eyes clouded. "But—you're not due to report till tomorrow morning."

"This is something special," he said. "They got a big case and nobody can handle it except papa." He held her close to him and smiled. "So long, honey. And take care of yourself."

"I thought *you* were going to do that today. I thought you'd stay home and that we'd go to the early show. There's a good movie."

"Sorry," he said, putting on his hat. "Maybe tomorrow, huh?"

"Mitch!"

He swung around and went up to her. "What is it?"

"Nothing. Kiss me, Mitch." He leaned forward and kissed her. She whispered in his ear. "Mitch—I think I felt it kick!"

He laughed. Her eyes were dancing. He had a swell wife and he was on the way up. He'd been on his toes and had brought in Andrea Minx for questioning. It wouldn't matter whether she was guilty or not. He wasn't supposed to crack a homicide single-handed, the way cops did in the magazines he occasionally read. It was enough that he had brought in a lead.

Even the sour-faced lieutenant had given Mitch his approval. "Go on home and get some sleep," the lieutenant had said, "and report back after you get some rest. You're going to stick with this case."

Mitch knew what that meant. It would be on his record. For the rest of his life, he'd be the guy who broke the Jarvis case, and did it the same night it happened.

He took the subway. On the whole, things looked pretty good. Andrea had been released, of course, but that didn't mean anything. She'd be there any time they wanted her, and they'd want her just as soon as the rest of the evidence was collected.

He thought back to the scene when she'd been questioned. A bare room with a table and some wooden chairs. A couple of homicide men watching, but letting Mitch do the work. Andrea looking like a scared kid who'd melt away if anybody touched her. She'd just fade away, like in the movies, and he'd be talking at a blank wall.

But he hadn't wasted himself feeling sorry for her. He'd had a job to do and she was merely the first hurdle. He'd tackled her the way he went for the first glass of cold beer at Hogan's.

Had she been having an affair with Jarvis? She'd blazed back at him. Of course not. Well, they'd been intimate, hadn't they? They'd been good friends, yes. Going to get married? Certainly not! Jarvis didn't want to marry her? Oh, that was different. She thought maybe Jarvis wanted to, then? He'd hinted at it, though she hadn't wanted him to propose. Had they scrapped over anything? No. No quarrels, no disagreements? Well, naturally they didn't agree about everything. What did they disagree about?

Andrea wouldn't answer that question. Mitch had pounded away at her and she'd admitted, vaguely, that Jarvis's family had something to do with it. Mitch had put on the pressure and finally gotten something damaging out of her. There were people who didn't want him to marry her. She'd been afraid— she wouldn't say why. But she'd been afraid something would happen.

"Who?" Mitch had slapped the word at her and she'd quivered and turned her head away. He'd stared at her clear profile and noticed the pulse beating in her throat. She was scared all right and he had her in a corner.

Suddenly, as she'd turned away, he'd remembered something from way back. Once when he was a kid, his father had taken him hunting up in the Adirondacks and they'd killed a deer. There were a couple of other men in the party and they were standing there next to the dead animal. It was tan, with a soft, fuzzy coat and with soft brown eyes that were almost human. Its long, graceful neck was stretched out on the snow and Mitch had felt funny about it. So many of them, and just that one deer. He'd even asked himself for a moment how he'd have liked to be the deer. Then, looking at his father and at the others in the group, he'd felt ashamed of himself. He oughtn't to feel that way about a deer. And so, to show himself he wasn't really soft, he'd walked up to the buck and kicked it, and then spat. They'd all laughed at him and he'd felt more ashamed than ever.

The scene came back to him forcibly. The group standing over the dead buck. The group surrounding Andrea Minx. He kept staring at the rapid, regular pulse beat, hammering in her throat. He had to tell himself that this was a homicide case, that she was right in the center of it and he had to crack her.

Then, after her long hesitation, Andrea had turned around and answered his question.

"I don't know," she'd said. "I don't know what I was afraid might happen and I certainly can't think of anyone who would harm him."

With that, Mitch had gone off on another tack.

"Where were you last night?"

"I had dinner with a friend of mine. Rose Ollenbach. She's a very old friend and she's about to go to Europe, for UNRRA.* And that's peculiar."

"What is?"

"Usually I stay home and sleep, from about six in the evening until midnight. I like to rest before the broadcast. I hardly ever go out in the evening. It just so happened, last night, that I did."

"Where did you have dinner?"

"At the El Paradiso."

"Just the two of you?"

"Yes. We left there around nine."

"I thought you claimed you didn't get home until ten-thirty."

"I didn't. We walked up Fifth Avenue. We had so much to talk about. Then I said I wanted to take a bus, and we stood in front of St. Patrick's and waited. Only we got talking again. It was around quarter after ten—maybe even later—when I finally left her."

---

* According to the Holocaust Encyclopedia (sponsored by the US Holocaust Memorial Museum), the United Nations Relief and Rehabilitation Administration (UNRRA) was created at a forty-four-nation conference at the White House on November 9, 1943. Its mission was to provide economic assistance to European nations after World War II and to repatriate and assist refugees coming under Allied control. The US government funded close to half of UNRRA's budget. The UNRRA oversaw numerous volunteer agencies.

"You went straight home?"

"Yes. I went upstairs and got my key from the broom closet and—"

Mitch had interrupted. "Broom closet? Why there?"

"Oh, I always leave it there. I used to lose keys and finally I made up my mind never to carry one. I hide them in the broom closet, outside my door. All my friends joke about it."

"They know you keep it there?"

"Yes. Why?"

"Go ahead," said Mitch. "So you got home."

"I told you about that last night. I opened the door and had the queerest feeling. I'm still frightened when I think of it. I don't know why." She'd put her hand to her throat, where the pulse was throbbing.

"Yes?" prompted Mitch.

She'd glanced around the room as if she were looking for somebody and couldn't find him. She kept doing that. She'd look up hopefully and then she'd swallow and start talking again, sort of scared, taking quick breaths, watching the bunch in the room as if she were giving a performance and had to hold her audience.

She'd held them, all right.

"So you opened the door," Mitch had said. "Go ahead."

"Yes. Stanley wasn't there and I immediately looked in the bathroom. When I opened the door, you have no idea how queer and chilly it seemed. Stanley was there, next to a carton. I told you how I picked him up and ran to the lamp, next to the window. When I realized Stanley was dead, I screamed."

"What was the carton doing in the bathroom?"

"I don't know. I didn't think of it at the time. It was pushed back, underneath the tub, and the top was clawed as if Stanley had been playing with it. He had a mania for ripping paper to shreds. But I don't know how the carton even got there."

"Was it the empty one that I saw in the middle of your room?" Mitch had said suddenly.

"The carton? I didn't notice, really. I was upset. I burnt my finger and I can't even remember how I did it."

Mitch had looked at the other detectives and stepped back. There wasn't much more he could do.

But he'd brought out enough. The hint of an affair with Jarvis. The impression that Andrea was holding out. The alibi that depended for confirmation on somebody who was on her way to Europe. It would be at least a week before they could get a deposition from the Ollenbach woman. Suppose she corroborated the alibi?

Suppose she didn't.

Mitch left the subway and walked over to the precinct. Fern Kent, who drank like a fish and didn't give a damn whether her father was dead or alive. Andrea Minx, who reminded Mitch of a deer and who looked as if she'd never harmed anybody in her life. How could you tell?

He marched into the precinct house and the lieutenant said there was a bunch of stuff for him upstairs, and to look it over and then come down. The boys in the detective room kidded him about walking into a homicide, but they were good-natured and Mitch could tell they were envious. He sat down at a desk. His jacket pinched and he rolled his shoulders, trying to ease the tightness.

He read slowly. The hit-and-run reports were there, but they didn't tell him anything new. Then he leaned forward and studied out the stuff on the Jarvis case. They were the follow-up reports, the D.D.5's on blue paper.* The original report was on white.

---

* Complaint follow-up forms are still in use by the NYPD and still referred to as "D. D. 5" forms. They are now color-coded—pink forms make no change to the classification of the charges, while blue forms can upgrade (or downgrade) the charges.

The boys had been busy. They'd interviewed Christie Mae and Lee Kent, who turned out to be Christie Mae's son.

Mitch stopped there and let it percolate. Peter Jarvis running around with Christie Mae, who is his dead wife's sister. And Christie Mae's son married to Peter Jarvis's daughter. It was too damn private. Didn't they ever go outside the family?

Mitch picked up another D.D.S. Jarvis's business associates, a few clients, a former partner. The cleaning woman at the hotel, the manager, a half dozen other people who might have some information. But none of them did. Mitch made a mental note to see Peyser, the hotel manager, and really put on the pressure. There was something about him.

The waiter at El Paradiso remembered Andrea and her friend. They'd dawdled over their coffee and he'd had to bring them their check to let them know it was time to go. They'd left around nine, so that much was okay.

The employees at the Hotel Quaker remembered Andrea. Anybody would. With a face like that, with her clear, singer's voice—sure, they'd seen her with Jarvis. But not yesterday. And that, reflected Mitch, was too damn bad. Maybe he could refresh their memories.

The complete file from the Medical Examiner's Office* was there, including the autopsy. Mitch took a long time to read it and didn't understand half of it. Charlie Corrigan used to say that the medical report told you whether the corpse was dead or alive, and Mitch figured that was about the size of it. Jarvis had been killed around ten or a little later. Mitch digested that. You

---

* The NYC Office of the Chief Medical Examiner (OCME) was founded in 1918 and serves to investigate deaths of all kinds, not just those related to crimes. New York's OCME was a pioneer in establishing serology and toxicology laboratories. It also examines evidence, a function then still part of the NYPD itself (as is evident from Jub Freeman's occupation).

could give it an hour's leeway. That meant Jarvis had been killed between nine and eleven. He'd been hit by a blunt instrument and Mitch couldn't understand the rest of it. Except that Jarvis was dead.

There was a second medical report. Mitch went halfway through it before deciding it wasn't his case at all. Then he happened to look at the top and saw it concerned an autopsy on a cat. Freeman's work, of course. Mitch still wasn't sure whether Freeman had a sense of humor or was a screwball. To play it safe, Mitch read the report again. It seemed that Stanley had not been shot, stabbed or poisoned. He'd been asphyxiated in a manner unknown, but there was no evidence of carbon monoxide and no marks to indicate manual strangulation.

Mitch went downstairs.

The lieutenant tapped a couple of typewritten forms. "I kept these down here, Taylor."

"Let's see," said Mitch.

The lieutenant handed him the papers. They were laboratory reports dealing with the spectrographs and the plaster cast of a cigar. Pictures of the cast had been compared with pictures of a dental impression of the corpse. The conclusion was that the corpse had not smoked the cigar.

"I don't say the laboratory hasn't got its place," said the lieutenant. "But this cigar business—I know damn well you can't tell who smoked a cigar just by looking at it. Now if it was gum, or something else that held a good impression—that would be different. But this—" He shook his head.

"Sure," said Mitch. "Anybody knows a cigar won't hold impressions good."

He coughed. He suspected that, if Jub Freeman took casts of a cigar, they meant something. If anybody was wrong, it was the lieutenant. Mitch had long ago decided that softening of the brain was an occupational disease that started when you got to be a lieutenant. There were exceptions, of course, but this guy wasn't one of them.

"They say you did all right last night," continued the lieutenant, "so let's forget this cigar business. It won't work out."

"That's right, Lieutenant," said Mitch.

"Now about this cat. I got two of my own. They're for the kids, of course, and it was the wife that got to calling them Butch and Mamie. But Butch isn't feeling so good these days. If there's going to be an epidemic of killing cats, I want it cracked down on right at the beginning. So I been thinking maybe you ought to go ahead on this cat angle."

The phone rang and the lieutenant reached for it. "Here's that cigar report." He picked up the phone and mumbled into it. "Lieutenant Tauner—"

Mitch parked the papers upstairs and then went out. It struck him that Freeman had had a pretty good idea. If you could find out who smoked that cigar, you might have something.

Except that the Minx didn't smoke cigars, and she was the one who'd done it. So Freeman was cockeyed, at that.

An hour or so later, Mitch left the office of the Captain of Detectives, Homicide Bureau. He'd checked over most of the evidence from the Medical Examiner's Office and then found that Homicide agreed with him. It looked like Andrea, but they'd have to wait for the deposition from Europe. Rose Ollenbach had sailed. In a week or so, after she'd landed, UNRRA would let the police department know how to reach her. Meantime she was a military secret.

Mitch saw the 400 Broome Street building directly across the street. He hadn't been in there since he'd attended police college, in the old days. Because of the war the college was no longer in existence. He decided to drop in, however, and see what the laboratory looked like. Freeman wouldn't be on duty today, but Mitch might be able to pick up a little extra information.

The acting captain in charge of the laboratory was sitting at a desk behind a brass railing. He said that Freeman was in. He was doing some work on the Jarvis case. He'd picked up a few clues last night and was trying to run them down. That was smart work about the cigar, added the acting captain. Just what he would have done if he'd been there himself. Freeman had gone over to the morgue the first thing this morning and established the fact that Jarvis had not smoked the cigar.

Mitch, who rarely entered into unnecessary arguments, agreed with the acting captain and wondered privately if a girl like Andrea had taken up cigar-smoking. Could be, because of the shortage. He wondered how he could find out what kind of impression her teeth made.

Science, reflected Mitch, brought up strange problems. You could get a fingerprint easily enough, but how the hell could you wangle a set of tooth marks? You couldn't ram your fist into a girl's mouth and tell her to chew. And even if you did, you'd get—or make—the wrong impression.

Jub came out in his laboratory gown and sat down with Mitch.

"I'm glad you came, Taylor, because there's a lot of stuff I couldn't put down in the report."

"Such as what?"

Jub lowered his voice. "I'm sticking my neck out, Taylor, and what I say is going to sound screwy. I can't even figure it out myself, but I'm pretty sure that the homicide and the hit-and-run are connected up."

"How do you dope that out?"

"By the spectroscope. I analyzed samples of paint from the accident and then I analyzed a scraping from the head wound.

The one should tell us something about the fender of the hit-and-run car, and the other something about the murder weapon. The surprise is that they both show evidence of the same substance."

"And that hooks them up?" asked Mitch.

"It certainly proves that the fender and the weapon have something in common."

"And what would that be?"

"I don't know."

"That's a hot one," said Mitch.

"Well, the spectroscope merely shows the metallic elements present in any particular specimen, and we haven't yet strung those elements together. However, we did get something else."

"What?"

"A substance with an asphalt base. We just identified it a little while ago from its physical properties, such as color, odor, density and solubility in certain solvents. So—we know we have something with an asphalt base, like road tar, but containing a lot of impurities in the form of tiny flakes. They look like small chips of paint and they're imbedded in this black asphalt substance. Trace elements are also present so that the substance is identified conclusively. But the funny thing is finding that same tar-like stuff and the same trace elements in all the specimens we have, regardless of whether they come from the homicide or the hit-and-run."

"Look," said Mitch. "You're a little over my head. All I want is to have you dig up something on Andrea."

Jub looked annoyed. "Give me something to analyze, and I'll analyze it for you. It's your case, Taylor."

"Yeah," said Mitch. Freeman had him on that, and Mitch went on in his thin, high-pitched voice, "That isn't what I mean. What I want is, whatever you analyze, check it with Andrea. Now the cigar, for instance—how do we know she didn't smoke it?"

"Sure," said Jub. "Just send me a cast of her teeth."

He was laughing at Mitch. Mitch knew that. He remembered the queer looks that Jub and Andrea had exchanged last night. He remembered how Andrea had kept looking for somebody. He decided to lay off Andrea.

"I can tell you this much," continued Jub. "Whoever smoked that cigar had one tooth out of line, on the right side of his mouth."

"I'll look for that," said Mitch. He stared across the room where somebody was trying to piece together the shattered fragments of a headlight. Seeing it slowly take shape, he had a sudden and complete confidence in everything the laboratory did.

"How about that fingerprint?" he asked. "The one on the insurance form?"

"Jarvis's," said Jub. "You called it last night."

"Any of Andrea's prints in the Jarvis apartment?"

"No. None of her prints and not even a hair from her head. The maid cleaned there last Wednesday. That means Andrea probably hasn't been in the place since then."

"How about all those other hairs you took?"

"A couple belong to Fern. They check with the ones I found on her bureau. The rest I haven't identified, except that nobody besides Fern was in both places. I'll keep you informed on whatever we find here. The big thing so far is what I told you at first— the possibility of the homicide and the hit-and-run hooking up."

Mitch started to object. Freeman said smoothly, as if he'd just thought of it, "They're both your cases."

Mitch stood up. If Freeman could make one case out of two, Mitch wouldn't give a damn who turned out to be guilty. He was willing to give up his Andrea theory in a minute, if that got him anywhere on the hit-and-run.

Freeman knew it, too. He and Freeman understood each

other pretty good. He wondered whether Freeman liked lieutenants.

II

The Lee Kent Gallery was a few steps off Fifth Avenue in the Fifties. Mitch had been in an art gallery once before, when Amy had decided she wanted an etching, but the place Amy had taken him to didn't have the swank of this one. This one had a big plate glass window with nothing in it except a very small painting, which Mitch didn't look at. He opened the door and walked in.

A dame wearing a neat blue suit smiled at him. "There's a catalogue on the table," she said pleasantly. "Just help yourself."

When she smiled, she reminded him of Amy, except that this dame was dark and Amy was blonde. Still, Mitch liked her for the resemblance and wanted to talk to her.

"Thanks," he said, in his tenor voice. He stood there, robust and chesty, and looked at the bad dreams hanging on the walls of the gallery. None of this stuff would ever make the Metropolitan, and instinctively he knew why. It didn't do things to you. Now take that madonna that Andrea Minx looked like— you saw it and it got you, and a year later you thought of it and got the same feeling. But this—it was wallpaper. Just wallpaper.

"Do people buy this stuff?" he asked suddenly.

She laughed at him. "If they didn't, we wouldn't be able to stay in business, would we?"

"Well, I guess there are all kinds," he answered. He stared at her instead of the pictures. She tried to look busy, writing something at her desk, but after a few seconds she got flustered.

"Really," she said. "Did you want anything in particular?"

"I'd like to see Mr. Kent."

Immediately she became businesslike. "Whom shall I tell him?" she asked.

"Detective Taylor."

"Oh," she said. She froze up and swept past him to the back of the gallery.

Mitch heaved a deep sigh and gazed at the pictures. He saw a man with three faces and a face with three men in it. It depressed him, thinking people wasted their time on this stuff. And in the middle of a war, too. He smacked his belly just for the feel of it. After that, the pictures didn't bother him so much.

Then the girl who reminded him of Amy came back.

"He'll see you now," she said, with the expression Amy usually had when she thought he was going out to Hogan's.

Mitch nodded and walked in.

He'd seen offices like this in the movies, but this was the first one he'd ever stepped into. There were cork panels on the walls, and the furniture was modernistic. The ceilings had paintings that were all angles and arrows and bright, circus colors. The place had plenty of front. Mitch wondered how much backing there was.

Lee Kent was sitting behind a big desk. He was tall and thin and starved-looking and he held himself stiff. His head was big, as if there were plenty of brains in it, but Mitch could have picked him up with one hand and shoved him clear across the room.

"Sit down," said Kent. "The police were here this morning. I didn't expect another visit."

"That was just routine," said Mitch quietly. "I'm the guy you socked."

Kent frowned and licked his lips. Then he pushed a small, carved cigarette box across the desk. "I've been worrying about that," he said. "Although I believe Fern explained. No hard feelings, I hope."

Mitch rubbed his jaw. "You don't look as if you packed much of a wallop," he said. "It must have been the way I backed into that light fixture."

"I'm sorry," said Kent awkwardly.

Mitch studied him. "You look as if you had a hell of a hangover," he remarked. "Tell me about it."

Kent spoke coldly. "There isn't much to tell. There was a little liquor and a lot of Fern. You know the ending."

"How'd it start?"

"Exactly what do you want to know?"

"Where you were all night," said Mitch. He didn't like the guy and he intended to make it tough. "Where you were every minute up until we smacked each other in the hall."

"That's not easy," said Kent. "I ran into Fern at Penn station. I was seeing somebody off on a six-fifty-three train, and she was on her way home. We started walking uptown and stopped at the first bar. I can't even tell you the name. Then—there were two drinks at the Astor Bar* and a couple more at Jack Dempsey's.† After that—" he shrugged. "Just an alcoholic daze. I never could drink like Fern."

"Is the divorce still on?"

"Certainly. We're not conventional people, you know."

---

* The Astor Bar was the watering hole at the popular Hotel Astor, on Times Square. Built in 1905, it was razed in 1967. According to historian William R. Taylor, "the Astor maintained its public reputation as an eminently respectable Times Square rendezvous, while its reputation as a gay rendezvous and pickup bar assumed legendary proportions" (*Inventing Times Square: Commerce and Culture at the Crossroads of the World* [Baltimore: Johns Hopkins University Press, 1996], xxiv).

† Jack Dempsey's Restaurant opened in 1935 on Eighth Avenue and Fiftieth Street, directly across from the third location of Madison Square Garden. In 1947, it moved to the Brill Building on Broadway, between Forty-ninth and Fiftieth Streets and changed its name to "Jack Dempsey's Broadway Restaurant," though everyone always referred to it as "Jack Dempsey's." It closed in 1974. Dempsey, a boxing champion of the 1920s, was a regular presence at the restaurant. He died in 1983, at the age of eighty-seven.

"You're people," said Mitch flatly. "And people that are going to get divorced don't go out on a bender together."

"Maybe I can explain. You see, Fern and I were brought up together. We're cousins. We were always together and we had a lot of good times and it was inevitable that I took her places. It seemed perfectly natural to us that we should get married. But somehow, after we were, we discovered it was not the great love affair we'd hoped it would be. We quarreled over unimportant things. You've seen Fern. She's positive, almost masculine in many ways, and not easy to get along with. The time came when we sat down and told each other we'd be better off going our separate ways. There was no hate. We'd been friends once and we could be friends again. Can you understand that?"

"Go ahead," said Mitch.

"That's all. I'm trying to explain our background, because the whole idea of what happened seems to bother you."

"What bothers me," said Mitch, "is who killed Peter Jarvis. You can have the rest of it."

"Then I don't have to go on?"

"You got as far as the drinks. Dempsey's, the Astor. Who'd you see and what did you talk about?"

"We didn't see anybody. I suggested a drink for old times' sake. We had a few, we grew sentimental and promised each other we'd always be friendly and harbor no ill will. We pledged that we'd go through with the divorce and then I took her home." Kent licked his dry, thin lips. "I stayed."

"Why did you run out when the police knocked?"

"Because I was scared. Anyone would be scared if the police knocked on his door at four in the morning. I didn't know what you wanted or why. I simply thought of how ridiculous the whole situation was. It seemed like a good idea to leave, and I did. In the hall, someone attacked me and I struck back. Then

I went out the fire escape and took a taxi home. This morning I heard Jarvis had been killed. If I'd known it was anything like that, naturally I'd have stayed and faced it."

"Sure," said Mitch. "You ran out on her last night. A little thing like letting her face the cops alone—that was all right, huh? Just so it wasn't homicide."

"I told you why I left."

Mitch coughed and rolled his shoulders to take the tightness out of his jacket. Then, in his high, squeaky voice, he went on with his questioning.

"How did you get along with Jarvis?"

"Not too well, but then no one did. Although we had no open break, I'd be a liar if I claimed I was fond of him."

"Do you know Andrea Minx?"

"Yes. She's a friend of both Fern's and mine."

"What about her and Jarvis?"

"Jarvis was attentive to her. They met last summer at my place in Connecticut. Fern and I were together then and both Andrea and Jarvis were up for an occasional weekend. Jarvis seemed to be quite smitten."

"And she?"

"I don't know. Andrea's a peculiar person."

"What do you mean by that?"

"Nothing. This is a serious matter and unfounded accusations would be out of place."

"You've got one?"

"No," said Kent. "And furthermore, I'm late for an appointment. Is there anything else?"

"Yes," said Mitch, more to be annoying than for any real interest. "With whom is the appointment?"

Kent hesitated before he spoke. "Andrea Minx," he said.

"Fine," remarked Mitch, getting up. "You can take me there."

In the cab they maintained a hostile silence. Mitch, staring at Kent's small, obstinate features, built up a case against Kent and knocked it down.

Kent had no motive that had come out, yet. He disliked Jarvis, but so did a lot of people. Practically the only thing against him was the way he'd scrammed when the police came. And even though Kent had explained why, the explanation sounded weak.

But there was too much in his favor. First of all, he had an alibi. He'd been with Fern all evening. With a divorce coming up, it wasn't likely that they'd collaborate on a homicide. In the second place Mitch had the evidence which Jub had turned up. Jub had hairs from Fern's bureau, Kent's hairs, and they didn't match any of the hairs found at the scene of the crime. And finally, Jub had said the cigar smoker had a crooked front tooth.

Mitch grimaced. How did you find out whether a guy's teeth were straight? The only way Mitch could think of was to ask for a look.

He turned to Kent and said, "Let's see your teeth."

Kent grunted at the unexpected question. "Huh?" he said.

"Your teeth," repeated Mitch.

Kent got sarcastic. "I'm sorry," he said, "but if you want me to hand them to you, I can't. They're not that kind."

"Cut the wisecracks," said Mitch. "We got a line on somebody with a crooked tooth, so let's look at yours."

"I'd suggest a visit to the manager of the Quaker. He has a very nice buck tooth that might answer your requirements. Personally, I have exceptionally straight teeth. See?"

He spread his lips and Mitch peered. The teeth looked all right, but Mitch was no dental expert.

"Who's your dentist?" he asked.

"Why do you want to know? To ask him whether my teeth are crooked?"

"Just tell me who he is, and let me do the worrying."

Kent wrote a name and address on a slip of paper. "He charges five dollars," he remarked, handing Mitch the notation.

"Thanks, but it won't cost me a cent."

"That's too bad," murmured Kent.

At Andrea's, Mitch watched contentedly while Kent paid the taxi fare and overtipped. They went up the stairs together and rang Andrea's bell. There was a long wait. The two men exchanged glances. Then the buzzer sounded and they walked in.

"You go on up," said Mitch, "I just remembered some work I got to do."

As soon as Kent had started up in the tiny elevator, Mitch went to the rear of the corridor. A big guy rose from the shadows and said, "Hello, Mitch."

"Hello, Charlie. She been out?"

Patrolman Charlie O'Connor shook his head. "About an hour ago she went down to the corner and bought a bottle of milk. That's all. She's probably been catching up on sleep. I guess she needs it."

"Yeah," said Mitch. "Well, stick around. I'm going down to speak to the janitor."

O'Connor watched Mitch Taylor feel his way down the darkened stairs to the basement. Taylor had put the finger on the Minx woman and he was riding high. Well, let him. O'Connor had a nice soft job: sitting in a corridor and waiting for Andrea Minx to go some place.

She wouldn't, of course. If she'd knocked off Jarvis, she'd be careful. She'd go down to the studio and come straight home when she was through. O'Connor wondered whether he could get into the place and see the broadcast.

He tilted his chair against the wall, leaned back and began re-reading the morning paper. There was only one trouble with a job like this. They figured you were on it every single minute, without a break. When was a guy supposed to eat? Or to go to the bathroom, huh?

Downstairs the small sullen man answered Mitch's knock and said, "Oh, it's you again."

Mitch squeezed into the doorway and took Lee Kent's picture from his pocket. It was the one Mitch had appropriated at Fern's, after she'd passed out.

"This guy you said called on the Minx last night," said Mitch. "Is this him?"

The sullen little janitor studied the photograph. "No," he said. "I told you—it was a big guy. Big all around."

Mitch pocketed the picture. "There was an empty carton in her room last night. Who brought it?"

"How would I know?"

Mitch didn't sound off. He wanted information. He might want more information tomorrow. So he had to take it from a snotty little guy, like this one.

"Did she get any packages yesterday?" asked Mitch imperturbably.

"Not that I saw."

"The carton still up there?"

"No. I threw it out this morning."

"Let's see it."

"I threw it out. On the sidewalk. You better consult with the garbage department."

"Thanks," said Mitch. "You'll do just as well." He turned around and marched out. He'd see what there was at the precinct, and then he'd go on home. He'd still have time to take Amy to that movie. Unless he stopped in at Hogan's. But he could skip that.

At the precinct, the lieutenant was about to knock off for the day. He called over to Mitch. "I want to see you before you leave. I'll be in the captain's office."

"Sure," said Mitch. This was going to be more about cats. He made a face and looked over the latest bulletins.

There was nothing about the hit-and-run car. Apparently it had disappeared into thin air. Maybe it was in a private garage somewhere, waiting for the police and repair men to forget there'd ever been such an accident. Or maybe it had gotten out of the state and had already been repaired in some out-of-the-way place that had never even heard of the New York City Police.

Mitch grunted. Jub had claimed the two cases were hooked up. Now if Mitch could get Andrea for the murder and Kent for the hit-and-run, that would be something. Hell—it would be a miracle.

He turned over the teletypes, keeping up to date on routine police work. Then Murphy yelled out that there was a message for Mitch upstairs. Mitch found a scrawled note saying that Simon Treeberg had died in the hospital that afternoon, as a result of internal injuries suffered in the accident.

He re-read the few words and thought of the old gent lying there on the sidewalk, with his leg busted and his eyes closed and his head in his wife's lap. Well, the hit-and-run was a homicide now, and with every hour that went by, the chances of turning up a car with a busted fender were a little worse.

Mitch shrugged. He'd done all he could, and a lot more than most cops would have. He'd called in the laboratory, hadn't he?

He turned and went down to the captain's office. The lieutenant was waiting there and his round, crafty face beamed at Mitch. Mitch sat down, expecting the worst.

"I've been thinking about the Jarvis business," began the lieutenant. "This Minx woman is a little weak on motive, but there's enough to get by. There's no weapon, of course, but that applies to everybody. What you need most is opportunity, isn't it?"

Mitch nodded. He wondered what the lieutenant was driving at. "That depends pretty much on what the Ollenbach girl is going to say," remarked Mitch. "If she left the Minx around nine or nine-thirty, then there's an hour or so unaccounted for and we're okay. But if Ollenbach checks the claim that they were together till around ten-thirty, then the Minx didn't have time to kill Jarvis because we know she was home by ten-forty-five, when she screamed."

The lieutenant nodded. "That's what I thought. The hotel people are pretty mixed up, so we can forget about them. How about that box? That carton?"

"I been asking about it. Nobody knows how it got there."

"Unless the Minx brought it," said the lieutenant. He had a sly smile, as if he was leading up to something.

Mitch swallowed. "Sure," he said. "She might have. But what for?"

"So," continued the lieutenant, "if you could prove, say, that she wasn't home at the time of the accident, you'd have a pretty good case, regardless of Ollenbach. The deposition wouldn't matter. You could say that the Minx was at Jarvis's, and that she killed him at the very moment of the accident."

"Yeah?"

"The whole trouble is that she screamed, and so she had to be home. How would you like to get around that?"

"It would bust her alibi wide open."

The lieutenant leaned forward. "Ever hear a Siamese cat yell?"

"No."

"It sounds," said the lieutenant, "like a person in mortal agony. That scream everybody heard—suppose it wasn't Andrea at all? Suppose she was at Jarvis's, and that the scream came from the cat!"

He leaned back complacently. The big idea was off his chest.

Mitch stared at the table. If she'd killed Jarvis and then come home, expecting to turn on a gas jet and pretend she'd been asleep all evening and had nearly been asphyxiated, she'd point to the dead cat and say there'd been enough gas to kill him. Sure. That was the kind of screwy alibi a dame might think up.

Mitch checked the facts. Two witnesses had claimed they'd seen her at the window—anyway, seen a woman. But there hadn't been much light and maybe they'd been mixed up. Witnesses usually were.

Say she wasn't there. As soon as she came in, she'd killed the cat. That would be the first item on her program, and she'd had the box there to use as a coffin. Then, before she'd had a chance to do anything else, the police had come and asked her about a street accident. No wonder she'd been so scared. She'd been thinking about gas and that was why she'd said she'd rushed to the window to air the room. She hadn't had the time or the presence of mind to make up a good, logical story.

Aimlessly, Mitch's right hand made endless, interlocking circles on a scratch pad. Yeah. That was a neat idea of the lieutenant's. It would work.

THREE

I

Andrea Minx finished her shower and wished the bathroom had a window, or at least were better ventilated. The mirror was covered with steam and the tile walls, coffee-and-cream color with the cream not well stirred, were coated with moisture. She dried her feet hastily, pushed open the bathroom door and stepped outside. The door of her one-room apartment was locked and the curtains obscured the view through the window, but she felt vaguely indecent, standing there naked in the center of the room.

She dried herself carefully, watching her flesh redden under the friction of the towel. She kept staring at herself, arms, stomach, legs, as if the wonder of it were not quite comprehensible. She found it hard to connect the familiar, physical fact of her body with the strange phantasmagoria of last night and early this morning. She kept repeating the words that described it, but they were empty. She was involved in a murder case. Photographers had taken her picture and reporters had swarmed around her when she'd left police headquarters.

It didn't seem real. It was more like a part she'd played. The words she'd spoken and the emotions she'd experienced weren't hers at all. They were bits of a comedy in which she'd had the lead, but the scenes had been written by someone else. She'd been Andrea Minx, the actress, and when she'd left the police it had been like leaving the theatre.

And yet, she was still the same Andrea, timid and with a deep abiding faith in her star. Andrea, the small-town girl, whose real name was Marx before she'd gone on the stage. Andrea who was so careful of her friends and who found it so difficult to partake of friendship because, once she gave it, there was no holding back.

She dressed slowly and then slipped into the long red negligee that trailed majestically on the floor. She combed out her hair and let it hang down over her shoulders. She looked about fifteen now. The police wouldn't harm anyone who was only fifteen. Everything was all right again. Why, she even felt hungry.

She realized she hadn't eaten since she'd left Rose Ollenbach last night. She'd tried a couple of times, but she'd gotten only as far as a restaurant door before her stomach began objecting. Even the milk she'd bought had set up a wave of nausea.

Well, she felt better now and she'd have some tea and toast. And maybe an egg, too. She needed all the nourishment she could take.

She wondered what the police really thought. Taylor, the detective who'd arrested her, had acted as if she'd killed Jarvis. And the other detective, the nice one who'd come to her room with Taylor—why hadn't he been there, when she'd been questioned? She'd kept looking for him. Somehow, he would have made her feel safe.

She sat down and stared at the batik wallpiece over the mantel. It had a complicated design in lovely, faded old pinks and greens, with a geometric tree which a geometric dragon was about to climb in order to grab a geometric man up in the top of the branches. Or at least, that was what she always imagined.

She kept staring at it, transfixed. After a time she shuddered. She mustn't, she told herself. She mustn't be afraid. Of anyone, ever.

Except that this time it was real. It wasn't just being nervous or timid or shy. It wasn't like her first visits to the casting offices, when she'd trembled because somebody might tell her to get out or might offer her a part or might do nothing at all.

She thought of the Andrea of those days, four years ago, who turned away and blushed every time a man looked at her in the subway and who kept her eyes fixed modestly on her plate whenever she was in a restaurant. No. This was different. She was sure of it. There was somebody or something.

If only Stanley were here. He'd have curled up in her lap and stretched his head, so that she could stroke the fur under his chin. Then he'd have purred conscientiously, just for her. He'd have told her the world was all right, that she was safe.

She bit her lips. Stanley, bridging the gap of her loneliness. There was no one left to whom she felt close. Jack, her brother, was in the army. So was Ford, and Will was in the Navy. And now Rose was with UNRRA and Stella with the Red Cross. All her friends swept up by the war and scattered across the earth, and she left here, doing what she could. Canteens and USO parties, in between her radio work.

But the loneliness had never been so bad. You could forget loneliness. And in other moods you could embrace it, even, and hug it close until it was part of living, one more emotion that you underwent in the process of growth.

But fear was different. You could never come to terms with fear, and you could never run away from it.

She stood up. The bathroom was beginning to air out and she had promised herself that she'd eat. She crossed the room, put a kettle of water on the stove and sliced some bread. She found a solitary egg in the back of the refrigerator. She inspected the shell for cracks and decided it would do for boiling. Then the bell rang.

Fright came back and swept her clean of all other thought and feeling. She stood stock still and told herself she wasn't going to answer it. Visitors meant danger. She wasn't safe.

But she knew it didn't matter. If it was what she feared, it didn't matter. The elevator would ascend. Footsteps would come down the corridor. The door would open.

She had no idea whether the footsteps would be different from any others. They might be soft, barely audible; they might be heavy and deliberate. She would have no means of recognizing them. And even when the door swung open, she would still have no inkling. She would see no monster marked with its terrible intention. No. She wouldn't know. That was why there would be no struggle. Just her limp body lying there for the janitor to find. Like Stanley. Like Jarvis.

There was no escaping.

Slowly, without volition, she crossed the room and put her finger on the button that released the downstairs front door. She counted to three, and then she pressed it.

With her heart thumping and her breath coming in short, labored puffs, she waited. She heard the rumble of the miniature elevator as it creaked upward. She heard it click to a stop and she heard footsteps march relentlessly down the hall. The knock was bold and precise.

She wanted not to answer. She listened intently, uncertain whether she really heard the sound of heavy breathing or just imagined it. Suddenly there came a weird, hissing noise and a long, sibilant breath. It was behind her. Panic-stricken, she whirled.

She laughed abruptly as she saw her singing kettle. And a voice called out her name. "Andrea? You there?"

It was only Lee. She answered almost gaily, "Just a minute. My water's boiling and my toast is burning. Oh! Everything gets done at the same time!"

She rescued the toast and moved the kettle to one side and then rushed to the door. Lee Kent, tall and intelligent and slender, with his hooked nose that seemed always to be sniffing out some half-formed feeling or idea, looked at her with a surprised, quizzical expression.

She laughed again in the blessedness of relief. He mustn't know how afraid she'd been. She must give no sign of her terror. Not to him. Not to anyone.

"Hello, Andrea. I hear you've been having a tough time of it."

"I guess I have," she answered, "though I've been too tired to think. All the questions they asked. For hours and hours and hours." She smiled apologetically. "But I'm glad you came. I'm glad to see someone I know. How is—everyone?"

He sniffed at the word and pecked it apart. "Everyone? I'm fine. Fern's fine. Christie Mae seems to be the only one who's taking it hard." He sat down, smiling, gazing around the room and liking the chairs and the couch and disapproving of the batik wallpiece, as he always did. "Look, Andrea. A detective by the name of Taylor was just at my office asking a lot of fool questions. I told him I had an appointment up here and he came along. If he asks about it, don't contradict me. I was intending to drop in to see if there was anything I could do, and so your name was the first one that came to my mind."

"Taylor? He's the one who arrested me."

"So he's responsible, is he? When this thing is over, I'm going to see if I can do anything about it. Talk about Gestapo methods! We have them right here."

"He was just doing his job," said Andrea gently.

"Think so? Well, I don't."

She smiled despite herself. Lee and Detective Taylor. The battering ram and the tortured, introspective creature who had broken down the first time she'd met him.

Suddenly she was aware of something queer in Lee, of his fixed, concentrated stare. For a moment she was terror-stricken. She wished she didn't have such a keen, almost psychic insight. She was never quite sure whether she was seeing through people or just imagining things. Then she looked down at her robe and she knew the reason for Lee's look.

"Lee," she said, "wait here while I put something respectable on." And, blushing crimson, she rushed into the bathroom.

His laughter seemed to follow her. "Don't bother, Andrea. Please. I only came for a moment to see if I could help. I'm going now. Unless—" he sounded anxious. "Unless you'll have dinner with me."

"Thanks, but I'm afraid I couldn't eat."

"Well, I'll be going then. Good luck, Andrea, and let me know if you want anything. Have you thought about a lawyer?"

"Don't be ridiculous. I didn't do anything and I don't need a lawyer."

"Okay—just a suggestion," he called out. Then the door slammed and she came cautiously out of the bathroom. She was alone again.

She went to the door and tried the flimsy, useless lock to which someone had a key. It was still closed and the latch had not been slipped.

She frowned and went to examine the toast. It was cold and slightly burnt. She put in a fresh piece and stepped to the stove.

Her egg was overboiled, of course. If only she could learn to do the simple things!

II

She sat down at the table and munched her toast, thinking of Lee and the evening she'd met him. Fern, who knew her slightly, had invited her to Connecticut for the weekend. It had all seemed so *New Yorker*ish. The white colonial house, the neighbors who dropped in for cocktails, the writing and painting crowd, the smart talk and finally Lee himself, art critic, dealer and collector.

There had been a buffet supper, and a tweedy young man kept following her and telling her she was the most beautiful creature he'd ever seen. He said she had the neck of a swan and the face of a Leonardo angel. She'd sneaked outside to avoid him, and she'd found Lee staring at the stars.

Maybe it was the cocktails or maybe it was just a mood and a moon that fitted together for a few moments and brought about a harmony unusual for two strangers. But they'd both felt it, an undercurrent, a subtle rapport.

Lee had started off prosaically enough. "Like it?" he'd asked. "The house?"

"It's charming."

"I wish I could give it to you. I hate it."

"I know you do," she'd said simply. "Why?"

"Because it's Fern's, I suppose." He'd snorted and looked up at the sky. "I don't mean that she paid for it. But she possesses it. Do you know Fern well?"

"I just met her once. I wasn't even sure whether I ought to accept her invitation."

"You have to do what Fern tells you. If she asked you up,

naturally you came. You see, she's a Jarvis. The Jarvises don't ask. They dictate. You should have known Tony."

"Who's Tony?"

"Her brother. The godhead. The apotheosis of all manly virtues and beauties." He'd sighed with a deep, satisfied relish. "I hated him."

"Why?"

"Because he eclipsed me. Because all his life he was better than I in everything I ever did."

"Where is he?"

"Dead. He died a hero's death on a Normandy beachhead. The medal ought to be along pretty soon. That will top it. Even in death he eclipses me. He makes me think of the days before I had my gallery. Scraping along on a few dollars a week, taking charity from Peter Jarvis. Fern may have understood, a little bit, but nobody else did. Shame and poverty. Squirming and crawling, just for the lack of a few coins. I'd die rather than go back to that. Am I boring you?"

"No, but do you think you should tell me all this? After all, you hardly know me."

"That's the only reason I can tell you, because you're a stranger. Only a stranger can appreciate the crazy, twisted, complicated lives of the Jarvis clan.

"You see, Fern's my cousin and Peter Jarvis is her father. He married my mother's sister and they begat a son, Tony the Paragon. All my days I've lived under the pall of Tony's perfection. Even my mother, who eats by the grace of Peter Jarvis's monthly check, considered the Jarvises superior to the Kents and, in particular, Tony superior to me. Possibly because I was fatherless. I wouldn't know. Shall I tell you why I married Fern?"

Andrea had looked up at Lee Kent's small, sensitive features, at his anxious, sniffing nose and ascetic mouth. She felt sorry for him.

He was in the throes of a self-pity that debased and unmanned him. She supposed he'd hate her tomorrow and avoid her. She might even have to go home on Saturday instead of Sunday, simply because he'd told her too many confidences. But he needed to unburden himself and the least she could do was listen.

"Why?" she asked dutifully, like the end man in a minstrel show. "Why did you marry Fern?"

"Because to marry a Jarvis is the next best thing to being one. Only it's not working out that way. Fern wants to break it up. She's merely waiting for me to say the word. She's strong and overpowering, but she's woman enough to want to be the jilted instead of the jilter. Let me tell you about Fern."

They had crossed the lawn and reached a small table and bench at the edge of the garden. Andrea sat down on the bench and Lee vaulted on to the table and balanced himself with one foot on the bench. He leaned back. Light from the house cut across his face and gave his skin an old, unhealthy texture, as if the sickness within him were marked there on his face.

"Fern's mother was the most wonderful being there ever was. She adored Tony, and so did my mother; Peter pampered him. Fern, of course, was jealous. At the same time, she worshiped and idealized Tony and wanted to be like him. In short, she wanted to be a boy. Psychiatry has a word for it."

Andrea knew the word and was glad Lee didn't say it. The ugliness of the picture he was painting, the bitterness of his reaction made her recoil. She wondered how much of it was true and how much was a product of Lee's own mind.

"Fern," he said, "did her best. She forsook dolls and played with Tony's trains and boats and mechanical sets. She trailed him home from school and trailed him to the ball game down the block. She raced him and challenged him on his own ground, and, being younger and a girl, she always lost, which made her more than ever want to be a boy. When she realized she couldn't be, she went to the opposite extreme." Lee smiled dryly. "She married me."

"Have you ever told this to anyone before?" asked Andrea suddenly.

Lee had bowed. "To myself, every single night. I see Fern and myself, the two of us overshadowed by Tony. Misery loves company and makes marriages. In a way it even made a good marriage, until Tony shattered its foundations by getting killed. If he'd lived, we might have accepted our humble existence under his shadow. Who knows?"

Andrea hadn't answered. She'd thought ironically of her envy of a few hours ago. Then she'd heard footsteps coming down the path and they'd both turned and faced Peter Jarvis.

His expression had made Andrea feel as if she'd been caught in an adulterous act.

"Most of the company's gone and I was looking for you," he said coldly. "I hope I'm not interrupting anything. But after all, Fern is my daughter."

"And my wife," Lee had added.

Jarvis's look had been murderous. "Is she?" he'd said. "Sometimes I forget."

Andrea had hated Jarvis that first weekend, but when he'd called on her in town a few days later, he'd been the soul of politeness and gallantry. At first she'd been amazed by his courtliness. Then, to her horror, she realized he was falling in love with her.

She'd tried to evade him and couldn't. There had been other weekends at the Kents. And then, when summer was almost over and she had decided to ask him point blank not to see her again, he'd changed his whole approach and become an insurance man. He'd told her he wanted to sell group insurance to the radio industry. He'd asked her to introduce him to the head of the station. She'd laughed and said she didn't even know him. But Peter Jarvis had insisted. All she really needed to do, he'd said, was to take him to the studio some evening and present him as a friend. After that, he'd manage.

She'd consented finally, with secret glee. First of all, once Peter had made his insurance contact, he wouldn't bother her any more. It was such an easy way to get rid of him. And then, just imagine Peter Jarvis prowling around WLT at three A.M., trying to drum up insurance prospects! There'd be the sound man and the engineer, who were always busy. There'd be Truffles, the drunk, a few cleaning women and the boy who smashed records because he was so sleepy he could never coordinate.

"Of course," she'd said. "I'll do that much." And it had been arranged for Monday night. Yesterday.

Cleaning up the crumbs and dishes, she reviewed her acquaintanceship with Jarvis. It gave her no clue as to why he'd been murdered. There had been nothing unusual in their relations save the sudden change in his approach.

"Maybe," she told herself, "that's the way he sells insurance. First he courts a prospect, and in the end he proposes a policy instead of marriage."

She laughed quietly. Then she glanced at the door and suddenly she was afraid again. She seemed to relive last night, when she'd come home and there'd been no Stanley. She seemed again to be leaning over his small, limp body, she felt again the coldness and the lack of air and she seemed to be running towards the window, wanting to shriek out her terror.

She knew why, now. She knew why she'd been so frightened. Someone had wanted to kill her. She was supposed to be home from six until midnight. She was home every evening. Someone *had* tried to kill her, and had killed Stanley instead. She was convinced of it.

She stared at the door. If someone had a key, the door might just as well not be there. She'd asked little Mr. Steegler, the janitor, to put a bolt on her door and he'd said he would, at once. She'd stop down there again and insist.

She touched her finger. It was still sore. She wondered how she'd burnt it. Was it possible she'd lit the stove and not even remembered? Of course not. That was quite ridiculous. Still—it *was* sore.

She dressed hurriedly and went down to the basement. She smelt something cooking in the janitor's apartment, something heavy and greasy which made her nauseous. She had an impulse to turn and run up the stairs.

The sullen little janitor opened the door. "Oh, it's you, Miss Minx."

"Yes. I was wondering about that bolt. You said you'd put it on, and really—after what happened, I need it."

From the rear of the apartment a woman's voice called to him. "Edward! Your dinner's ready."

He didn't answer. He looked at Andrea and said, "You look pretty, Miss Minx. Real pretty." There was a long, painful pause. "I got a letter for you somewheres. I'll put it on your table when I come fix the bolt."

"Let me have it now."

His small, dark eyes bulged. "No," he said. "I want to go into your room."

She turned swiftly and fled up the stairs.

III

The street was deserted. She stared up at the dim sky, hazy with the reflection of city lights. It was cloudy and there was a coolness in the air. She went to the corner and turned towards

Broadway. The lights and people reassured her, and she walked uptown for a few blocks.

Someone was following her. She didn't know who. She could pick out no particular person in the thin crowd that strolled along the avenue. But she felt him. Like a shadow. There was no reason why anyone should follow her and she had noticed no one in the darkness of the side street. But she knew.

She didn't need reasons. Faced with the need for a reason, she was helpless. But things came to her, suddenly and with certainty. Like the conviction that someone had wanted to kill her. It didn't have to be rational. It merely needed to appear in her mind with that curious, definite finality.

She turned and headed back, scanning the faces of the people she passed. There was no one she could pick out. Maybe, even, she hadn't seen her shadower. But she knew he was there, out of sight in a doorway, going through the pantomime of pretending to hail a taxi, fusing with that small group laughing at some private joke. She couldn't pick him out, but she knew he was there, stalking her.

She stopped at the newsstand on her corner and bought a paper. She glanced at the headlines. She saw her own picture on the front page under the caption, "Radio Singer Held. Beautiful Andrea Minx Friendly with Slain Insurance Man." In the left-hand column she read that a tropical storm was gathering off the Atlantic coast.[*]

A couple went by and headed toward West End Avenue. She

---

[*] A major tropical storm devastated New England, the mid-Atlantic states, and especially the Jersey shore in September 1944. Dubbed the "Great Atlantic hurricane," among other victims were 248 sailors lost when the U.S.S. *Warrington* was sunk by the blow about 450 miles east of Vero Beach, Florida. The first storm warnings for the US were disseminated by the Weather Bureau (now the National Weather Service) on September 13, 1944; thus, this dating is consistent with the earlier mention of Monday, September 11.

followed. With someone in sight, maybe there would be less danger.

She walked hurriedly. Before turning the corner, she looked back. A man was halfway down the block. She ducked around the corner and began running. At least he couldn't catch her before she reached home.

Upstairs, she found that the janitor had finally put the bolt on her door. She barred it and picked up the letter he'd left. It was from a friend of hers upstate. Andrea read it through rapidly. Gossip and news of people she'd almost forgotten during her four years in New York.

She unfolded the paper and scanned the murder account. It seemed strange and remote. It couldn't really be herself she was reading about. Still, she supposed the publicity would help her career. She might get a chance on a daytime program of one of the bigger stations.

It was curious how little she cared that Jarvis was dead. He had been someone she had not wanted and yet hadn't had the strength or the callousness to send away. Now it had been done for her and she felt the freedom from an encumbrance.

Except that she wasn't disencumbered. She looked up, expecting to see Stanley get up from her bed, utter a mild plaintive squeak, stretch himself and come over to be stroked.

She missed Stanley more than Peter Jarvis. It was terrible to feel that way, she supposed, but she did. She'd been fond of Stanley. And now she was connected with him, too closely. She was obsessed with the sense that it was she who was supposed to have died. And instead, the evil thing had merely burnt her finger.

She thought of the detectives who'd asked her about an accident last night. If it hadn't been for that, if she hadn't chanced to tell a couple of policemen that she was scared and was expecting Jarvis, she never would have been involved.

She was not overly worried about the police. She was innocent, and therefore she was safe. But she was not safe from the other thing.

She wished she were tired and could sleep, but she was still too wrought up. Besides, she'd slept most of the day. She wondered whether they'd say anything to her at the studio.

She got up and went to her bureau. She wanted that light blue handkerchief with the print design. It wasn't in the top drawer where it was supposed to be. But then nothing ever was. The location of any article of dress which she hadn't worn in the last day or two was always a minor adventure.

She began rummaging. In the bottom drawer she felt something heavy and metallic. Wondering what it was, she pulled it out and found herself holding an automobile wrench. How had that gotten—

Suddenly she noticed the stain. She started to tremble violently. She was panicky now, for she knew she was holding the weapon with which Peter Jarvis had been killed, and she knew that the stain was blood.

But how had the thing got here? And why? And why on earth did anyone want to hide it in her drawer?

She heard the elevator come up, creaking and jerking in all its aged bones. She was always afraid it would drop or get stuck. She supposed she ought to walk up. The elevator was dangerous.

She heard it stop and she heard the footsteps come down the corridor. She gripped the wrench hard and pressed it against her dress. She kept staring at the door. When someone knocked, the wrench seemed to jerk out of her hands and hit the carpet with a thud. She drew in her breath and didn't move.

Whoever was outside knew now that she was home. The knock was repeated. She had to get rid of the wrench somehow.

She couldn't put it back in her drawer. Suppose it was the police and they searched?

She ran to the closet and whipped the door open. A canvas bag was hanging from a hook. She'd been filling it with some of her old clothes which she was sending to a thrift shop. They'd promised to call for it. She stuffed the wrench inside and whirled.

She saw the knob move and she heard a key turn slowly in the lock. Only the bolt protected her now.

She stared. Her knees felt weak and her muscles were paralyzed. She mustn't faint. Oh, no—that would be too much. To faint now?

A heavy blow made the door quiver. The bolt gave slightly and seemed to bend. She opened her mouth and began screaming.

Charlie O'Connor called up the precinct station. "Patrolman O'Connor reporting. I'm at Andrea Minx's house and something happened. I don't know what, but all of a sudden she starts screaming. I ran up there and she was claiming someone tried to bust into her room. I don't know if anyone was really there or if she just made it up....Sure I looked through the place, but there wasn't anybody around."

He tapped the wall with one finger and hoped nobody would find out that he'd been around the corner getting a sandwich when the thing had happened. They never figured that a guy had to eat once in a while.

He listened carefully to what the desk said, and he answered with pride, "I investigated thoroughly. I looked around the place and there was nothing. And while I was there, a guy come from some thrift shop and picked up a bag of junk. But he was okay.... Sure, I checked him. All he took was that junk."

Patrolman O'Connor hung up. He'd be glad when his relief showed up. He was beginning to get bored. The Minx had gone for a walk and bought a paper. It had been a cinch to trail her, and she hadn't even known he was there. But, except for that scream of hers, nothing had happened all day. Not a thing.

FOUR

I

The following afternoon, Mitch got around to seeing Christie Mae. She had a two-room apartment in the same sort of place as Jarvis's. But where Jarvis's suite looked like a few hundred thousand others, Christie Mae's was so crowded with fancy junk that the shortest line between any two points was around a coffee table.

Christie Mae herself did all right for her age, although she probably worked pretty hard at it. Nobody ever grew hair just that color, a kind of blue-gray that was a little lighter than her eyes. She still had a good build, but she was beginning to fight the wrinkles. She hadn't given up, though. Her eyes danced and she had a trick of twisting her mouth as if she'd just finished getting kissed, and liked it.

"I don't know what you can possibly want," she said, as soon as Mitch had introduced himself. "There were detectives here yesterday and they asked about everything."

"Sure," said Mitch, settling himself in a comfortable chair, "but that was just routine. Those boys didn't really understand.

What I want is to have a nice, friendly talk and find out all about Jarvis."

She picked him right up. "All?" she asked. "How would I know all?"

Mitch sized her up and took a header. "He didn't leave you his money just because he liked the way you made salad dressings."

She smiled as if she approved of his approach. "How do you know? You never tasted them, did you?"

"Salad dressings," said Mitch in his high, piping voice, "are not in my line. But Peter Jarvis was murdered and I want to know what he was really like."

She twisted her lips. "I can tell you, Mr. Taylor, but I doubt whether it would be wise. Perhaps I know too much."

Mitch squirmed. He had a hunch she could keep this up all afternoon, and have a hell of a good time at it.

"Mrs. Kent," he said, "you're an attractive woman and I can see why Jarvis went for you. But you're thinking you got to protect yourself. You have to be careful what you say, because how do you know I won't spill everything to the papers that you tell me?"

"Would you?" she asked hopefully. "Would you really? So far, that Andrea Minx has gotten all the publicity. And just because she's an actress, too."

Mitch coughed. It looked like he'd got off on the wrong foot again.

"That's because she's in it up to her neck," he said dryly. "But you—you're innocent."

"How do you know?" she flashed.

Mitch saw his opening at last and he dived right through. "Maybe you're not," he said. "Tell me, huh?"

She twisted her lips again.

"I'll let you judge for yourself. Cigarette?"

"I only smoke cigars," he answered.

She got up and walked over to a kind of a desk with a bookcase on top of it. "I can supply that, too. Shall I tell you a secret? Sometimes I smoke them myself." She offered him a box. "My private stock."

"Thanks," he said. He took a cigar, bit off the end and stuck it in his mouth. He hated cigars, but maybe this one was going to be evidence.

"You haven't asked me where I was last night," she said, smiling.

"You were home," answered Mitch. "You turned the radio on at nine and kept it playing till midnight. You turned it down twice, around ten, when you got a couple of phone calls."

"I have such nice neighbors," cooed Christie Mae. "I wonder whether they listen that carefully every night."

"They did on Monday. Of course, they don't know whether you were here or whether you went over to Jarvis's and lent your apartment to a friend. Who phoned you, Mrs. Kent? That's something we haven't checked."

"I really don't remember," she said. She smiled, as if she wanted to be accused. She probably had an idea the whole thing would be romantic. He wished he could pull her in, just to show her how wrong she was.

"You haven't told me about Jarvis," he remarked.

"No. And to be perfectly frank, I don't want to."

"Why?"

"It isn't nice to speak ill of the dead."

"For the love of Mike!" exploded Mitch Taylor. "Jarvis was murdered and I want to find out who did it. I have to know what he was like and who hated him and who loved him and who had reasons for bumping him off. I come to the one woman who knew him, and you tell me it isn't nice to answer questions!"

"Have you asked Andrea?"

"You don't like her, do you?" demanded Mitch.

Christie Mae's mouth went hard. It didn't look now as if it had just been kissed. Mitch had no idea why she'd started off by playing, but she wasn't playing now.

"No," she said. "I don't like Andrea. She was thirty years younger than Peter and trying to make a fool of him. I told him what I thought, and do you know what he answered? That he was trying to sell her an insurance policy."

"He was," said Mitch. "He kept a little book with all his prospects, and how much he thought they were worth. He had her down for five thousand."

"He may have wanted to sell her a policy," remarked Christie Mae, "but only from force of habit. He tried all my friends. He was suave and courteous and polite about it, but completely without conscience. He worshiped the almighty dollar. The only principle he had in his whole makeup was the kind on which you pay interest."

"He did all right by you," said Mitch.

"You think so? Mr. Taylor, I've been a widow for almost twenty years. When my husband died, there was a little insurance money and that was all. I went out and got a job. I worked as the receptionist at a funeral parlor. Does that shock you?"

Mitch blinked. He wondered why he was supposed to be shocked, but he didn't bother figuring it out. She'd started off now. She had something she wanted to get off her chest, and he'd see to it that she did.

"It's no fun," said Mitch sympathetically.

Christie Mae snorted. "If it had been up to him, I'd still have been at the funeral parlor. But Helen—my sister, who was Mrs. Jarvis—wouldn't stand for it. She shamed Peter into helping support me. I didn't accept for myself, but I had a small boy and

I owed him an education. I didn't like to live off Peter Jarvis's bounty, but I had to."

"Sure," said Mitch. She was putting it on kind of thick, but he could string along.

"When Helen died, I wondered whether Peter would have the gall to stop my check. I didn't ask him outright. But Helen died from an overdose of sleeping tablets, and I could have spread the story that he'd killed her, that his carelessness was responsible. It would have hurt him in a business way, you see. So when the check came, how much do you think it was?"

"I wouldn't know," said Mitch. "But I'll bet he cut it."

"Exactly. And when I spoke to him about it, I discovered that he'd never given me any more. Helen had always made up the difference by skimping on her house money and her clothes budget. I told Peter at the time—"

She stopped suddenly. Mitch said, because he knew it would infuriate her, "Well, he made up for it now, leaving you the money."

"Nonsense!" she snapped. "He did that merely to spite Fern. He didn't care about me any more. I was broken. But he'd never been able to manage Fern and he didn't want to make her an heiress. And besides, I'd earned it."

"How?" asked Mitch.

"Not the way you think," she flamed. "I may have been a kept woman, but I was never his mistress. I was kept pure as the driven snow." She lit a cigarette and puffed vigorously. "He made sure he got his money's worth out of me. Sending me around to meet people so that I could invite them to dinner for him. He used to give me a list. Then a week later he'd call on them to sell insurance.

"And not only that," she went on, "but he humiliated me in every possible way. He supported me and he wanted value for his money. I had to run his errands because a fashionable errand girl made him feel important. Besides, he wanted people to think I was his mistress. That made them talk, which was personal publicity and good for business."

She tamped out her cigarette and began laughing. "And with it all, I loved him. God help me, but I loved him!"

She stopped speaking. She looked old now. The sallow flesh in her cheeks seemed to have pulled away from the dabs of rouge. Her blue-gray hair had lost its life. She had fat little cheeks and strings of dyed hair that clung lifelessly to her skull, like junk and cinders on top of a dump heap on a wet day.

Mitch moistened his lips. "Did you kill him?" he asked.

Christie Mae laughed. "Wouldn't you like to know?" she said. Then she buried her face in a pillow and began weeping.

Mitch didn't get it. In a way, she was putting on an act. But there was more to it than that. Jarvis had treated her like dirt and she'd had no one else, so she'd given in to him. A widow for twenty years—that does things to a woman.

She hadn't spilled any of this yesterday, to the boys who'd questioned her. She must have held back until it was all ready to pop, and Mitch happened to be there when it did. He wondered whether it put any new light on the case.

After a while she sat up. "I don't know why I've been telling you all this," she said. "You must think I'm awful."

"I think you've had some tough breaks."

"I suppose I have." She tried to smile at him and didn't get very far. "Would you like some tea, Mr. Taylor?"

He wasn't exactly a tea drinker, but he had a feeling she'd talk some more if he stuck around, so he nodded and said "Sure." She went inside. He stared glumly at a dish of candy.

When she came back with the tea stuff, she'd swept up the powder and wrinkles and looked pretty much the way she had when Mitch had first arrived.

"Lemon or milk?" she asked politely, pouring the stuff out of a fancy tea pot.

"Straight," said Mitch. Then he motioned towards the picture of a soldier that stood all by itself on the mantelpiece. "Who's that?"

Christie Mae's hand jerked slightly, but she kept on pouring. "That's Tony Jarvis, Fern's brother. He was killed in France."

"Oh," said Mitch.

"I wish you could have met him. He was the only decent one in the family. Peter was hard and hating and disliked. Fern, wild and impulsive and drinking too much. Lee engrossed in his pictures and caring about little else. Myself—I'm nothing to be proud of. But Tony—"

She turned now and looked at the picture of the dark, gay, handsome soldier. "You can see how good looking he was, but you can't see his brains or his charm or his personality. If he were only here now!"

Mitch put his teacup down. His cigar had gone out and he felt the end of it to make sure there were no embers. It seemed safe enough and he stuck it in his pocket. He'd send it down to the lab to compare with the cigar butt that Jub had taken. Christie Mae was a queer old duck. You never knew.

"You got your son," said Mitch tactfully. "That's plenty to be thankful for."

She glared at him and forced a smile. "Yes," she said thoughtfully. "Of course. There's always Lee."

"What about him?" asked Mitch.

Christie Mae leaned back. Whatever she was thinking, he'd have to drag it out of her, inch by inch.

"I saw him yesterday," remarked Mitch. "He's got a swank place."

"Yes, hasn't he?" said Christie Mae in a strained tone. "And he's built up that business entirely by himself."

Then the doorbell rang and she got up. Mitch had his back to the door. He didn't turn around. He heard a familiar voice burst out, "Oh, Christie Mae darling, I'm so glad you're home. I've been hiding from the police all day and—"

Fern Kent shut up suddenly. Christie Mae must have given her the high sign.

Then a man's deep, dry voice finished her sentence. "She hides because she's scared that if the police ask her any questions, she'll accuse Andrea. As if anybody'd take Fern seriously!"

Mitch stood up as they walked in. Fern said, "Why, Detective Taylor! You certainly get around! I'd like you to meet a friend of mine. Mr. Boganov—Mr. Taylor."

Mitch nodded and Boganov glowered. He was a big guy. He'd have been big even in a roomful of cops. He had curly hair, sallow, pasty skin, thin angry lips and a nose that pointed in the general direction of his left ear.

"We were having tea," murmured Christie Mae. "Will you join us?"

"Thanks," said Fern. "Emil will, but make mine a highball. Or I'll make it myself."

"The hell you will," said Boganov. He bent down and sampled one of the chocolates.

Fern swung around. "Why, Emil!" she said. But she didn't go into the kitchen and she didn't get her highball. She sat down and beamed. "He's trying to reform me. He's trying to make me stop drinking. And he's getting away with it because he looks like Tony."

"Nonsense!" said Christie Mae. And for once, Mitch agreed with her. There wasn't much resemblance between the Adonis on the mantel and the Boganov on the couch.

Boganov glared and even disliked his chocolate. He put down his half-eaten piece and tried another.

Fern turned to Mitch. "What were you finding out?" she asked abruptly.

"We were talking about your father," answered Mitch.

"Oh, him!" said Fern contemptuously. "Does it really matter?"

"Fern!" exclaimed Christie Mae in shocked disapproval.

Fern laughed. "Why pretend, Aunty? Sometimes you're positively mid-Victorian. Everybody knows that Helen was a saint and Peter was a bastard, and the police may as well hear it from us. I can't carry off the role of a dutiful and loving daughter and I'm not going to try. Peter always favored Tony and approved of everything Tony ever did, while he had nothing but criticism for me. He hated me and I hated him. And I still do."

Boganov took another piece of candy and stood up. "What I like about Fern," he remarked, "is her tact. That and her sweetness. And while I'd like to stay and watch her performance, I have to get back to work. Besides, this is a family affair and I don't belong. Thanks for the candy, Mrs. Kent."

He nodded at Mitch and started for the door. Fern followed him. Mitch heard the murmur of voices and Fern's sharp, delighted laugh. Then the door slammed and Fern returned alone.

"How are you getting on with the case?" she asked. "You can't be doing too well, because you arrested Andrea and then let her go." She sat on the arm of Christie Mae's chair and ruffled her hair. "Aunty—Aunty," she said teasingly, "fancy getting involved in a murder. And you with gray hairs."

"I wish you'd be serious," said Christie Mae. "And I wish you'd behave as if you were grown up. You insist on treating the whole thing as if it were some kind of a game."

"Well, in a way it is. The police are on one side and we're on the other. Isn't that right?" She turned to Mitch. "What's your first name?"

"Mitch."

"You can call me Fern. What makes you think Andrea did it, Mitch? What motive could she possibly have?"

"When you've handled as many cases as I have, you don't bother so much with motives. That's the way civilians approach it. But we find out first who did it, and then the motive falls right into line. Now take a case like this—a young girl and an older man. There are a dozen reasons she might have had. Maybe they were in love and he was going to throw her over. Maybe he had something on her and was threatening to expose her. I don't know, and I don't worry about it."

"Well, I think you're wrong," said Fern. "If you knew what I did, for instance, if you knew all the things locked in my mind that I've never even hinted at, you might find motives which would give you a brand new slant."

"For instance?" said Mitch.

Fern smiled. Christie Mae said quickly, "You're just joking, Fern. You're pretending, the way you always do."

"That's what you think," said Fern coquettishly. "But boy, could I tell things!"

"I've told them already," said Christie Mae quickly. "Before you came. You mean me, don't you?"

"Of course not," said Fern. "I wouldn't accuse you for anything in the world."

"Then maybe you should. You think I wasn't home Monday evening, don't you? And you think you know who was here."

Fern's pale green eyes looked startled. She was sorry now that she'd spoken, but she didn't know how to stop what she'd begun.

"Furthermore," continued Christie Mae, "you're annoyed because I got all the money and you didn't get a cent."

Fern jumped to her feet. "You—what?"

"Didn't you know?" asked Christie Mae quietly.

"You mean I don't get *anything*?"

Christie Mae nodded and Fern exploded angrily. "Oh, the rotter! The dirty, mean double-crosser! He promised he'd see me through the divorce and take care of me till I got married again. And he never made any provision at all. Oh, the stinker! Then I will tell!"

"You don't have to," said Christie Mae. "I'll spare you the trouble."

Fern gaped. Mitch looked from one woman to the other. He didn't know what they were scrapping about, but he realized there was more to it than their surface words. They were talking all around something about which he hadn't the slightest idea. And all he could do was sit there and not get in the way.

"You mean the phone call," said Christie Mae. Her lips gave a funny little twist, as if she didn't give a damn, "I haven't the least idea who made it, because I wasn't here. I was up at Peter's."

"Christie Mae!" exclaimed Fern. "You couldn't! You weren't!"

Christie Mae shrugged. "I had reason enough to kill him. Mr. Taylor knows all about that."

"Sure," said Mitch. "Tell me—did you leave a cigar butt up there?"

Christie Mae nodded wearily. "Yes."

Fern jumped up. "Oh, this is ridiculous! I wish you'd shut up."

"Please," said Christie Mae. "I think you'd better run along, Fern."

"And leave you to make a fool of yourself? I should say not." Fern bounced up out of her chair and bounced back. "Oh, Christie Mae—I'm sorry for what I said before. Just because you got all the money—I don't mind, really. I guess you deserve it."

"Helen wouldn't have stood for it," said Christie Mae. "I'll see that you get what she would have given you."

Fern leaned back, speechless for once in her life. Mitch grabbed the opportunity to get a word in.

"You admit you were up there," he said to Christie Mae. "What happened? Who came in?"

"I'm sick of it all!" exclaimed Christie Mae abruptly. "Peter was my business and mine alone. I don't want to drag anybody else into this. It was me—just me. Do you understand?"

She whirled and walked over to the window. Her stride was quick, springy. She tapped on the window pane once or twice and then she swung around.

She looked younger now. Her color was high and her eyes were sparkling, as if she were happy for the first time in years. Even her voice had a new, clear energy.

"I told you why, before," she said. "He'd humiliated me and I hated him. It was something between Peter and me. I'd wanted to so many times, I'd thought about it so many times. I—"

Her voice choked and she had to stop. Then she drew up her shoulders and raised her head. For a moment, she was almost majestic.

"I killed him," she said quietly. "Do you hear? I killed him!"

Fern gaped. For maybe a half minute, Mitch didn't speak. He stared at Christie Mae and she seemed to wilt under his eyes. The emotion was too much for her; she couldn't hold it.

"What did you hit him with?" he asked in his high, piping voice.

"Does it matter?" she asked. "The how and the why?"

"What did you hit him with?" repeated Mitch.

"A bronze bookend. The one on the table."

"There was no blood on it."

"I washed it off."

"There was dust all around it. Those bookends hadn't been touched in a week."

"You're lying!" she exclaimed.

Mitch walked over to the table with the candy dish and helped himself to a piece of chocolate. On the edge of the dish he saw the nougat which Boganov had bitten into and hadn't finished. It had nice tooth marks, so Mitch picked it up casually. The first chance he had, he dropped it in his pocket.

"The person who smoked that cigar had a crooked front tooth," he continued, "and you haven't. And Jarvis wasn't killed with a bookend. You can sign a confession if you want, but it'll be a phony and so full of holes we'll drive a wagon through it. You were home all evening, Mrs. Kent. You didn't go out. And if you claim you did, you'll make a hell of a lot of trouble for us and a fool out of yourself."

"You don't believe me?" she asked in a low voice.

"No. We get screwy confessions all the time. Mostly they're just for the publicity. Every once in a while, though, we get one like yours."

"What kind is that?" she asked in a low, weary voice.

"Where they're trying to protect somebody else. But it won't work, Mrs. Kent." He glanced at Fern and met her small, frank eyes. Then he looked at Christie Mae again. "If you still want to confess, call up the D. A.'s office and tell 'em you want to make a statement. But me—I'm not interested."

He felt sorry for the old dame. She'd been knocked around plenty and now she'd tried to make the supreme sacrifice, and all she made was a mess. In an access of sympathy, Mitch realized he ought to get out of here and leave her alone with her thoughts.

"If you get any more ideas," he said, "just call me at the precinct. Detective Mitch Taylor. All right, Fern. You coming along; or staying here?"

She practically danced up to him. "I'd love to come, Mitch. Will you take me out for a drink?"

"Sure," he said. The last he saw of Christie Mae she had dropped her head against the side of the couch. He hoped she'd cry herself out.

II

It was raining when Fern and Mitch Taylor crossed the lobby of the hotel. Fern glanced through the doors and said, "Damn! I suppose we'd better not go to the one in the building, but there's a nice bar down the block. I'll show you."

Mitch turned up his collar and let her take his arm. He couldn't make her out. She skipped along next to him as if this were her first date. She hated her father and walked out on an aunt who'd just tried to confess a murder. She slept with the man she was about to divorce and ran around with another guy. She drank like a fish and sparkled with health and energy. She dropped enough hints so that he could have arrested her as an accomplice after-the-fact, and she'd have been flabbergasted at the possibility. She took the case as if it were a surprise party in her honor and she enjoyed every minute of it. She had a frank, disarming look and she popped off with whatever came into her mind. She thought a detective was thrilling and she had no conception of the seriousness of the whole business.

He didn't get it. He didn't know whether she was dumb or deep, and whether she was putting on an act or just had the knack of getting as much zest out of a mudhole as from a swim at the beach. No matter how he looked at her, she didn't add up. When he thought she was involved in a homicide, she giggled at him, and when he laughed with her, she reminded him that he was a cop working on a case. And so he went into the bar with her as much to try and find out what made her tick as in the hope of getting any information.

It was a snappy place, with curved mirrors in the corners and comfortable, upholstered chairs grouped around low tables. She called the waiter by his first name and ordered a double scotch. Then she turned to Mitch and said, "Well, did she tell you?"

"Tell me what?" asked Mitch.

"Don't be difficult. Whether she slept with Peter, of course."

"If you couldn't find out in ten years, how do you expect me to learn it in ten minutes?"

"Oh, she'd tell you. She still treats me as a child and thinks I shouldn't know about things like that. But boy—what I could teach her."

"Maybe," said Mitch, "but don't try."

"Did you ever stop to think of what twenty years of celibacy does to a woman?" asked Fern. "Christie Mae's husband died when Lee was two, and she hasn't had a man since. Unless she had Peter. I wish I knew."

"Why does it bother you so much?" asked Mitch.

Fern drank her double scotch and ordered another. "It's a loose end, that's all. I'm inquisitive and I have to know."

"You think it would give Christie Mae a motive for murder, don't you?"

Fern's light green eyes looked at him guilelessly. "Oh, she wouldn't need that. But she's such a period piece out of the Victorian age. Lee and I urged her to get married, lots of times, but she wouldn't. Do you know why she refused?"

"Sure. Lots of women stay faithful to the memory of the man they've been in love with."

"Nonsense!" said Fern. "You're as bad as Christie Mae. Do detectives ever read psychology?"

"We've got to have a working knowledge of it."

"I don't mean that. I mean Freud and the subconscious and things like that."

"If you think I've got time to read books," said Mitch, "you don't know much about the department."

"Then I'll tell you something about Christie Mae. She wanted Peter and wanted to marry him, but not because she was in love with him. She wanted him because she was jealous of my mother."

"How could she be jealous, when your mother was dead?"

"I'll try to explain," said Fern expansively. "My mother was the most wonderful person that ever lived. She was generous and full of good will, a sort of saint, always doing things for others. And although lots of people hated Peter, they kept up with him for her sake. He sort of lived in the after-glow of her personality.

"She was two years younger than Christie Mae, but she was so much finer and stronger and everything. They'd always been very close, and when Christie Mae's husband died, Mother couldn't do enough. Christie Mae must have hated it. Here Mother had two children and she only had one, and her Lee was nothing compared to Tony, and Mother had a husband and money and Christie Mae had neither. You see? Mother was prettier and happier and better in every way, and Christie Mae wanted to be what Mother was. So after Mother died, what better than for Christie Mae to step into Mother's shoes, to get her husband and actually *be* Mother. Why, I bet she even wanted to be Tony's mother instead of Lee's."

"A book tells you all about that?" said Mitch.

"You're impossible!" exclaimed Fern. "You can't be that stupid."

"I'm trying to solve a murder," said Mitch laconically. "Whether Christie Mae was jealous of your mother doesn't interest me. All I want to know is where Christie Mae was on Monday night."

"Well, do you know?"

"Sure," said Mitch. "She was home."

"Is that what she told you?"

"She told me, and I checked up on it. And then she tries to pull a phony."

Fern frowned. "I suppose I should have stayed there to comfort her. But somehow, the whole thing was disgusting. She couldn't even convince herself, so how could she convince you?"

"She told me plenty."

"What?"

"She told me who she thought killed Peter."

"And who was that?" asked Fern quietly.

Mitch shook his glass and let the ice tinkle. Fern asked too many questions, and when you didn't tell her something she took it as a personal insult. Still, you didn't get reactions unless you threw a few ideas around, and Mitch wanted Fern's reaction. After all, you never knew.

"Who?" asked Fern again.

"Lee, her son, of course. Who in hell else?" He made a face and said in his high, squeaky voice, "That's mother-love for you. She wouldn't want to take the rap for anyone except her own son, and if I hadn't known Lee was with you all night, I'd grab him and grill the hell out of him." He smiled at Fern. "Maybe I will anyhow, just for the fun of it."

"Can I come along?"

"No."

Fern pouted and finished her drink. "Have you got much money?" she asked suddenly.

"What do you want?"

"I feel like drinking. If you've got plenty, we'll stay here. Otherwise you can come back to my place and drink out of a bottle."

"The way you drink," said Mitch, "we better get out of here."

It was still raining and Fern called a cab and gave her address. On the way she said, "It's funny, isn't it, Christie Mae getting all that money? I was afraid Peter would marry Andrea and leave everything to her. That's why I wanted to break it up. And it was all useless, wasn't it?"

"What was useless?"

"Wanting him to give Andrea up," said Fern. "You know, Andrea was much too nice for him."

The bed was still unmade and the kitchenette was still a mess. Fern threw a cover over the bed and brought out a bottle and two glasses.

"Are you married?" she asked.

"Sure. So are you."

"Oh," said Fern. She smiled and rumpled his hair in passing.

"What are you going to do," asked Mitch, "about money?"

Fern shrugged. "I don't know. Lee's giving me money now. He isn't making too much at the moment, but he will. If I ask for a lot I'll get a lot. And he can always sell the house."

"Is there much money in art?"

"If you're clever there is. Lee started off by being a kind of critic. He also did a little painting and wrote articles. Peter used to tell him he'd be broke all his life. And then Lee sold a painting for five hundred dollars that he'd bought two years before for ten. Peter was impressed by that. Buy cheap and sell dear—anyone who could do that was all right. Peter was so impressed with the percentage of profit that he set Lee up in business. But Lee didn't repeat often enough and so Peter went back to his old contempt."

"Didn't Lee resent it?"

"Of course he did. He resented everything about Peter. Peter used to try and get him drunk whenever there was a party. He wanted to disgrace Lee."

"Kind of a private feud?"

"Oh, no. Peter was like that with everybody, except when he was trying to sell them insurance. His favorite trick with me, for instance, was to try to catch me in lies. He'd ask me where I was going or with whom, and then he'd call up to see if I was there or not. If I was, he'd make some excuse and not mention it again. But if I wasn't—as usually happened—he'd tell me I was dishonest and unworthy of trust and all that sort of thing. And the funny part of it all is that Mother thought he was wonderful. And he was—to her. I wish it would stop raining."

"What did you mean earlier this afternoon when you said there were things locked in your mind that would give me a new angle?"

"Oh, Mitch darling, I was just joking." She smiled at him. "Do you like this dress?"

"Sure. It looks nice."

"Oh," said Fern. She filled her glass and then dumped some more into Mitch's. "You're not drinking much." Her face was close to his as she leaned down to pour. He didn't look at her. Her cheek grazed his as she stood up.

Mitch lifted his glass and didn't drink. Fern was nice. A little heavier than Amy, but with weight in the right places. And she was practically asking for it.

She'd slept with Lee on Monday night and probably with Boganov last night. She had a few hours off and she was making a play for Mitch.

She couldn't be trusted. She'd blab about him and think he was nuts about her, and if he didn't do what she asked, she'd write in a complaint and his promotion would be off. He wasn't going to chance that, just for a few minutes with Fern. Besides, he had a kid coming. He had responsibilities.

"I've only been like this since Tony died," said Fern affably. "I was at Peter's the evening the telegram came. He was going to take Christie Mae out to dinner. I'd stopped in to give him some bills and he'd told me that once a man saw his daughter married, he was supposed to be quit of all financial responsibility. He said a man who couldn't support his wife had no real manhood. I told Peter he didn't know the half of it, and he said I had a dirty mind.

"Somehow, the remark hit me wrong. Peter had said a lot of nasty things to me in the course of my life, but he's not usually that crude. I told him that if Tony were here, he wouldn't dare say things like that."

Fern lifted the bottle and started to pour some more liquor into her glass. Then she noticed her glass was still full. Her hand shook a little and she put the bottle back on the bureau.

"Then the doorbell rang," she continued. "It was a telegram from the war department. Peter read it and handed it to me. When I looked up, the bellboy was still standing there. Peter's lips were moving, but there was absolute quiet. I thought I'd gone deaf. There weren't even street noises.

"I said, 'You'd better tip the boy.' I heard my voice and then the other sounds came back. Peter gave the boy a half dollar and looked at the telegram again.

"'It says Corporal Anthony P. Jarvis was killed in action,' said Peter. 'What is it that we always called him? You know—his nickname.' It took me a couple of seconds to realize that Peter couldn't think of Tony's name. It was an awful shock. I thought Peter had had a stroke or something, but it wasn't that at all. I told him and he said, 'Oh, yes. Tony. He was my son.'

"Then I told Peter he'd better tell Christie Mae to call it off for the evening. He said no, he had an important client to see. And then he smiled and said maybe it would be a good idea at that. It would create sympathy and he would have a better chance of selling the policy.

"I started drinking the next day. Really drinking, that is."

Mitch got up. It was tough on Fern, but what could he do about it? He was here to ask questions about a homicide, and now he was all tangled up feeling sorry for a kid whose brother had been killed and who was becoming an alcoholic.

Mitch raised his glass and gulped down the contents. To a soldier, he told himself. Lee hated Tony and all the others had loved him. Well, whatever Tony had really been—to a soldier.

Fern smiled. "Lee told me how he socked you out in the hall. I thought you'd be able to handle him better than that. Lee isn't so big."

"I bumped into that lamp fixture."

"It was a funny evening, wasn't it, Mitch? I have a confession to make. I didn't really pass out. I just wanted to get rid of you so I could phone Lee and tell him the good news. You're awful easy to fool."

"Thanks," said Mitch.

The laughter bubbled out of her and she curtsied deep and low. When she stood up, she pirouetted gracefully. Her dress swirled around her and she held her stance, one leg across the other, one toe pointed gracefully.

"I studied ballet once," she said.

"It's quite a trick."

She approached him demurely and her pink lips pouted at him. He didn't move, but he let her come and plant her mouth on his.

They held it for about a half minute. She was educated, Mitch kept telling himself. She knew how, and she wanted it.

When she moved away, she wasn't smiling any more. Mitch smelt the alcohol on her. He'd only had one full drink, to a soldier. The rest of the time he'd gone easy. He didn't like drunks, particularly women drunks, but he could see why Fern went for the stuff. With a guy like Peter for a father. With her marriage on the rocks and then the news about Tony. If she took it out in drink, you couldn't really blame her. She'd snap out of it one of these days.

"Like my dress?" she said.

Mitch stared at her, feeling the pulse beat in his temple. "Sure," he said.

"I hate it," she said. She reached down the side, zipped something and yanked the dress off. She didn't have much on underneath, but what there was she kind of sidestepped and then she was standing stark naked in front of him.

He felt funny, being all dressed that way when she wasn't. He tried to think, but his mind was fuzzy and nothing came clear. Amy's name kept flitting across his mind. He was on his way up, to a promotion. He couldn't take chances.

Fern wouldn't talk. But if she did, he could kiss his promotion good-by. But she wouldn't talk. And to walk out on her now would be a dirty trick.

She frowned slightly, as if she didn't quite understand. This wasn't the way things happened. A guy like Mitch didn't stand there in a daze, unable to make up his mind.

He made it up suddenly. He grunted, muttered something at her, grabbed his hat and marched straight past her and out of the apartment.

Fern—she was dynamite.

III

Mitch walked a couple of blocks in the rain before he could even think straight. Then he looked at his watch. It wasn't even five. He felt as if it were a couple of weeks since he'd seen Amy.

Suddenly he had a craving to speak to her. He couldn't go home yet because he still had another stop to make, but at least he could hear her voice.

He went into a phone booth and called his number. Amy's voice said, "Hello?"

"Hello."

"Oh, Mitch!"

"Yeah. That you, Amy?"

"Of course it is. What's wrong, Mitch?"

"Nothing. Nothing at all. I just wanted to see how you were."

"That's sweet of you. I'm fine, darling. I've been doing some mending. And I remembered what it was I couldn't think of yesterday."

"Yeah. What?"

"About the holes in your socks. There are so many of them that you must have a nail in your shoe. I wanted you to look. Will you?"

"Now?" asked Mitch.

"Of course not. I mean when you get home. You sound as if you were in a daze. Did anything happen?"

"To me? No. Nothing."

"It doesn't sound like you. Will you remind me to ask you to look for the nail when you get home? And the faucet leaks. You'll have to fix that again."

"Sure," said Mitch. "Look, Amy, I don't know just when I'll get back. You know how these things are. But if I get home in time, maybe we can make that movie. Are you listening?"

"You said maybe we could make that movie."

"Yeah. Well, I guess that's all, then. So long."

"Good-by, Mitch."

He hung up and went outside. He felt better now. Cleaner, and his mind was beginning to work. And as he got his thoughts straight, one thing became more and more certain. He had to see Lee Kent.

Mitch's number-one candidate was still Andrea, but in this

game, he told himself, you've got to cover everything. That was the one thing Charlie Corrigan had always impressed on him.

"The difference between the guy that stays a flatfoot all his life and the guy who gets to the top is that the one of them gets his case and lets it go at that, and the other one keeps on cleaning up all the angles. If it's a big case, you never know but what the lawyer on the other side is going to turn up something you didn't bother with, and make something out of it. Then where are you, huh? You're there on the carpet listening to the lieutenant."

So Mitch wasn't letting anything slide, just because he had Andrea Minx on ice. He was following up every lead he had, and that meant Lee Kent. He ought to see this hotel manager, too, and find out how crooked his teeth were, but that could wait. Lee Kent was more important.

First of all, if Christie Mae had done all that to protect her son, she had a reason. She knew something that Mitch didn't, and it had made her think Lee was guilty. And even though he had an alibi, there was another possibility. Maybe Lee and Fern had committed the crime jointly.

Mitch didn't think much of the idea, but he was going through with it. A guy and a girl who are getting divorced don't commit homicide together. When you're nuts about each other, like Judd Gray and Ruth Snyder,* maybe you do, but not the

---

* May Ruth Brown met and married Albert Snyder in 1915 when she was twenty and Snyder was thirty-three. They settled in Queens, and in 1918, they had a daughter. In 1925, Brown began an affair with Henry Judd Gray, a married corset salesman who lived in the New Jersey suburbs. She began to plan the murder of the physically and emotionally abusive Snyder, enlisting Gray's help, and, according to Gray, made seven attempts to kill Snyder. In 1927, Snyder was found in his home, garroted with a picture wire, his nose stuffed with chloroform-soaked rags, and his head beaten with a sash weight. Brown claimed that a burglary had occurred, but the police found her behavior inconsistent with this tale. She and Gray were arrested for murder and, at a sensational trial, they turned on each other, each accusing the other of the actual killing. Both were convicted, and in 1928 both were electrocuted by the State of New York, Brown's death occurring only ten minutes before Gray's.

Fern-Lee combination. Still, there were enough signs pointing in Kent's direction to put him next on the list.

Mitch called the gallery and the girl told him Kent had gone home early, so Mitch took the bus over to the apartment on East Eleventh Street and went upstairs.

Lee Kent greeted him coldly. "Oh, it's you. What do you want now?"

Mitch looked around. It must have cost plenty to fix up this place. It had that new, modern furniture that Amy always said she wanted to get, and Mitch knew you couldn't buy it on Fourteenth Street. There were some more of the bad-dream paintings and a few carvings and then some stuff that he recognized vaguely as being Indian.

"You got a nice joint," said Mitch. "This where you and Fern lived?"

"The Kent love nest," remarked Lee sardonically.

"Mind if I look around?" asked Mitch. "I don't get a chance to see this kind of thing often."

"Admission free," said Kent. "Do you want a conducted tour, or do you prefer to wander?"

"Either way," said Mitch affably. "You may as well tag along, though."

"I was just getting ready to go out when you rang the bell. You won't be too long, will you?"

Mitch strolled into the bedroom. The walls were silver and there was only one picture in here. He didn't like it. The bed would sleep four people, if they weren't too fat, and any extras would find it comfortable on the big bearskin rug. There was a full-length, three-piece mirror, like you found in the clothing stores, only this one had a table built into it. Fern's vanity table, Mitch supposed.

He looked at himself in it, examining the shine across the back of his shoulders.

"I never can get a suit that fits right," he said. "They're always tight on me."

"You should have your clothes made to order."

"On my salary?" said Mitch.

"I have mine made at an uptown place. Nelson's. Only thirty dollars."

"Say!" said Mitch. "I didn't know you could get it that cheap. What kind of stuff does he make?"

"Everything I own comes from there," said Kent. He opened a closet door. "Plenty of variety, you see."

Mitch stepped into the closet and examined the rack. There was no tan suit.

"Well, I won't keep you if you got some place to go," said Mitch. "I saw your mother today. She was plenty upset."

Kent led the way outside. "Yes, I know. She was fond of Jarvis, in a way."

"You weren't?"

"We didn't get along," said Kent. "I told you that."

"Yeah," said Mitch. "The question is how well you didn't get along."

"Find out for yourself," said Kent. "You ought to do something to earn your salary, besides asking me questions and pestering Andrea. Tell me—what possible motive could she have?"

"I wouldn't know," said Mitch, "unless she told me."

They were silent as they rode down in the elevator and marched outside. In the rain-swept doorway, Lee halted.

"Seen my dentist yet?" he asked abruptly.

"One of the boys stopped in. Picked up a cast of your teeth and took it downtown, but it didn't tell us much." Mitch stared gloomily at the rain. "A guy like that could pull a fast one easy. How would *we* know if he gave us the wrong teeth?"

"Any time you want," said Kent irritably, "I'll come down to headquarters and bite a piece of cheese for you."

"Clay," said Mitch.

"Clay," repeated Kent. "Glad to oblige, though I'm not fond of the taste."

Mitch decided he was being kidded in some subtle, high-hat way. To change the conversation he said, "This damn rain."

"September's the month for it," said Kent. "The equinox."

Mitch snorted. "Yeah. But why can't it rain the days I can stay home and relax? It never happens that way." He stared at the sky, a stocky man of medium height, chesty, speaking in a high-pitched voice, seeing the whole universe in personal conspiracy against him.

"Which direction you going?" he asked.

Kent looked down, uncertain about something, sniffing vaguely. Finally he said, "I'm going uptown. I have my car here. Can I give you a lift?"

"Thanks," said Mitch. "You can drop me off at a subway station."

Lee led the way to a black Plymouth sedan, 1940 model. A street lamp shone down on it and turned the rain drops into quicksilver. The paint had dulled from the weather, but the right front fender gleamed.

Kent climbed in and switched on the motor. Mitch followed and slammed the door. His eyes were bright, hopeful, but he held himself back, waiting to calm down, staring fixedly through the moving windshield wipers.

When he spoke, his voice was deeper than usual. He gave no other sign of tension.

"You got a brand new fender," he remarked.

Kent nodded. "Yes. I was lucky to get it, in these times." He swung into the middle of the street and eased to a stop at the first traffic light. With the gear lever in neutral, he turned towards Mitch.

"I don't usually have the luxury of a car in town," he said, "but I used it to bring some of my pictures down from the country. I didn't like to leave them in an empty house. It's inviting theft."

So what? thought Mitch. So Kent had a car in town, like a few hundred thousand other people. Why all the explanations?

"What did you need the new fender for?" he asked.

"I smashed up the old one. I don't change them for amusement."

"Oh," said Mitch. "Had an accident, huh?"

Kent nodded and started the car as the light changed. Mitch breathed slowly. He crossed his legs and then uncrossed them as he felt the dampness of the cloth on his knee. Stranger things than this had happened. You investigate one case, and another one falls in your lap. Andrea for murder, Kent for the hit-and-run.

Charlie Corrigan always said, "Keep your eyes open, and you get the breaks when you don't expect 'em. I cracked a ten-year-old murder by helping a kid fish a nickel out of an iron grating."

It was possible. Why not? Mitch began to feel certain of it. Boy, but would they fall over dead if he brought in the guy who'd smashed into Treeberg!

"What happened?" he asked casually.

"I skidded into a lamp post. There was a little rain and some of the streets were wet. Still, I don't know how it happened. Fatigue and inattention, I suppose. My only accident in ten years of driving."

"Where?"

"Uptown, on Convent Avenue.* Luckily the street was deserted. I'd have hated to hit anyone."

---

* On the west side of Harlem, running between 140th and 150th Streets.

"Who did the repair work?"

"You seem too interested," smiled Kent. "I injured no one and damaged no one's property except my own. I felt like a fool, but scraping a lamp post that belongs to the city is no crime, is it?"

"Who fixed your fender?" asked Mitch again.

Kent jerked the car as he shifted gears. "Why do you want to know?" he demanded irritably.

"There's a hit-and-run accident I'm interested in."

"If I'd hit anyone, I'd have reported it," said Kent sharply. "As a matter of fact, a cop came and looked over the damage and let me go. It was my fault and I had the trouble and expense of getting a new fender. I daresay the whole thing is filed away somewhere, for posterity to find when they read my biography. 'On September twelfth, 1945, Lee Kent skidded into a lamp post and sprained a finger. Several days later, a nameless detective showed a morbid interest in the event.'"

"You sprained your finger, too? Which one?"

"Third finger, left hand. It's getting along nicely, thanks."

"Who fixed the fender?" demanded Mitch for the third time.

Kent sighed. "You're persistent. Some place on West Fifty-Fourth street. Or maybe Fifty-Fifth. I'm not sure. The receipted bill is there in the glove compartment. You'll find it if you look."

Mitch opened the compartment and rummaged. The bill was there all right. Tip-Top Garage, West Fifty-Fourth.

Somehow, Mitch was sure, then. A guy makes up a story to explain the new fender. Convent Avenue instead of West End Avenue, Tuesday night instead of Monday. Maybe Kent had actually had an accident or maybe he'd heard of one. Anyhow, he'd probably woven a few facts into his story and made up the rest. That's the way most lies went.

Mitch glanced at Kent's small, tight features. Kent was tricky. Sure. But with all his brains, he didn't know about the police laboratory.

"You can drop me at the next corner," said Mitch quietly. "Over there by the subway entrance."

Kent swung towards the curb and came to a stop. "Thanks for the ride," said Mitch.

Kent nodded. His thin, sensitive lips widened slightly in a smile. "Not at all," he said.

Mitch got out and slammed the door. As the car slid uptown on the shiny, black pavement, Mitch took out his memo pad and jotted down the license numbers.

He took a crosstown bus and trudged the rest of the way in the rain. The garage specialized in repair work, but it was after hours now and the place was almost empty. A light was burning in the dingy front office. In the old days, there'd have been a collection of uniformed chauffeurs lounging around on the broken-down chairs. But now the place was deserted except for a guy in a straw hat poring over a bunch of bills. The going was heavy and his square, unshaven face looked irritable.

"Yeah?" he said, all set to take it out on Mitch. "What do you want?"

Mitch showed his badge. "I want to find out something about a fender you replaced. Party by the name of Kent."

"Look," said the garageman. "He got a bill. The price is on there. It's the regular ceiling price, listed in the book. What the hell is he yapping about?"

"Keep your shirt on," said Mitch. "This isn't an OPA case.* If

---

* The OPA was the Office of Price Administration. During the war, the federal government implemented an elaborate system of price controls to reduce or eliminate profiteering. Wage and price controls were introduced again in the United States for two brief periods in 1971 and 1973, when Richard Nixon imposed them.

you charged him double and put the list price on the bill, that's between you and Kent. I'm working on the accident he had."

"What about it? Where do I come in on an accident?"

"I want to see his old fender."

"It's in back somewhere. What do you want to do with it?"

"Borrow it and look it over. We'll send a truck for it, you'll get your receipt, and then the fender comes back here just as soon as we find out what we're after. We do everything except supply you with a new set of diapers."

The garageman got up without speaking, switched on an overhead light and started for the rear. "I got it some place."

He located it in a corner of the repair shop. The whole side of the fender was crumpled in and there was a knife-like gash that had almost cut it in two. Mitch stared. This was it, all right. He could feel it in his bones.

"That cut must have been opened up in some other accident," said the garageman. "Somebody just bent the pieces back together and painted over the joint, but the whole business is rusted underneath. Been rusting away for a couple of years. Look—you can see for yourself."

He parted the two pieces and showed the flaked, rusty edges. Mitch examined them. "Yeah," he said. He was less sure as he scratched Kent's name and then his own on the fender for identification.

"You give 'em this when they come," said Mitch. "I'll phone now."

He was bothered as he returned to the front office and picked up the phone. Maybe the garageman knew what he was talking about and maybe he didn't. Well, Jub had said to send along the evidence and the lab would do the rest. So it was up to them. Why should Mitch worry?

He gave his badge number to the operator and his call went

through free. When he was connected with the research lab, he said, "Is Jub Freeman there?"

"Gone for the day," answered the technician on duty.

Mitch grunted. "This is Taylor, Two-One Squad. On the Jarvis case. I got something to check up on."

He gave the necessary information. While the technician repeated the garage address, Mitch slipped his hand in his pocket and fingered the bitten half of nougat and the hunk of cigar.

"There's something else," he said. He glared at the garageman and the garageman glared back. "I can't talk private right now," continued Mitch, "but you'll know what I want with this stuff. A cigar, and some tooth marks."

The garageman went back to his bills. Mitch brought the phone close to his mouth and gave his explanations in a low voice. When he hung up, the garageman spoke in a monotone, without glancing at Mitch.

"How much longer you going to be on that phone?"

Without answering, Mitch made a second call, to his precinct. He gave a routine report to the lieutenant and then said he wanted to find out whether Lee Kent had brought in a tan suit, possibly with blood stains, to any of the cleaning establishments in his neighborhood. The appropriate local precinct could check.

Mitch put down the phone and glanced at his watch. He'd put in a day's work all right. He'd just about have time to get a bite to eat and make the show with Amy.

Later on in the evening, sitting in the theatre and holding Amy's hand, Mitch kept wondering about that hit-and-run. It was almost too much to hope for. Two cases out of two. Naah—he never got breaks like that. The way things went with Mitch, he'd do all the work and then the Minx or whoever was guilty would walk into headquarters and confess. It would happen on Mitch's day off and he'd be some place where he couldn't be reached, and he wouldn't even hear about it until the next morning.

Well, what the hell. All he was interested in was his promotion. He began figuring his salary, whether it would take care of the kid and whether they'd have to cut down on expenses or not. When the whole audience rocked with laughter at some crack that had been made on the screen, Mitch realized he hadn't even heard it.

He squeezed Amy's hand and she squeezed back. With a wife like her, he didn't have any real worries. She was all right. By and by he began to pay attention to the show. It was one of those murder stories. The cop wanted a promotion so he could be hot stuff and marry the girl, and he thought he'd get promoted by solving the case.

Mitch snorted in disgust. You got promoted because you had a rabbi. That was what counted. What made the movies hand out this kind of tripe? Didn't they know any better?

Presently Amy leaned over and whispered. "What kind of a day did you have, Mitch?"

"Lousy," he muttered. "Same old merry-go-round."

He settled back grumpily and stared at the screen. Gradually it caught and held his interest. Now a guy like that, with something happening to him every minute—that was the life. But all Mitch ever did was interview a bunch of screwballs.

Avidly, enviously, he watched the picture.

FIVE

I

Late that same afternoon Jub Freeman entered the 1910 version
of American baroque where he lived with his aunt. He ascended
in the remodeled elevator cage of false mahogany, tramped
down the imitation lapis-lazuli corridor and, with a sense of
emerging finally into the fresh air, turned the key to his apartment and entered the living room.

It was a room you could neither duplicate nor disregard. It
had been constructed laboriously with the pieces of Aunt Ella's
life, and the lives of her forebears. The brown plush couch might
be hard at first contact, but it was soft with the memories of Ella's
great-aunt, the one who had sallied forth after Chancellorsville
to nurse the Union wounded. The wooden rocker wasn't inviting, but Ella had climbed it when she was three, and for the last
fifty years it had been part of her home. What it lacked in comfort, it made up for in sentiment. And so it went, piece by piece,
through the plush chairs, the carved bookcases and the strange
and varied collection of tables, foot-stools, cabinets, desk.

But the room derived its character not so much from the

furniture as from the mass of pictures, books, samplers, prints, clocks, ornaments, souvenirs and bric-a-brac. Every object was mellowed with history and Jub's boyhood was rich with their stories. The silver cup, for instance, had been given Ella by the hospital where she worked before coming to New York. The pipe rack had belonged to her husband, the mounted coins were souvenirs of the Columbia exhibit of 1893,* and the old musket had accompanied a patriotic Freeman in the course of a half dozen skirmishes with the British redcoats.

Aunt Ella was sitting in the wooden rocker when Jub came in.

"Hello, Aunt Ella," he said. The dimple came and went as he bent down and kissed her, lightly, for she was a fragile, meek woman. Despite her years, she was not old. She had no wrinkles and never would have. She had been about forty when he'd first been orphaned, and she would remain about forty until the day she died—if she was human and some day would actually cease to exist—Jub doubted it.

"Have a good day?" she asked.

"Fair. And you? Anything new in bedlam?"

"No, nothing." She smiled, as she always did, at his allusion to the pre-school nursery where she worked.

"Anything happen at the lab?" she asked. "How is the Jarvis case going?"

"Still a puzzler. One of the boys finally broke down my substance X. It's plain ordinary house paint. Road tar with paint in it—I wish I could figure it out." He shook his head and stared into space, his forehead wrinkled and his sharp features poised, as if he were waiting to grab the idea that didn't come.

"Jub," said Aunt Ella, "sometimes I think you lead an unnatural life. Spending your time studying a bit of paint and worrying

---

* A world's fair held in Chicago to celebrate the four hundredth anniversary of Christopher Columbus's voyage to America.

over where it comes from. When you visited my nursery you said all the babies looked alike. If you can't tell *them* apart, how can you tell paint?"

"With a spectroscope. And if I had samples of your babies, I bet I could classify them, too."

"Heaven forbid!" exclaimed Aunt Ella. "What do you do about your paint now?"

"Rack my brains for another week. Fuss and fume and flutter."

She looked at his solid, substantial bulk. "Flutter!" she said. "You!"

He grinned amiably and then he caught the fragrant odor emanating from the kitchen. "What's that?" he asked. "Bread?"

Aunt Ella nodded guiltily. "Yes. I came home early and had nothing else to do. I thought I might as well bake."

Jub stared at her, uncertain whether to accuse her of overtaxing her energy or whether to accept the results in good part. He decided on the latter.

"If this date of mine weren't so important," he said, "I'd call it off and eat the stuff right now."

Aunt Ella smiled in relief. "Her name's Andrea, isn't it? It's a nice name."

"She's beautiful," said Jub. "I only saw her once, for a few moments. If she's as nice as I think she is, I want you to meet her."

"I saw her picture in the paper," remarked Aunt Ella placidly. "It said she'd been going around with Jarvis. He was much older than she, wasn't he?"

Jub laughed. It was as near to a rebuke as Aunt Ella was capable of reaching. He put his hand on her shoulder and whispered.

"I'll tell you something. I go round with an older woman myself. In fact, I'm in love with her."

"Is she related to you?" asked Ella. "Your aunt, for instance?"

"Could be," said Jub. He went into the bathroom to wash.

An hour later, ringing the downstairs bell at Andrea Minx's house and waiting for the answering buzz, he felt embarrassed. He wasn't sure whether he had a date or was working on a case.

Either way, this was dangerous business. If it was ever discovered that he'd gone to dinner with a suspect, and an attractive one at that, there'd be hell to pay. To the police mind, there would be only one possible interpretation.

Well, the hell with the police mind. Jub was an individual human being and he had no intention of restricting his whole life to conform to a set of departmental rules. If his superior officers knew what he thought of the police mind, they'd confiscate his shield and suspend him in nothing flat. One of the first things that Jub the cop had learnt was to keep his mouth shut. He had discovered that he could get away with most things so long as nobody knew his reasons. The average cop, if he happened to see an infraction on the part of one of his fellows, kept his mouth shut. Among themselves, the police subscribed to a philosophy of live and let live. Like the inmates of a jail, they were banded together against the rest of the world.

Still, Jub was taking risks and he knew it.

The buzzer rasped and he opened the front door and went upstairs. He hadn't seen Andrea since the night he'd been here with Mitch Taylor, but he'd thought of her often, and always she appeared in his mind as she had at that first moment. A dark scared thing, graceful and unexpected, with her hand pressed against her mouth and her brown eyes slowly widening. The light from the room had been shining obliquely, illuminating one side of her face and leaving the other in darkness. But there had been no props and no warning. She had been as natural as water and as unaffected as sky.

Jub sighed, straightened his shoulders and rapped on the

door. He heard her voice, vibrant and quick with some under-current of emotion. "Who's there?" she asked.

"It's me. Jub Freeman."

There were footsteps and the sound of a bolt sliding back. Then a lock snapped and the door swung open.

Looking at her that first swift moment, Jub was disappointed. Somehow she was not made of moonbeams and dew, as he'd been dreaming. She was flesh and blood, and her delicate air was shyness and fright and hormones and glands and neurons.

Then she smiled and the animation of her face transformed her. She wasn't the Andrea he'd imagined, but he liked her.

"Hello," he said.

"Hello. Won't you come in?"

"Thanks." With his peculiar, rolling gait, he marched inside and waited for her to sit down.

"I had the bolt put on," she said. "I guess it seems silly to you."

He gulped and wanted to say, "Please—forget it. Be yourself. You're beautiful and you don't have to put on an act. Not for me." But all he said, in a dull, flat voice was, "No. Not silly."

"I wish I understood what's happening. You heard how somebody tried to break down my door, didn't you?"

"I saw the report," said Jub. He didn't mention what they'd said about it. That she was seeing things under the bed. That a guy had taken a bag of junk for a thrift shop and she'd watched him as if he were walking off with her right arm.

"I hoped you'd come," she said. "I wanted to explain so many things. Taylor, the detective who arrested me—he made it sound all wrong. He kept asking the same questions over and over again. Why was I worried about Jarvis? Why did I think something had happened to him? I couldn't answer because I didn't know. I never do have reasons. I just know."

"I get hunches," said Jub. "With you, it would be intuition."

She smiled impulsively. "No. Let's call mine a hunch, too. It sounds so much more substantial."

Jub studied her. She raised dark, luminous eyes and met his gaze unflinchingly. He didn't think she was the kind who took fright at nothing at all.

"Well?" she smiled. "Am I?"

"Are you what?"

"Dizzy. Cracked. Hysterical. Seeing people behind doors. That's what you were wondering, isn't it?"

Jub stared at her. Mind-reading? Hardly. Just a logical inference, such as any intelligent person might make.

"Listen," he said. "I've been working on this since Monday night. I'm woozy with it. I thought we'd have dinner and a drink and talk things over. Andrea, you're scared, aren't you?"

She nodded. "Yes."

"Why? What's wrong?"

"Wrong? I hardly know, but you can't imagine what it's like. I don't have a persecution complex, and yet I think someone is following me. I've received no threats, and yet I'm being threatened every single minute. Have you ever lived with fear?"

He got up and crossed the room and took her hand. The fingers that grasped his were cold. He looked down at her. Her dark eyes, intent on his, seemed to lose their hunted look. He released her hand.

"Feel any better?" he asked.

"Well," she said, and she was laughing at him. "Well—no."

He shrugged. "If you don't, I do. What are you afraid of?"

She caught her breath. Nobody had the right to ask her this, for it was not a thing you could put into words. You're scared because you're scared. It sounds silly when you say it.

"I'm scared of being murdered," she said at last.

"By whom?"

"I don't know."

"I think you do."

"Well—" There was another long hesitation, and then she came out with it. "By Jarvis."

Jub's voice was flat, cold; it gave no indication of his surprise. "Jarvis is dead."

"Yes, but I'm afraid of him. There's no one else I can think of. I have to be afraid of a person and a name, don't I? Well, I call him Peter Jarvis."

"Why Jarvis?"

"Because everything starts with him. It's something he began and it's still going on."

"If it comes from him," said Jub, and he was groping for some idea that eluded him, "then Fern is the person to see. Fern ought to know, somehow."

Andrea looked at him sadly. He had a feeling that there was something on her mind, that she could supply him with a piece of information which would change everything, and that she wasn't going to tell. He waited a long time, but she didn't speak.

"Andrea," he said suddenly, "let's try to figure this out. There's something missing. There's got to be. You scream because your cat is dead, and Taylor ropes you in on his accident. We come up here on the accident, and you send us out on a homicide. I take the evidence of the two cases and put them in the spectroscope, and presto—they connect. Who's Simon Treeberg?"

"I never heard of him."

Jub frowned. Maybe she hadn't heard of him. Maybe Mitch Taylor was right and Andrea had killed Jarvis and managed to hold out on the police. Jub knew he shouldn't trust her simply because he liked her and was attracted. He was playing with fire. And yet he did trust her, completely, which was no way for a cop to behave.

"And this man who tried to see you while you were out. The big guy that the janitor mentioned—who is he? You've thought about that, haven't you?"

"Yes, but I haven't the least idea. He sounds like my brother, Jack, but Jack is in uniform and he's at Camp Benning, in Georgia."

"All I can do," said Jub, "is to work on the case of the cat. It's the only concrete thing there is. Jarvis was killed without clues, but Stanley—let's investigate Stanley. Did anyone dislike him?"

"Jarvis did."

"Why?"

"He just didn't like cats. He didn't like animals or people or anything or anyone except his own self. I disliked him from the moment I met him. I wanted to break with him, but I couldn't do it short of an insult, and I never can bring myself to hurt anyone deliberately. Besides, I guess I had fun trying to deflate him. Thinking back, I can't understand why I was willing to go out with him even once. I suppose it was on account of Fern and Lee."

"Do you know them well?"

"Fairly well, although I only met them last June. I spent a few weekends at their place and I've seen Fern quite often. But I don't feel intimate. I couldn't ever, after that first weekend. It was so queer."

"In what way?"

"You'll laugh at me," she said gravely, as if she dared and doubledared him to. "It will sound silly."

"Why? Did your intuitions tell you that Peter Jarvis was going to be murdered?"

"Oh, no. Nothing like that. But everything was so tense. Lee and Fern were thinking of breaking up, and Peter Jarvis had come there to see that they did." She shuddered violently. "Ugh! I was thinking about the cat."

"Stanley?"

"No, not Stanley. It was a kitten that grinned. The Kents had just gotten it—a funny, stupid, awkward little thing. Half its face was black and the other half white, with a red splotch right in the middle, as if it had stuck its face in a bottle of red ink and couldn't lick it off. A calico cat. It hadn't solved the problem of feet and it was always right underneath you. Jarvis kept knocking it out of his way with his cane. He had a habit of prodding things, as if he were too fine to touch objects directly."

"What happened to the cat?" asked Jub.

Andrea made a face and shuddered again. "I hate to think of it. It gives me the willies, and I always felt that somehow he did it on purpose. I didn't see it happen. I was at the other side of the house, and I heard a scream and came running. Lee dashed out at the same time, and there we saw Fern and Jarvis. She was having hysterics. She'd been cutting flowers and she had her scissors in one hand, open, and she was yelling at Jarvis and trying to attack him. He was holding her off with his cane, like a fencer, and he had such a queer, cold smile, as if he were enjoying it and wanted to get through her guard and poke her in the stomach.

"Lee grabbed Fern and she calmed down at once and gave him the scissors. I remember thinking that maybe it was good, the way she turned and clung to him, because they were so near to breaking up."

"But what was it all about?" demanded Jub. "Where does the kitten come in?"

"The kitten? Jarvis slammed the car door on it. It was simply horrible. I lost control of myself, too. Lee put his arm around me and squeezed the two of us. Fern and me. We were bawling all over each other, like a couple of babies. Then Jarvis walked past and said, 'You'd better tell the maid to clean it up.'

"Fern and I looked at each other, and then Lee took us inside and fed us drinks. Later on, Jarvis tried to convince me that Fern had told him to close the car door and he'd just pushed it without even looking. But that's impossible."

"Think he killed Stanley, too?" asked Jub quietly.

"I don't know. Why would he?"

"Let's start with Stanley again. You came home and opened the door. Did you notice anything on the way in? Anything at all?"

"No. I was thinking of Rose Ollenbach and how I wished I could go abroad, too."

"All right. You came in and looked for Stanley and he wasn't there. The bathroom door was closed and you wondered whether he was locked in. Had you shut the bathroom door before you'd left the house?"

"I don't know. I've shut him in before and have had no recollection of it, so that was my first thought. That I'd gone and done it again."

Jub smiled, "Don't look so forlorn about it. Now the carton— had *that* been in the bathroom earlier in the day?"

"I don't remember. The way it was placed, underneath the tub, it could have been there a week, or it might have been put there just a few minutes earlier. I wish I could be more helpful."

Jub licked his lips. "You said you rushed across the living room to open the window. Are you sure it was closed?"

"Oh, yes. I hardly ever open a window. I even sleep with it closed. I remember their making fun of me up in the country. Peter Jarvis claimed I was afraid a strange man might come in."

"Suppose you show me exactly what you did," said Jub. "The window was closed, like now. The lights were out. I'll turn them off and then you can come in. If you go through the motions, maybe you'll remember something that's slipped your mind."

"I'd rather not," said Andrea. Then she shrugged and stood up. "I'm just being superstitious, I guess."

She walked to the door and opened it. Jub switched off the lights. He watched Andrea's silhouette.

"All right?" she asked faintly.

"Yes."

"I walked in," she said. She took a breath. "I said, 'Stanley?' There wasn't any answer. I turned on the lights, like this." She pushed the wall switch and the bridge lamp near the window flashed on. "I noticed the bathroom door was closed and I went in. Stanley was there, next to the carton, looking as if he were asleep. I picked him up. It was cold and suddenly I felt—I don't know. Frightened, as if I couldn't breathe."

She'd said that before. The cold. The fear of not being able to breathe.

"Yes?" said Jub.

"I started for the light. In the middle of the room I dropped the carton and almost fell over it. Then I rushed to the window, like this."

She darted past him and flung herself on the bed and pulled up the window. "Jub, must I scream again?"

"No, don't scream. Sit down now. You must have brought the carton into the bedroom at the same time that you brought Stanley. That explains why it was in the center of the floor. But who put it in the bathroom and why?"

"I don't know. I don't remember. The next day I asked the janitor and he said he knew nothing about it. It scares me."

"That's enough," said Jub abruptly, "Put your hat on and let's go eat."

II

Toying with her drink in a comfortable, crowded restaurant, Andrea Minx seemed like a different person. There was no hint of fear, no journeying into the dark corners of the mind where intuitions produced their vague, half-formed, tortured knowledge. She was merely a dark lovely girl, with black hair and brown eyes, poring over a menu and intrigued by everything she saw.

"I'm hungry," she said. "For the first time in days, I feel as if I'd like to make a pig of myself."

"Try it," said Jub. "I doubt whether you can put over the effect, but try it."

She smiled and raised her glass. Casually, still smiling, she glanced past him. Then the smile froze on her lips and slowly she lowered her arm.

"Jub, don't look now. But Mr. Steegler, the little janitor—he's sitting outside in the bar!"

Jub started to turn around, and didn't. "Are you sure?" he asked.

Andrea nodded.

"Tell me about Steegler," said Jub quietly.

"I don't know a great deal," she said. "When I came looking for a room, he was awfully nice. He couldn't do too much for me. Anything I asked for he ran out and got. Then one day Mrs. Steegler knocked at my door."

"I didn't know he was married."

"Oh, yes. She's twice his size and she's always shouting at him, but he disregards her and talks about her as if she weren't there. But that day she came up—she walked in and told me I'd taken sufficient advantage of him and I should stop. I was so flabbergasted I didn't know what to do. I said that if she thought I wasn't behaving fairly, I'd be glad to leave. And that was her turn to be flabbergasted. She practically collapsed in a chair and I had to give her tea to revive her."

Andrea laughed, a carefree, tinkling sound that seemed to come from her whole body.

"Try it on Taylor some time," said Jub. "A tea party might drop him into the hollow of your hand."

"Oh, no—not him. He's smart." She glanced past Jub and narrowed her eyes. "Steegler just moved over," she said. "He took his glass and slid out of sight, at the other end of the bar."

"He followed us down here, of course," said Jub. "He wouldn't pick a place like this for any other reason."

He gazed thoughtfully at Andrea, wondering how she felt about all this. But despite her appearance of fragile shyness and despite her constant fear, she hadn't collapsed and the police had got practically nothing out of her. And now she exuded a quiet, stubborn confidence. Because she'd thought someone was following her, and now she saw that she'd been right? Maybe. And if she'd guessed that, did it mean she was also right in supposing that someone was trying to kill her?

"Go ahead with your story," said Jub.

"Well, after that I didn't see much of Steegler, except that I'd come home and find objects moved, as if someone had been in my room. Books, chiefly. But nothing was ever taken."

"Did you speak to him about it?"

"I came home unexpectedly once and found him sitting in my room, reading. He apologized and said he often came there. He asked if I minded. I told him it wasn't exactly the thing to do, and he said he was so interested in my books, he liked to read what I did. And then he said it was such a good place to go when he wanted to get away from his wife. I remember his exact words.

"'The atmosphere is so different,' he said, 'so much cleaner and more wholesome.'"

"And he kept on?"

Andrea nodded. "Yes. He even brought tidbits for Stanley. A sort of bribe, I guess."

"The way to your heart is through Stanley," remarked Jub. "I wish he were still around."

"I wish he were, too," she said, lowering her long lashes. "You know, Steegler must have come and taken the body. It was gone when I got home."

"I took it," said Jub.

"You! Why?"

"I wanted to find out how he died. But I've never been quite satisfied with the report. It said asphyxiation. But from what? I don't know. They treated the whole thing as a kind of joke."

"Asphyxiation—that means gas, doesn't it?"

"No.—Gas would have meant carbon monoxide in his lungs, and there was no trace of that. It was just suffocation. Asphyxiation is the fancy word." He leaned back while the waiter changed their plates. "I think I'll go speak to Steegler."

"You won't make a fuss, will you?" asked Andrea anxiously.

Jub grinned at her and the dimple sliced along his cheek. "No. No fuss." He turned and walked to the bar in the front section of the restaurant.

Steegler had moved into a corner. At sight of Jub, he turned away and lifted his arm to hide his face. Jub sat down on the stool next to him.

"Hello, Steegler."

The little janitor looked up without answering, and then returned to his glass.

"What are you doing here?"

"Having a drink," muttered Steegler sullenly.

"You followed Miss Minx. Why?"

"Me?" Steegler's small, dark eyes glanced anxiously in the direction of the door. "Me? You got me all wrong."

"Waiting for somebody?" asked Jub.

"A friend of mine. I came down with a friend. The bartender'll tell you that. He just stepped out."

"Who?"

The little janitor's eyes darted at Jub and shifted away. "Just a friend."

"Who?" repeated Jub.

"What do you want to know for?" mumbled Steegler. "I got a right to be here, haven't I?"

"The hell you have. You followed Miss Minx. Now beat it."

Steegler looked worried. "I didn't follow her. I didn't even know she was here."

Jub reached over for Steegler's glass, lifted it and set it down out of his reach.

"Get out of here," said Jub quietly.

Steegler didn't move. Jub signaled to the bartender and said, "This man wants his check."

The bartender looked from Jub to Steegler. There was something wrong here, but the bartender couldn't figure it out. He shrugged and pulled a check from under the counter. Steegler paid, without leaving a tip, and headed for the door.

Jub watched him go. Steegler, he figured, would be scared off for a while. If he had anything in mind, he'd postpone it until the police were giving him less attention. Jub's main purpose was therefore accomplished.

But there was another angle Jub had to think about. Steegler had a perfect right to sit at a bar; if he chose to make an issue of Jub's behavior, Jub was sunk. The wise thing was to check on Steegler. If nothing else, it ought to be easy to get him on a violation of the multiple-dwelling law. Remodeled houses like the one Steegler ran were never a hundred percent.

Mitch, however, was the man to handle that. Besides, it was his case and he ought to hear about Steegler. In Jub's opinion

Steegler was more eccentric than dangerous, but Jub had no intention of gambling on a hunch. No matter how he looked at it, he had to get something on Steegler.

Jub rose and strolled to the lobby of the restaurant. He leaned against a wall and glanced outside. Little Steegler marched past, puffing on a cigarette and glancing jerkily around him. Then he disappeared.

Jub waited. Was Steegler mixed up in this? How? Why? And how to connect him with Jarvis? Had Steegler brought in the mysterious carton? And if so, what for? And did he really have a friend with him?

Jub frowned. He had found a new pawn. He stood there, wondering what use he could make of it, until little Steegler came into sight again, marching nervously past the restaurant door.

When Jub returned to the table, Andrea looked up with a question written on her face. "What happened, Jub?"

"Nothing," he said, sitting down. "He said he'd just happened to come down here. I kicked him out."

"Jub, while you were out there I remembered something else. Jarvis was giving him money."

Jub digested the news. "Jarvis," he remarked, "might merely have been tipping him."

"Five dollars?" asked Andrea. "I saw Jarvis give him a five-dollar bill, once. And that was only part of it."

"What do you think it was for?"

"I wondered," said Andrea, "and I decided maybe Jarvis was keeping track of me. It sounds absurd, but he was jealous. I think he paid Steegler to tell him who called on me and who took me out."

"Could be," said Jub. "Now look. Let's forget about the case and enjoy ourselves. No mention of Jarvis or murder or anything remotely connected with it until we leave here. You start. Tell me where you come from and how you happened to get into radio and whether you like movies and all the nonsense you can think of."

She smiled gaily. "All right. I'm just a small-town girl who wanted to be an actress. I came here four years ago, with a letter of introduction to a producer, and I thought I'd be famous in a year. I haunted casting offices until my money gave out. Then I got a job.

"It went on like that for years. I'd save up a little money and then make the rounds of the theatres, and then I'd be broke and have to start all over again. But I got to know a few people and somebody told me to try radio. I had a part in a soap opera for a little while. By that time I was beginning to realize I wasn't going to burn up the world, the way I'd dreamt."

"It's still inflammable," said Jub.

"Yes, but I'm the one who's being burnt."

"We weren't going to talk about that," said Jub. "Remember?"

"I'm sorry. I was up to my first radio part, wasn't I? It wasn't much and it didn't last very long. Then one day I woke up with a feeling. My intuition again, you'd call it. I went to the studio. I only had about three lines that day, but I had a feeling, and I was happy. I was humming to myself, and suddenly I noticed the director looking at me.

"'You sing?' he asked.

"'Beautifully,' I said.

"'They're looking for somebody with a voice who can fill in on one of the early morning programs, as M. C. The girl that does it is sick. You might try.'

"'When?' I asked. 'And where?' And that's me."

"Success story," murmured Jub.

"It seemed that I had the right kind of voice, and they let me fill in. There's a drunk by the name of Truffles who helps with the program. He used to be in burlesque. I have to give a few commercials and do some ad-libbing. Most of the program is recorded, but occasionally I sing. Now it's your turn."

Jub smiled and told her about Aunt Ella.

"But how did you happen to get on the police force? That's what I can't understand."

He shrugged. "Neither can Aunt Ella, but I have a badge to prove it."

Jub knew what Andrea meant. That he wasn't cut to pattern. That he was more intelligent and progressive and individualistic than she thought a cop could be.

Well, she was right. But he was a scientist doing scientific work, and that was what counted. Since he was neither God nor the commissioner of police, he accepted the department as it was and strove merely to get along with it.

He looked up and found that Andrea was laughing at him.

"What is it?" he asked.

"Nothing. I was just laughing at your dead-pan look. Whenever you don't want to talk about something, you get that look."

"I didn't know I was so transparent."

"Now you're trying to put me in the wrong," she said. "I should have stood on my legal privilege and refused to answer."

"Some day," said Jub, "I'll let loose. You'll be sorry you started me and it will serve you right."

"I won't be sorry," she said. Her eyes were shy and misty and she lowered them modestly, in a gesture that was pure flirtation.

The waiter bent down over the table. "You're Mr. Freeman?" he said. "There's somebody asking for you."

"Me?" Jub gulped and stood up, wondering who could possibly know he was here. He said to Andrea, "I'll be right back," and followed the waiter to the front section, past the bar.

The big man in a blue suit had to be a cop. He glowered and said, "Freeman? I'm O'Connor, Two-One Precinct. I'm tailing the Minx girl and I let the janitor come along with me tonight. I left him in here while I went to the corner to eat. He says you kicked him out."

"Then *you've* been following her," said Jub. "She thought somebody was after her and she spotted Steegler. I figured he was up to some kind of monkey business and that's why I told him to beat it. You know anything about him?"

O'Connor scratched his head. "Well, he's pretty anxious to help and he asks a lot of questions about Miss Minx, but I don't know. You think he's all right?"

"I'd be careful of him," said Jub. "He's been hanging around her a little too much. You might ask Mitch Taylor to see if he can get anything on Steegler, just in case. I was going to do it myself, but if you want to—"

"Sure," said O'Connor. "Something to put in the report."

"Yeah," said Jub. "The report. I was wondering whether you expected to tell 'em I took her out to dinner."

O'Connor gave Jub a blank stare. "Did you? You know, Freeman, it never would have crossed my mind to put down a thing like that."

"Thanks," said Jub. "And about Steegler—if I find out anything, I'll let you know. I'll admit it's just a hunch, but—"

He smiled and went back to the table, walking in his queer, rolling gait, like a sailor climbing the slope of a deck. Soon after he had sat down, Andrea said she was tired. She wanted to rest up and reach the studio early to study a new sequence. Jub called for the check.

The evening was ending far too soon. He wanted to see more of Andrea, to watch her in restaurants and theatres and living rooms. He wanted to see her in full sunlight and in the shadows of a darkened street. But most of all he wanted to see her in normalcy, without the background of murder and police reports.

Andrea. It was a nice name.

He left her upstairs, in front of her door. "Let's do this again," he said, "some night when you're not working. We'll start early and end late, and we'll forget all about the case."

"I'll try," she smiled, "but I'm not sure whether I can really get it out of my mind."

"And meantime," said Jub, "it might be wise not to see anyone even remotely connected with Jarvis."

"Anyone? There's only Lee and Fern. And Lee, at least, is harmless."

"Not Fern?"

"Oh, yes, but she's so efficient that sometimes she frightens me. The way she drives, for instance—she's like a man."

"Drives?" said Jub, thinking of the hit-and-run. "Has Fern a car?"

"No, but Jarvis had and she used it whenever she wanted."

Jub said nothing. Andrea smiled and held out her hand. He took it and then she slid free and, with a queer, self-effacing motion, she seemed to melt away and disappear behind the door. Jub stood there until he heard the bolt slide shut. Then he turned and walked down the stairs.

O'Connor was sitting in the hall. His chair was tilted back and he was reading a magazine. At sight of Jub he looked up and grinned. Jub called good night and marched outside, into the rain.

He wondered whether he should have told Andrea that the man who was following her was a cop. It would have eased her mind, but it also would have tipped off a suspect to the fact that the police were watching her. Which would have been a dirty trick on O'Connor.

III

Jub went straight to the Hotel Quaker and asked a spruce, broad-shouldered clerk with a Charlie McCarthy smile* whether the place had an official garage. Down the block he was told. He went.

He found a night man in a turtle-neck sweater racing motors and jockeying cars around the main floor. He glanced at Jub and decided to race one more motor and to inch one more car around a post. Then he climbed out, patted the fender of a big limousine, and limped forward.

"Yeah?" he said from a distance. He had a long neck, a weather-beaten face and a high, arched nose. "Yeah?"

"Does Peter Jarvis keep his car here?" asked Jub.

The night man snorted. "Did," he answered, "before he got bumped off. What about it?"

Jub showed his badge. "I'd like to have a look at it."

"I thought you fellows would be around long ago," said the garageman. "It's upstairs, on the fourth."

He elongated his neck so that it popped an inch or two above the line of the sweater. He could have gotten a job as a circus freak and doubled his salary, but apparently he preferred to race motors and curl fenders around the pillars of a former livery stable.

Jub stepped into the big elevator. "Did he drive much?" he asked.

"Plenty. He must have been using black-market gas, the way he took that thing out. But he didn't try to get rid of any

---

* Charlie McCarthy was the name of the wooden dummy used by the ventriloquist/comedian Edgar Bergen. Dressed in top hat and tails, McCarthy often made wisecracks and risqué remarks, in contrast to the bland Bergen. The duo were hugely successful radio performers and made numerous appearances on stage and television.

coupons* around here. I got a brother got lost on a tanker two years ago. Anybody pulls funny stuff and I turn 'em right over to the OPA." The elevator ground to a stop on the fourth floor and the night man switched on some lights. "That's her. The black Plymouth in the second row."

Jub walked over and studied the car. There were fender dents, but nothing severe enough to indicate a major accident. Still, there was no proof that the hit-and-run car had sustained any real damage. Maybe that was why it had never been picked up. One of those freak accidents in which a car escapes with practically no marks. Frowning, Jub reached inside and tried the lights. They both worked and neither of them looked new. Still, you can always install a second-hand unit. He bent down and examined the headlamps. One of them had been hit, at some time or other.

"When was the car used last?" asked Jub.

"Monday night. The night he was killed. Big tall guy brought it back, around midnight."

"Was he alone?" asked Jub, thinking of the man who had tried to see Andrea.

"I couldn't tell you. He left it downstairs. I just happened to get a quick look at him as he stepped out. I had another car on the elevator and didn't take much notice."

Jub stared at the fenders. He wanted to get rid of the night man and have a private session with the car.

"Got a flashlight?" he asked. "I'd like to examine the tires."

"Downstairs. I'll go get it, if you wait."

"Sure," said Jub. "Glad to." He put his hands in his pockets and tried to look bored. But as soon as the elevator had disappeared, he took out his penknife and went to work. He scraped

---

* Gas coupons, used to ration gasoline. There was a brisk black market in such items.

paint liberally from the fender dents and wrapped up the samples in the envelopes he always carried with him. He had just folded up the last one when the elevator returned.

Jub made a show of examining the tires. After a while he stood up and returned the flashlight.

"Thanks," he said. "I guess that's all."

The garageman stuck the flashlight in his overalls and started on the trip down.

"Find anything?" he asked.

"Can't tell yet. I'm glad I saw it, though. And thanks for the help."

"Glad to do a favor, any time." The garageman slid the doors open and stared at the street. "Still raining," he remarked.

"You're telling me," said Jub. He turned up his collar and went out.

He brought his paint chips straight to the laboratory. He wanted to compare them with the batch he'd collected at the scene of the hit-and-run. He had, of course, no logical expectation that they'd match. Andrea's scream and a pair of spectrographs were the thin links between the homicide and the accident. Andrea had explained her scream, and as for the spectrographs—so far, they proved nothing beyond a coincidence. And yet, Jub clung to the notion that the two crimes were part and parcel of the same thing, and when he'd made the suggestion to Mitch, Mitch had accepted the idea without question.

Why? Jub told himself there had to be something else. Maybe a piece of evidence which both Jub and Mitch had seen and forgotten, as far as their conscious memories went. Jub, walking along the wet pavement, squinted and tried to visualize the bit of missing evidence in his mind's eye. But it wasn't there. All his brain could produce was the image of a girl with dark, luminous eyes which she lowered in a kind of naive modesty. Andrea. Why bother with inductive reasoning?

When Jub rang the night bell at the laboratory door, Detective Gerrity opened up.

"Hello, Jub," he said. "What's the trouble? Can't you keep away from this place?"

Giordano, who was on duty with Gerrity, answered from the door of the first big room. "You know he can't. He's an eager beaver. Likes work and always comes down here around midnight, when the moon's out."

"Sure," said Jub. "I want to be an inspector and have my own car."

"Wrong again," chirped Giordano. "You don't get to be an inspector because you work. Not in this world. What's up?"

"Treeberg and Jarvis cases," answered Jub. "I found a car that might have been in the hit-and-run."

"You, too?" said Gerrity. "We're getting them wholesale."

Jub spun around. "Why? Who else?"

Gerrity laughed boisterously. "Taylor. He's getting to be our best customer. Pretty soon he'll need the services of a whole laboratory all to himself."

"What's he got this time?"

Gerrity made a face. Giordano said, "You know that cigar you found at Jarvis's? Well, Taylor wants to match it up, so he sends us a second cigar and asks if it's the same kind. That first one was a seven-cent cigar. Remember?"

"Yes," said Jub.

"Well, I took one sniff at this one and it said six bits."

"Don't tell me you're getting to be a tobacco expert," said Jub.

Giordano grinned. "Well, I read the label on it, too. And now Gerrity's trying to swipe it so he can find out what a good cigar tastes like."

"Sure," said Gerrity. "I want the cigar and he wants the little fancy chocolate. That guy's always hungry."

Giordano picked up a half-eaten nougat and sniffed at it.

"Candy," he said. "See the nice tooth marks on it?"

Jub studied the nougat. "Not bad. Where'd he get it?"

"He didn't say. All he wanted was to make a plaster cast and compare it with the one from the Jarvis cigar."

"Well?" said Jub impatiently. "What did you find?"

Giordano opened a drawer and took out photographs of a pair of plaster casts showing tooth alignments. There were red ink marks pointing to the differences. "Two hours' work," he said. "Like it?"

Jub grunted. The two casts were about as alike as cat teeth and cow teeth.

"You said something about a car," he observed.

Gerrity nodded. "Kent's car. That guy Taylor is a humdinger. He found out Kent had been in an accident. Skidded into a lamp post, ripped his fender apart and had to buy a new one. So Taylor got the old fender and sent it down here."

"Well, spill it."

"We're thorough," said Gerrity. "We even found a damaged lamp post on the block where Kent claimed he'd skidded. We got paint from the lamp post and from the old fender." Gerrity made a face. "You tell him, Giordy. I can't."

"The samples from the lamp post and the old fender checked," said Giordano sourly. "Couldn't find a better match-up. Kent told the truth. He hit a lamp post."

"How about the paint from Treeberg's car? Did you compare that, too?"

"Sure. And it looks like Kent's car was never even near that accident. Incidentally, there was no trace of tar on that fender of Kent's."

Jub emptied his pockets. "Well, here's my candidate. Jarvis's car. The fenders were scratched up and I scraped off some samples. They're in these envelopes."

"I don't get it," said Gerrity. "How could Jarvis be involved in the accident? He was dead by then, wasn't he?"

"He wasn't driving his car," said Jub. "Somebody else was, and I wish I knew who."

Giordano picked up one of the envelopes. "You better come through with something, Jub. Ever since you dreamt up that dizzy one about the homicide and the accident being hooked up, we've been taking an awful lot of kidding."

"Well, what of it?" demanded Jub. "Do you believe the spectroscope, or the kind of folk-lore they dish out across the street?"

"Stop wasting time and let's get busy," said Gerrity. The three men marched into the back room and checked their apparatus.

To Jub, it was more exciting than the wildest gun battle. Microscopic bits of paint, yielding up secrets which no eye was keen enough to discern. Vertical lines on a gray band, mysteriously spaced, giving up information as surely as if they had voices with which to speak.

"I was involved in an accident with a lamp post," one of the spectrographs had said. "I was never near Treeberg's car."

It gave you no double-talk. The lines were there. You compared them with the lines of another spectrograph, and you knew. They were the same, or they weren't.

Aunt Ella could never understand it. "They're just things," she always said. "People are interesting. Somehow, I never trust your science."

"But you believe my results," he'd say. "You never question them."

"Because I believe you."

Aunt Ella didn't understand. He wondered whether Andrea

would. He wondered whether any woman could understand the intense, fevered absorption that he was experiencing now.

The bare walls of the laboratory were not romantic. The desk was messy with papers. The reference volume of spectrographic charts was as dry as a trigonometry table, but it concealed a mystery as profound and elusive as the final puzzle of a human mind. Jub picked up the photographic plate and stepped into the next room.

"How do the new samples look?" he asked. "The ones from the Jarvis car?"

"Judging by their physical properties," answered Gerrity, "they have an asphalt base, same as the others. But that doesn't tell us much. There must be thousands of cars with smears of tar on their fenders. The point is, what trace elements we find in the tar."

"Well, the spectrograph will answer that, as soon as we develop the plates."

The three men went into the darkroom. There, standing in the dim, familiar light and listening to the steady patter of Giordano and Gerrity, Jub felt at home. Andrea's features seemed to take shape in the blackness. He smiled at her, unseen.

"Let's take a look at 'em," said Giordano. "What the hell are you doing in the dark, anyhow? Making love to a negative?"

Jub snapped on a light. "You ought to study photography," he said dryly. "They say there's money in it."

"He's not interested in money," chirped Gerrity. "Commerce is beneath him. Come on—let's look at these things."

They marched back to the laboratory table, set up the glass viewers and spread the prints. Three men hunched over a long green table, peering at diagrammatic pictures as feverishly as if they were choice pornography. Three men, silent except for the swish of paper and their steady, deep breathing.

Suddenly Gerrity let out a yell. "Hey—look!" he exclaimed. "These two—the samples from Jarvis's rear fender and the ones deposited by the hit-and-run car—they match! You got it, Jub! Jarvis's car is the one we're looking for—it's the hit-and-run car!"

"Wait a minute," said Jub. "You're going too fast. It ought to match up with Treeberg's car, too. It ought to have traces of that red paint from Treeberg's car. It has to check both ways. Let's see now—here's the sample."

He placed the spectrograph on the glass viewer. Three pairs of eyes stared intently. Then three heads rose and three pairs of shoulders shrugged.

"Hell!" said Gerrity. "Not a thing. But by golly, we got something."

"What?" asked Jub.

"I don't know. But Giordy and I are going up to that garage right now, and if there's any red paint on that wagon, we'll find it."

"Then you can give me a ride home," said Jub. "But I'll bet you a month's pay you don't connect that car up with the accident."

Neither Gerrity nor Giordano took the bet; but if they had, they would have lost.

IV

The next day there was a driving rain and the wind began mounting. New York twitched slightly and stirred in its sheath of concrete at the announcement that a tropical storm was creeping up the coast and would be off-shore by evening. Jub had visions of emergency duty, of a long night spent uselessly at a precinct station.

He had no phone. If you have a phone you can always be reached. But Aunt Ella's privately listed number was not known to the department and only in the event of a radio broadcast could Jub be called out, once he was off duty. Consequently as soon as he had left the laboratory, he felt comparatively safe.

On his way uptown he called Andrea. Her low voice was the voice of Andrea Minx, the radio singer, and it seemed far removed from the shy, dark girl who'd had dinner with him last night.

"I just called to see how you were," he said.

"Oh, I'm fine," she answered eagerly. "I feel so much more rested. As if the worst were over."

"I think it is. Just weather the storm for me, and be careful about going out."

Her laughter seemed to bring her closer. "I'll stay home, Jub. I don't expect to go to the studio before midnight, and the storm may be over by then."

"I wish I could stop in and see you."

"Maybe tomorrow."

"Fine. I'm off all day and I'll call you. And Andrea—"

"Yes?"

"You don't have to worry about Steegler any more. He won't follow you."

"Why not?"

"Taylor checked him and dug up a minor charge. Nothing important, but enough to keep him quiet."

He didn't tell her what the charge was. Molesting young girls. That was why Steegler had been so scared at the prospect of any personal investigation.

Jub hung up and stepped out into the rain. He felt as if he could raise his two hands and fling the whole storm back into the sea. His blood bubbled through his veins and his mind was clear and keen. No power on earth could thwart him. He thanked whatever gods there were for the chance that had brought him to a police laboratory and dumped him in the middle of the Jarvis case. He had the tools, the knowledge. Sooner or later he'd find a piece of evidence that would clear Andrea beyond all possible doubt. He felt serene and confident.

He came home whistling and almost blew Aunt Ella off her feet.

"Jub," she said, "you act as if you'd just done something brilliant. What happened? Were you promoted?"

"Better than that," he answered. "I called a girl and she said she'd see me tomorrow. Aunt Ella, if people are as nice as I think they are, we ought to have more of 'em."

"Thanks," she said, "but I think we have quite enough. And if you saw what a nuisance they are before they grow up, you'd want fewer instead of more."

"Bad day?"

"Yes. The weather seemed to affect them. They cried all day long. Fifty bawling infants. Sometimes they can be trying, although they *are* cute."

"Well, I hope they're all battened down for the night."

"Jub, you sound so unfeeling."

"I said battened—not batted. You know—safe in their downy beds. Which reminds me—I'm going out tonight."

Aunt Ella smiled knowingly. "Will I meet her soon?"

"It's not Andrea. I'm going to see the other girl tonight. Fern Kent, and it's straight business and not pleasure. Otherwise I wouldn't think of leaving you all alone. You don't mind, do you?"

"Of course not. Aunts aren't made of glass and gossamer; they can take care of themselves."

"Sure. They're the heavyweight champs," said Jub.

He left immediately after dinner and took the subway downtown. New York was excited at the prospect of the storm and there was an atmosphere of sharp expectancy. Jub caught snatches of conversation. "I was up in New England in thirty-eight, when we had that hurricane—" "Took that tree up by the roots and planted it a hundred feet away, where it's growing yet—" "Maybe we'll get a real hurricane—".

He got out at Sixty-Sixth street and fought the rain up Broadway. The wind was still rising, in a malevolent, irascible series of gusts and squalls. Jub kept close to the line of buildings, but the rain spattered and seemed to bounce up in little geysers that aimed with uncanny accuracy at his knees. He found Fern's house and strode into the lobby. He shook water from his coat, wiped his eyes and then shrugged the whole business off with a final roll of his shoulders.

"She's sure blowin' up," said the elevator man. "I wonder whether she's going to knock down some of them tall buildings."

Jub considered the remark. Elevator operators are the front men of modern urban civilization. A stranger can spend two weeks in New York and never make a friend or speak to anyone except the elevator men. They are the first people you meet in the morning and the last ones you see before locking your apartment door. They are the principal medium through which all major rumors are broadcast. In criminal work they purvey the initial, on-the-spot series of clues. Their accounts are usually unreliable, inaccurate and distorted. And yet the very distortion marks them as individuals of distinctiveness, marked out by their idiosyncratic peculiarities.

So Jub considered the remark and gave it a worthy answer. "Could be," he said soberly. "You better be careful. Third floor."

The elevator man shrugged and went through a routine of pretending to look at the ceiling while he judged his landing. He made it neatly and Jub stepped out.

He marched sturdily down the tile corridor and rang Fern's bell. With his finger on the button, it occurred to him for the first time that she might be out. He frowned and felt the wetness of his coat.

A voice called out.

"Who's there?"

"Freeman," he said.

"Just a second." He heard the sounds of quick movements and the slam of a closet door. Then Fern let him in. She was wearing a yellow print dress with short sleeves. Her quick energy and her frank, boyish face made her an unexpected island of light in the drab room with the two rain-splattered windows.

"Oh, it's you," she said. "I was afraid it was that goof Taylor. If he ever dares come back here!" She tightened her lips and let the threat remain unfinished. "Well, come in out of the rain."

"Thanks," said Jub. "Where can I hang this wet stuff?"

"Just throw it on the floor. A little water doesn't hurt." But she took his hat and coat and hung them in the bathroom.

Jub looked around and saw the same dirty kitchenette, the same rumpled bed with a checkerboard spread tossed hastily over it.

"What a night!" exclaimed Fern. "It's too nasty to go out and I was hoping somebody would come. You're not going to ask me a lot of questions, are you?"

"Not particularly," said Jub.

"Good. Have a drink?"

The bottle came out of the kitchenette and she filled two glasses.

"Water in mine," said Jub. She obliged, and then clinked her glass against his.

"To the police," she said. "What makes them so stupid?"

"We're doing this one the hard way," he said.

"I don't see why. You had a good lead in Andrea. You arrested her and then you muffed it."

"She wasn't arrested; she was merely held for questioning. And since she didn't have the answers, we let her go."

"If she hasn't got them, who has?"

"You," said Jub.

Fern took a big gulp of whisky. "I've told everything I know. In fact, I'm an open book. I couldn't hold anything back if I wanted to."

"Not even the name of the man who drove your father's car the night of his death?" asked Jub.

She looked startled. "Why ask me? I'm not his chauffeur."

"A big, tall guy."

"Sounds like Lee, except that I know it wasn't. I thought you weren't going to ask questions."

"All right. Let's talk about the weather."

"You win," she said, tossing her head. "Only let's get it over with. It's all I think about, anyhow. Shall I tell you something? I dream I know who did it, and I keep seeing his face. He has a different name every night, but it's always the same person."

"Who?"

"Taylor. Is that funny?"

"You don't like him; you wish he were guilty and so you dream that he is."

"Yes, but that isn't the reason. It's something else. Besides, his questions were stupid." She grinned cheerfully. "Go ahead— let's hear yours. Where do you start?"

"With the weekends you had Andrea up in the country," said Jub. "Tell me about them!"

"I wouldn't know where to begin. Peter killed a cat, and Lee and I decided to split up." She leaned back, with a quiet, thoughtful expression. "It's a funny thing, but I'd been wanting to leave Lee ever since Tony died. Lee didn't seem to care about Tony and I didn't think I could live with a man who felt that way.

And then, when I finally got Lee to suggest we call it quits, it knocked me for a loop. Somehow, I hated to give him up."

"So I gathered, from his presence here the other night."

"Oh, that," said Fern. "I needed a man. That was all. But Lee goes deeper. When he finally told me he wanted to leave me, I couldn't believe it. I didn't sleep all night. I got up about six in the morning and went for a walk in the woods. I saw the sun rise and—oh, hell! I sat down on a rock and bawled like a baby. Then I decided that if Lee really wanted it that way, he could have it. But I'd make him suffer.

"There was one way I could get at him. Through his gallery. If you'd known Lee a few years ago and seen how he had to crawl and grovel, just because he had no money, you'd know what I mean. He'd do anything rather than go back to that."

"How did he start his gallery? Who gave him the money?"

"Peter, my father. He put ten thousand dollars into the business. He wanted the right to withdraw it on demand, but Lee had sense enough not to accept under those conditions. It was finally arranged that Peter could take his money out only with my consent."

"And you threatened Lee with that?"

"Of course not," said Fern sharply. "I'm not that kind of a skunk. All I wanted was a little money. I told Lee that if he'd support me decently, he could keep his damn gallery."

"In other words," remarked Jub, "Lee had a nice motive for killing Jarvis."

"How ridiculous!" exclaimed Fern. "With Peter dead, Lee naturally expected me to inherit, so it made absolutely no difference. Regardless of whether or not Peter was alive, I had complete control over the money."

"Did Lee make any overtures to you about coming back to him?"

"You ask the damnedest questions," said Fern. "If you'll finish your drink, I'll fill it up again."

"I'm a slow drinker," remarked Jub.

Fern filled her own. "Nobody can keep up with me. How long do you suppose I'll go on drinking like this?"

Jub didn't answer, and Fern strode impatiently to the window. A gust of rain slapped against the pane and the window banged. She fastened the lock.

"The storm," she said. "It does things to you, doesn't it?"

"Yes."

"Those were awful weekends," she went on. "I thought Lee was falling in love with Andrea. Undoubtedly Peter was. Poor little Fern was left out in the cold. Believe me, I won't forgive Andrea for that." She turned around and smiled. Her greenish eyes were almost colorless, but they were clear and frank and friendly and her face was pert, fresh. "Are you going to stay here all night?" she asked.

For a moment Jub wasn't sure that he'd heard correctly. Then he gulped. "I hadn't planned to," he said uncomfortably.

"I make awfully good scrambled eggs for breakfast."

Jub got up and took her two hands in his. He didn't want to insult her with a straight refusal. "I've got to report in, to the nearest precinct," he said. "Everybody in the department is on call, because of the storm."

"Oh. That's rotten, isn't it? But couldn't you, somehow—"

She left her sentence unfinished. Jub said, "If I disobey orders, it's pretty serious business."

She pulled away from him and he returned to his chair. The window rattled and for a moment he thought it was going to blow in. Something crashed on a roof outside. Another squall of rain slapped against the glass panes. The wind howled in angry, muffled fury.

"It scares me," said Fern. "It gets me all mixed up. You, the storm, murder—"

"If you know who killed your father," said Jub quietly, "why don't you come out with it? You'll feel a lot better."

For an instant, as Fern looked at him, he was certain he had touched off something in her mind. Did she really know? Had he made a wild, lucky guess?

Then she laughed sharply. "Oh, hell!" she exclaimed. "Don't hand me a lecture. I don't know who killed Peter and I don't care. I'm going to get drunk. When you get drunk, you forget. If it weren't for the storm you'd stay with me, wouldn't you?"

"Sure," said Jub.

"Why do people like me happen, anyhow? I've got something rotten in me, something of my father's. It would be all right if I were all rotten, but I'm not. I've got something of good, too, from my mother, and the two parts don't mix." She filled her glass again and looked at Jub. "What time do you have to report?"

"Pretty soon," said Jub.

Fern emptied her glass and went into the bathroom. Jub leaned back. He was getting nowhere fast. He was in an impossible situation with a nymphomaniac. She knew something and so far he hadn't been able to get it out of her. He wondered how to approach her.

He sipped his drink. The door opened and Fern came back. She was wearing a blue flannel robe and she had nothing on underneath. She looked like a precocious child. Light hair and pale, inquisitive eyes. Small, clear, startled, green button eyes that showed nothing of the conflict inside her.

"Well," she said. "I wish you'd get out of here."

Jub stood up. "Look," he said. "You're doing things all wrong. If I go, you'll hate me and hate yourself, and if I stay, it will be the same thing. You'll get drunk, and in the morning you'll wake up and you won't be any further along with your problem. You know who killed Peter Jarvis, don't you?"

"Of course not," she said. And then she added, in a low, infuriated voice, "Make up your mind!"

Jub walked over and took his hat and coat. Then he stared at Fern. Maybe she knew and maybe she was just dramatizing. It was a hell of a night outside, but it was worse in here. Whatever he did would be wrong.

The doorbell rang and Fern said sulkily, "Go and open it."

Jub dropped his hat and coat on the chair and walked to the door. The man outside had his hat pulled low on his forehead and his coat collar was turned up. He was big and husky and had thin, violent lips and burning eyes. His nose was flat and crooked.

"Come on in," said Jub. "We were just talking about you."

The violent man jerked. Jub turned around to look at Fern. She had let the folds of her robe fall apart and she was standing there in a queer, lewd innocence, as if she had no conception that anything was wrong with her appearance.

Jub heard the big guy draw in his breath with a hiss. Then he struck. Jub rolled with the blow and the big guy hit with his other fist. It exploded behind Jub's ear like a bolt of lightning and he went crashing to the floor.

It was the end of the world and all around was storm and deluge. The ark pitched on troubled waters and Noah stepped out on deck and stared.

"The lousy heel!" Noah said, and kicked at Jub.

An angel with golden hair flew down to his rescue. "Go—quick!" she said. "He's a cop."

Noah said, "I don't give a damn if he is. What were you doing—"

It was like a song with a refrain. Noah and the angel were harmonizing, while the storm beat down and the ark tossed and the doves went looking for an olive branch and couldn't find it. "He's a cop—I don't give a damn if he is—What were you doing—"

Jub tried to join the chorus, but he wasn't in good voice tonight and he got the words twisted. "Go—quick—you're a cop. Bop the cop till he drops." But he was out of tune and the door slammed in his face.

Fern was bending over him. He was lying on the floor and he felt dizzy.

"You tripped," she said. "You'd better lie down."

"Who was that?" he demanded, climbing shakily to his feet. "Who?"

"The guy that was just here."

"Nobody was here. You tripped and fell. Lie down, Jub. I'll take good care of you."

She was trying to keep him here while Noah ran away. Jub reached for his hat, planted it on his head, grabbed his coat and stumbled towards the door. He shoved his arms through his coat and started sprinting down the tile corridor.

He heard the elevator, but he didn't wait for it. He found the stairway and raced down, hugging the banister and half-sliding, half-staggering. At each turn, he bumped his chest on the newel post, and then he reached for the banister and went down the next section.

The elevator man yelled at him as he went charging across the lobby, but Jub paid no attention. He erupted into the street.

The storm was at its height. The wind knocked him off his feet and he fell to his knees. A bucket of water splashed across his face, but it cleared his head. He got up and fastened his coat. A couple of hundred yards away, heading east, he saw a big guy. Jub lowered his head and bucked the wind.

A piece of wet newspaper came sailing at him. He ducked and the edge of it slapped at his ear and made it tingle. A For Rent sign and a bit of planking flew past. The wind lifted him off his feet and his legs couldn't find the sidewalk. He looked up and the rain stung his eyes. Noah was far ahead, sprinting through the storm and deluge, seeking his ark.

There wasn't any traffic. A pair of headlights flashed in the distance but no car came. Jub thought of using his gun. If he fired in the air, nobody would hear the shot except Jub.

He saw the big guy cross the avenue. He was leaning forward at an impossible angle. He was leaning against gravity and gravity wasn't bothering to pull. The wind was too much. Then Jub reached the corner.

He went up to his ankles in water. A stalled truck was parked in front of a bus sign, but nobody cared and the driver wouldn't get a ticket. The streets were deserted. There was nothing but the wind and the rain and the flying objects you had to duck. There was nobody except Noah, hurrying ahead.

Noah turned because the wind hit him wrong or else because he sensed he was being followed. Jub couldn't see his face, but Noah rammed his hat lower on his head and increased his speed. Across Broadway. Downtown on the other side of the street, towards the subway station.

He was fast. He stretched his long legs, swung his arms and knifed ahead. He ran steadily, with the even, tireless stride of a marathon runner. He sped past the subway station without a side glance and tore on.

Jub was puffing. His muscles were sluggish with exertion and he fought for breath. His side ached. The storm, the blow, the chase. He was exhausted and unaware of where he was going or how or why. He simply followed a man. And then the man reached a theatre marquee and darted inside.

Jub reached the ticket office, shoved some money on the counter and raised a finger. One. One ticket. He was too breathless for speech. The girl stared at him and opened her mouth. Her eyes were fixed and unblinking and they widened slowly. She wanted to scream at Jub's appearance and she was holding herself back.

In the void, a ticket jumped up from the feeder machine. Jub didn't hear the click. There was a tremendous clap of thunder. If the girl gave him any change, he didn't see it, for something else was happening. The world was giving up its dead.

They came tramping out of the theatre, hundreds of slow, shuffling feet, hundreds of fixed and emotionless masks. They were drunk with the scenes they had just witnessed and they were transfixed in the mood that had lifted them from the drab insecurity of their lives and lent them an hour of escape. Now they refused to return and therein lay their death, that they were narcotized and incapable of normal feeling. They simply erupted in a common daze, and when they came out they saw the storm and wanted to go back to their dreams.

It was all very simple. The show was over and the audience was coming out. And it was all very complex. They were warped and giddy with illusion and they had an excuse to return to their make-believe. They turned, they pushed, they milled. They expanded into the small cramped lobby and threatened to break the glass and bulge the walls and stampede in their panic.

Jub pushed forward. Twenty feet ahead of him, caught solidly in the crowd, towered a tall man with thin angry lips and burning eyes. He turned and saw Jub, saw the wet and the blood and the anger on Jub's face, and he smiled.

Jub couldn't yell. To yell would excite the mob and start a riot. And Jub couldn't push through. The bodies were too dense, the slow shuffling procession that came out and circled and went back was too precise and too powerful. All he could do was let himself be carried along. All he could do was float with the current and watch Noah, watch him slide past the ticket man and vanish inside the theatre.

Jub should have stayed with Fern. Noah wouldn't have bothered them. Jub could have been lying quietly in her arms and asking her questions. "Who killed Peter Jarvis?" "Why, Noah killed him. Jarvis was bad and had turned away from his God. He was evil. Come closer to me, sweet love."

Andrea was sweet love. Noah had tried to see her the night of the murder. He'd used Jarvis's car and had somehow killed Stanley. But who was Noah? Did it matter?

Of course it mattered, because Andrea was afraid of him.

Jub wiped blood from his face. Noah could stay in the theatre or sneak out through any of a half dozen emergency exits. By the time Jub reached the manager and showed his badge and stated what he wanted, it would be too late.

Jub let himself be carried along. Nobody even tried to collect the ticket he had never needed to purchase in the first place, since his badge would have gotten him inside without paying. But he hadn't thought of that. Punch-drunk, with his mind temporarily blunted, he'd automatically stopped to buy a ticket.

The air inside the theatre was close and stale. The crowd muttered, packed itself densely in the rear and trickled into the aisles. Jub squeezed forward slowly and determinedly and sought the lavatory. There he washed up and made himself presentable. For weeks afterwards he kept wondering what picture had been playing and why its appeal had been so strong.

When he returned home, Aunt Ella had already gone to bed. Jub let himself in quietly, went straight to his room and changed his clothes. Then he sat down in a brown plush chair and opened a book. Outside, the wind was beginning to drop.

He sat still for a long while, not thinking, but shaken by his experience and wanting to get back to normal. Occasionally he glanced at his book, but most of the time he just sat there, thinking.

Who was the big guy he'd followed? Fern knew. Fern had told him to go away because Jub was a cop. Fern would be drunk now. Or maybe the big guy had come back and was with Fern.

He'd keep, though. Fern hadn't been joking. She knew. Jub couldn't handle it himself. He could call Homicide right now, or he could wait until tomorrow and inform Taylor. It was Taylor's case.

Jub leaned back, thinking. The storm had died down and there was no longer any rain. It must be late now. Andrea would be down at the studio.

Jub reached out and turned on the radio. He kept it low. Andrea's voice came over sweet and stirring, and he seemed to see her smiling faintly into the microphone. The last thing he remembered before dropping off to sleep was the impression that Andrea was talking to him. Just to him.

SIX

I

In the morning, Jub called Mitch Taylor and gave him the latest information.

"The guy got away," concluded Jub, "but Fern knows who he is."

"Fern?" said Mitch. "I'm not going near that dame. Not for anything."

"Don't be a jackass. Find him and bring him in. He's right in the middle of everything."

"I can find him all right," said Mitch. "Whenever I want to. His name's Boganov and he's Fern's boy friend."

"You know about him?" said Jub in surprise.

"Sure. He's okay. I saw him the other day. You're not trying to rope in a new suspect, are you?"

"The old ones haven't panned out so well. You ought to be glad of a new angle."

"I've got too many of them already. You heard the latest?"

"What?"

"Kent. His Connecticut place burned down last night. I'm

going there this morning to meet the insurance investigator. Want to come along?"

"You bet your life I do," said Jub.

"Then meet me at the station. Grand Central, ten-fifteen."

It was Jub's day off. He was due at the laboratory at five that evening and he'd be on duty with Callender until nine the following morning. Only a rookie or a crackpot does work on his own time. Jub supposed he was a crackpot, but he couldn't help it. He believed in the laboratory and he couldn't pass up a chance to give it a boost.

It had inflamed his imagination ever since he had first heard of it, and in his age of innocence he'd imagined that it was routine practice to call for scientific help whenever the circumstances so indicated.

He remembered the first time he'd used the laboratory. He'd been patrolling his Queens beat late one night when somebody yelled out. A moment later Jub had heard the sound of an object crashing and then another yell. He'd started running in the direction of the noise.

He'd had to circle the block and he'd been rounding a corner when he'd practically collided with a man sprinting in the opposite direction. The man immediately turned and tried to dash across the street. Jub tripped him neatly and grabbed him by the collar. After a few pointed questions, Jub had continued his trip with the suspect in tow.

He'd arrived just ahead of the first radio car and had discovered that an apartment had been broken into. The tenant was still too excited to be clear on the details, but he stated that he'd come home and surprised somebody in his apartment. The prospective thief had made a dash for the fire escape and gotten away. But, on the landing below, he'd tangled with some flower pots and knocked over a collection of geraniums.

Jub had examined the point where they'd hit. There was plenty of loose earth, shattered bits of pottery and several footprints.

Jub had stated a perfectly obvious fact to the radio cop. "If this is the guy, he'd probably got dirt and fragments of the flower pot on his shoes and in his trouser cuffs. The laboratory can tell us for sure. They can take a cast of those footprints, too. Want me to call 'em?"

Jub could still see the astonishment on the face of the radio cop. "Call in the laboratory, for that?" And chiefly because of a state of shock induced by the suggestion, he'd adopted it.

At the trial, a laboratory technician had gone into an accurate description of how earth and bits of pottery found on the suspect's clothes matched the earth and pottery of the flower pots, and could match nothing else. The judge's learned instructions had pointed out that, since the suspect had pleaded not guilty, the only evidence against him was circumstantial and scientific. The jury had acquitted.

After the trial, the lieutenant had remarked to Jub, "What you should have done is crack down right off and got a confession. Remember that, Freeman. The old way's always the best."

Jub had said, "Sure, Lieutenant. I'll remember." But he hadn't explained what he'd remember and he'd gone away thoughtfully. In the course of time he had learnt that there were high-ranking officers who, if they knew of the laboratory's existence, had only the vaguest idea of its purpose.

As for the ordinary cop, Mitch Taylor was typical. Why he'd called in the lab in the first place, Jub didn't know. Apparently the idea had begun to percolate that science was useful in hit-and-run cases.

Mitch had been skeptical enough in the beginning. And yet,

just yesterday he'd brought in a fender, a second-hand cigar and a chewed piece of nougat. And if that wasn't progress, Jub didn't know what the word meant.

As he crossed the crowded lobby of Grand Central Station, he spotted the short, chesty detective standing at the train gate. He greeted Jub cheerily and headed down the platform.

"They wouldn't give me a car," chirped Mitch. "I told 'em I'd have a big load of evidence to take down to the lab and I needed a squad car, but the lieutenant just laughed at me. Probably wants to use it himself, to go round the block." Mitch spat. "The trouble is you don't get any cooperation."

"Tell me what happened," said Jub, taking a window seat in the rear car. "You're not going all the way up here just because you like fires."

"Well, the insurance people let us know about it and the lieutenant said I ought to go up. It seems that Kent had a pretty big policy, on account of the paintings. That's a laugh, too, if you'd ever seen the things."

"How much?" asked Jub.

"Twenty-five thousand."

"Where was Kent when it happened?"

"At his office. It started late yesterday afternoon. If you ask me, the insurance angle is just routine. We've checked up on Kent. He hasn't been to the country in almost a week, and the last time he was there he took out the most valuable of his paintings. They tell me he's only claiming for twenty grand."

The train started moving. Jub thought of what Fern had told him last night. That she intended to milk Lee dry. Suppose Fern had made heavy demands on him. Suppose he'd figured that Jarvis's death would bring Fern plenty of money and relieve Lee of all obligations. That was a possible motive, since both Lee and Fern had assumed that Fern was the heir.

And Andrea and the cat? How did they fit in with the theory of Kent's guilt?

Jub grimaced. They didn't.

"What do the insurance people think?" he asked.

"Arson," answered Mitch. "They haven't come out with it, but that's what they got in mind. Now why would he want to burn down his house? And how could he do it when he was here in New York?"

"There are plenty of ways of doing it. A clock system. A time bomb. Some chemical eating through a container and then leaking through to form a combustible. Or he could hire somebody to set the fire. There are ways, but I guess an insurance detective knows what to look for."

"Well," said Mitch, "it looks to me like a waste of time. All this chasing around, and for what? Charlie Corrigan, who was one of the best men the department ever saw, used to say that if you didn't break a case in the first twenty-four hours, you never would. And that makes it Andrea."

"She had no reason," said Jub. "And besides, she's in danger herself. Somebody killed Jarvis and wanted to kill her. The question is why anybody would want to get both of them. I can't figure it out."

"Theories!" exclaimed Mitch. "You can beat your brains out, wondering."

"If you want facts," declared Jub, "I gave you some over the phone. Boganov. He's the big guy who tried to see Andrea the night of the murder and who brought back Jarvis's car. You said yourself he was Fern's boy friend, and that ties him in. The minute he saw me last night, he socked me. And as soon as Fern told him I was a cop, he got scared and ran away."

"Jealous," said Mitch. "That's all. He goes to see his girl and finds you there. He's got a temper. The guy I want to see is Peyser, the hotel manager. Somebody said he had a crooked tooth, but I never have the time to go see him."

"How about Boganov being at the garage and at Andrea's house?" asked Jub. "What brought him there?"

"Maybe it was somebody else. I'll get hold of a picture of him and show it to the janitor and the garage man. There's no sense going after him till we know. And he didn't smoke that cigar. Your own laboratory said so."

Jub rubbed his jaw. "I've got a feeling," he said. But it was a helpless one.

The taxi driver who took Mitch and Jub to the Kent place was a volunteer fireman and he discussed the blaze with authority.

"When a frame house like that starts to burn," he said, "you can kiss it good-by. She started around half-past four, I guess, but we didn't get out there till five. Some guy at the sawmill happened to see it and turned in the alarm. You know what started it?"

"That's what we come to find out," said Mitch. "You tell us, and we can go home."

"I'll tell you," said the driver. "It was mice. They get inside the house and gnaw on a wire, and there's a short. More fires from short circuits than anything else."

"How do you know he left the current on?"

"Because the pump was working when we got there. We could hear it down in the cellar. She'd turn over a few times and then stop, and then she'd turn over again and quit. Something wrong with it."

"Maybe the fire," said Jub.

"Yeah. I guess it was the fire. You should have seen her. The wind blowing and giving her as nice a draft as you want. We didn't even try to save the house. Too far gone. What we were worried about was the lumber."

"What lumber?"

"Sawmill near by. It's an old one that they fixed up when the war started. They turn out oak planks for them P-T boats.* So we figured we'd let the house go and just keep the fire from spreading. We worked mostly on the garage. Saved that all right."

"Him and the storm," said Mitch to Jub. "Rain wetted it down and he watched."

"What's that?" asked the driver, turning around. "Oh— thought you were talking to me. Well, here she is."

Three or four cars were lined up in the circular gravel driveway that swung to the edge of the ruin. A long rectangular lawn stretched to one side. Elsewhere, a stand of young forests was closing in. From some place on the far side came the shrill, intermittent racket of a sawmill.

There was little left of the house beyond twisted bits of metal, charred timber and a pile of rubble. The springs of a bed were draped over the blackened end of a rafter. Sections of the collapsed roof had fallen clear, into the shrubbery, but most of the house had caved into the cellar. Two or three boys, under the supervision of a tall, sour man in a gray suit, were rummaging gingerly among the smoldering ruins. A few of the neighbors stared glumly and doubtless wondered whether they'd ever be burned out themselves.

"That'll be him," said Mitch, pointing to the man in the gray suit, and the two policemen introduced themselves.

"My name's Gideon," said the insurance detective. The invisible mill let loose a blast of sound and he had to yell to make himself heard. "Got here a few hours ago and I'm pretty near through."

---

* Motor torpedo boats used by the Navy in the war. Famously, John F. Kennedy captained PT-109 in 1943, when it was sunk by a collision with a Japanese ship; Kennedy was hailed as a war hero for heroically saving his crew. The incident was the subject of several books as well as a 1963 film titled *PT 109*.

"What do you make of it?" asked Mitch.

"Well," drawled Gideon, "it's still kind of hot in there and I can't shift the ashes yet. And I can't get samples of stuff down at the bottom of the heap, where things are liable to get smothered and not be entirely burnt. And I haven't checked on what kind of an electrical system was put in and whether they used approved material. I got to know all that, and it'll take me a couple of days, anyhow."

"Then so far there's nothing?" said Jub.

Gideon pushed back his hat. "I wouldn't say that. For one thing, that fire was too hot. Practically melted the furnace down to nothing."

"Couldn't the fuel from the tank do that?" asked Jub.

Gideon shrugged. "It could, but the trouble is, I can't be sure. There's none of the ordinary signs of arson, but I'll show you something."

He walked over to his car and picked a small metal dial from the seat. "Thermostat," he said. "Set at sixty-five. Why?"

"Was the furnace on?" asked Jub.

Gideon nodded. "The switchbox says so. Now you wouldn't think he'd leave the furnace on, would you? It doesn't get cold this time of year."

"It can, though," said Mitch. "He was going to be in town for a week or two. He couldn't tell if there was going to be a freeze."

"Sure," said Gideon. "But sixty-five? When you close up a house and leave the furnace on so the pipes won't freeze, you set your thermostat as low as you can. At fifty-five, so's you don't waste oil. But sixty-five? Why?"

"Is that all you got?" asked Mitch. "Just a thermostat he didn't set the way you expected him to?"

"No. Something else is bothering me. Down in the cellar, right next to the furnace, there's a section that looks as if it used to be a coal bin. You can see the place where the timbers marked it off."

"Yeah?" said Mitch.

"Well, where the door was, there's a brick wall, and I'd say it was new. Somebody sealed up that coal bin and did it in the last couple weeks."

"Find anything in it?"

Gideon made a face. "No. Want to have a look?"

"Sure," said Mitch.

Jub did not accompany them. He figured that Gideon was thorough and knew his business. And yet, all he'd discovered was a hot fire, a bricked-up wall and a thermostat set above the minimum. And nobody could charge a man with arson on the basis of that.

Jub strolled over to the garage. It was a white frame structure with space for two cars. The approach to it sloped up and had recently been resurfaced with a prepared tar product which was still black and gleaming.

Jub stooped and picked up a few samples. He stuck them in one of his inevitable envelopes and marked it. Then he sauntered inside the garage.

The rear was stacked with the accumulated junk of several owners. Garden tools, broken chicken wire, lumber, rusty pails, new pails, a few lengths of pipe, half-empty bags of cement, of lime, of fertilizer. A couple of empty paint drums.

Jub looked at the drums. They'd apparently been used to transport the tar product, parts of which would consequently have picked up traces of paint.

He thought of a spectrograph and of what it had told him. A half dozen men had worked long, tedious hours, grumbling and not knowing what they were after. They had tested and retested the physical properties of a tar-like substance until the

probability of error was at a minimum. And this was the culmi-
nation of all their slow, laborious effort. Straight from a book of
charts to the discarded rubbish in the rear of a garage. To Mitch,
it would be meaningless; to Jub, the scientist, it was climax.

His heart was hammering as he took out his penknife and
scraped off a few samples. He grinned and stroked the envelopes
into which he slid them. He scrawled identifying phrases and
ended them with a flourish. He patted the pockets into which
he put them. He felt as if he were slamming home the breach of
a great siege gun.

Ready—fire!

When Jub returned to the ruin, Gideon and Mitch Taylor
were talking to a tall, thin man and an attractive, middle-aged
woman.

Mitch said to them, "You haven't met Mr. Freeman, have
you? He's been working on the case with me. Mr. Lee Kent and
his mother, Mrs. Kent."

They nodded briefly and then Gideon resumed his
questioning.

"You left the thermostat on, didn't you?"

Lee Kent nodded. "I always do. You never know what kind of
weather you're going to get, in September."

"At what did you set the thermostat?"

Kent frowned. "I haven't the least idea. As a matter of fact, I
don't think I set it. I just threw the switch."

"You don't know at what temperature?"

"No. But the thermostat must have stayed at whatever
temperature it had been in the spring, when we turned the
furnace off."

"There's a corner of the cellar been sealed off, hasn't there?"
asked Gideon.

Kent nodded. "Yes. I did the job myself."

"What for?"

"The house was going to be empty all winter. In the past, we've been troubled with either rats or squirrels—I never could find out which. But they come through that corner of the cellar, and I figured that bricking it off might avoid a lot of damage. It was my first try as a mason."

"Convenient to have bricks and cement lying around, wasn't it?"

"They were left over from a chimney that we put in last spring."

"Hm!" said Gideon. And there, reflected Jub, went the arson case.

In the long silence that followed, Jub said affably, "I hear it was a nice house. It must have been a shock when it burned down."

"I liked the place," said Kent. "I'd put a lot of work in on it."

"Yes. I noticed you'd just resurfaced the approach to the garage. When did you do that?"

"August. There was a muddy spot and nobody would send a truck with such a small amount of material. Jarvis and I brought it over in the two cars, in some old paint containers. I did most of the work myself. Why?"

"I have a driveway of my own that needs surfacing. I didn't know you could get the stuff."

"Oh, you can buy it all right," said Kent. He started to say something else. Then the sawmill went into action. Kent shrugged and turned away.

II

Standing in the photograph room of the laboratory, Jub adjusted a light to a sharper angle. Callender, peering through the lens which was set at a fixed focus, muttered with contented fussiness, "A little further. No, too much now. There—hold her."

It was six in the evening and they had the place to themselves.

"I want to take some spectrograms for the Jarvis case," Jub said. "You don't need me, do you?"

"No," said Callender. "More of them?" He looked up with a vacant stare. "I wish I had your patience." Then he moved the light a fraction of an inch and studied the effect.

An hour or so later Jub returned to the camera room, sat down at the desk and spread his data in front of him.

He'd found exactly what he'd expected to find. According to the spectroscope, samples taken from Jarvis's car and Jarvis's wound showed substantially the same substances as the sample from Kent's driveway, but Jub felt no thrill at the discovery. His only emotional reaction was a headache.

To a certain point he could figure it out. A car had crossed that resurfaced strip in front of the garage and kicked up a few bits of tar with its traces of paint. The stuff had stuck to the fender, and when the fender had hit Treeberg's car the bits of tar and paint had been deposited on the area of contact.

That much was easy, but it was only the beginning. First of all, what cars had been driven over that patch of resurfacing? Kent's must have, and Jarvis's undoubtedly had. But how many others? And which were they and who had driven them and where were they Monday night? And since Kent's original fender didn't show the tell-tale substances, did the whole structure of evidence break down? And why in the name of all the gremlins that plagued the laboratory did Jarvis's head wound match up? And what was the real connection between the homicide and the hit-and-run?

Jub couldn't dope it out. He had an accumulation of evidence that staggered him. The trick was to pick out the few bits that were significant and then string them together in a new way.

A couple of cigars, plaster casts of teeth, hair ends, tar and paint chips, fragments of glass, spectrographs by the dozen. Threads from a tan suit, a blood-flecked towel. A carton that didn't belong. A dead cat and the suspicion of arson. A big tall guy who'd visited Andrea, used Jarvis's car and socked Jub, and whom Taylor had seen and exonerated. How did it all fit together?

For a long time Jub sat there, thinking. The laboratory had proved that Boganov, the big tall guy, hadn't smoked the cigar. But on the same evidence neither had Lee nor Fern nor Christie Mae. Was there anyone else? Mitch kept talking about Peyser and never did anything about him.

Jub looked up and found that he was alone. He rose and walked into the darkroom. For an instant, as he opened the door, he saw Callender bent over the big sink. Then the door closed and everything was in darkness, save for a small red pilot light.

Jub felt his way to a table and sat down.

"It all goes back to that cat," he said. "That's the only thing that isn't mixed up. There's a hit-and-run, but Kent's fender doesn't match and Jarvis's fender, which does, had dents that are hoary with age."

Callender, timing the developer bath, said, "I forgot to set that damn timer. It works fine when I remember it, but what the hell can I do to remember to use it? That's about fifteen seconds."

"On the Jarvis murder," continued Jub, "there were so damn many amateur astrologists running up and down the elevators, on account of that lecture, that we'll never trace anybody. Fern knows, or thinks she knows, but she's as liable to come out with the wrong name as the right. And whatever she knows, I don't think she can prove it. Just her word. So that brings us back to the cat."

"That's about it," said Callender. He switched on a light and took his prints out of their water bath. "Not bad," he said, examining the first one. "That ought to do the trick. What did you say about a cat?"

"The cat and the carton," said Jub. "What the hell do you know about cats?"

"Used to have the best mouser on the block," said Callender slowly. "Got so there weren't any more mice around, so she up and left us. Either that or somebody stole her. Anyhow, I never did get her back." Callender made a rumbling sound, as if he were cranking up his mental machinery. "Name of Jezebel," he finally said. "She used to line up the bodies on the front porch. For every five I counted, I gave her an egg to eat. She loved eggs."

Jub stared spiritlessly. "Did she have kittens?"

"Loads of them. I gave 'em away till everybody I knew had a cat. Then I took 'em in a bag and drowned 'em. Then the creek dried up."

"That must have taxed your ingenuity," said Jub. "What then?"

"I asphyxiated them."

"How?" asked Jub. The word snapped out like a whip.

Callender turned slowly. "How?" he repeated. "Plain ordinary gas. I put 'em in the oven and turned on the gas. With the windows open, of course. I had to wait till my sister was out of the house and Jezebel had gone visiting. Not that she seemed to care, though. She lacked the maternal instinct."

"Stanley was asphyxiated," said Jub, "and the first thing Andrea noticed in the bathroom was the lack of air. But she'd have smelt gas. And besides, the autopsy would have showed it. So that wasn't it."

"Maybe the cat just died," said Callender. "Natural causes. Can happen, you know."

"It was asphyxiation. How would you asphyxiate a cat in a room?"

"You pump out the air," said Callender. "Then everything dies."

"Don't give me that stuff about a pump. What's your favorite gas? For killing?"

"Never thought about it," said Callender slowly. "Sounds morbid. But carbon monoxide is the usual favorite. Colorless, odorless, deadly. Mixes with the air and permeates evenly. I wonder what did happen to Jezebel." He bent down over the drier and took out a print. "Yeah," he said. "She's real nice."

Frowning, Jub led the way out of the darkroom. If you could get carbon monoxide in a tank, say, and release it in the room. Except that you couldn't buy it. And the autopsy would show it. Carbon dioxide might be different. But—

"How would you get carbon dioxide?" he asked Callender suddenly. "And what do you use it for?"

"You freeze it," said Callender, "and use it to keep ice cream. Friend of mine burned his hand touching the stuff."

Jub leapt up. "Wow!" he yelled. "You got it!"

Callender scratched his head and stared. He wasn't sure whether or not he was being kidded. If he'd said something clever, he wanted the credit for it. But if Jub was spoofing, he didn't want to fall for the trick.

So he scratched his head and said cautiously. "Sure. I always do." Then he noticed the light in Jub's eyes and he realized he'd said something important.

"I'm going to figure something out," said Jub excitedly. "Carbon dioxide. It's about one and a half times as heavy as air and would sink to the floor. How much of it do you need to displace the air in a room about nine by six, huh? And how much will saturate it to what height, and what's the normal leakage through windows and doors and how fast does—"

His voice trailed off. He sat down and began calculating on a sheet of paper. His pencil moved rapidly. Whenever he reached the end of a series of figures, he drew a sharp, slashing line and uttered a cluck of satisfaction. Then he bent down and began scribbling another set of digits.

When he'd finished his tabulations he picked up the telephone book and jotted down names and addresses of ice cream plants. They'd be the logical places to start from. He had a big day ahead of him. He felt elated.

In the morning he went straight from work to the first address on his list.

"Police department," he said, showing his badge. "I want to find out whether you sold anyone some dry ice last Monday, the eleventh. It would probably go to an individual rather than a regular customer, and you'd have sold him from fifty pounds up to a hundred, packed in a carton."

All morning long he worked at it, and it fairly screamed at him. Andrea had had a feeling of suffocation and an impression of coldness upon entering the bathroom. When she'd lifted the carton, she must have touched a bit of dry ice and burned her finger. She'd thought the burn was from heat, but actually it was from cold. And, though she hadn't realized it, she'd done the one thing that had destroyed all evidence of the method. She'd let in fresh air. Furthermore, carbon dioxide is heavier than air and will sink to the floor, and that was where Stanley had been. He'd clawed open the carton and asphyxiated himself. So the thing was beginning to make sense and Andrea was coming into the clear. For that much, at least, Jub was grateful.

But there was something radically wrong. Assuming that

someone had opened the door, brought the carton into the bathroom and then departed, what had his purpose been? Last night's calculations showed Andrea wouldn't have been killed in any case. The carton had held about fifty pounds, and fifty pounds wouldn't begin to saturate a room. Even the cat, with a smattering of chemistry or a little luck, could have climbed the sink and weathered the crisis in safety. So the crime had been bungled. And yet it was folly to assume that the killer had committed such a fundamental error.

Jub didn't get it, and he had a tight, perplexed pull to his mouth and a glint to his eyes as he went from plant to plant and asked his questions. And always got the same answers. No. No dry ice had been sold on Monday, except to the regular accounts. Now Friday—that was different. The storm had blown down electric wires, and people with food-freezing units out in the suburbs had put in a hurry call for dry ice. There had been plenty of purchases on Friday. But Monday? Nobody.

Around eleven-thirty Jub walked into the front office of the Old-Fashioned Ice Cream Company and put his question to the girl at the desk.

"I really don't know," she said. "If you'll wait a moment, I'll call somebody who can tell you." She mumbled into the phone and then turned to Jub.

"Mr. Boganov will be right out," she said. "I'm sure he'll know."

Jub stiffened. Boganov—that was the name of the big guy who'd assaulted him. Mitch Taylor had said so. Could there be two Boganovs? There could, of course, but—

A door opened and Noah, the big, violent guy, came through. He blinked at sight of Jub and tightened his lips, but he gave no sign of recognition.

"You wanted to know something about dry ice?" he asked.

"I think we'd better sit down some place where we can talk," said Jub. "Unless you want to come to headquarters."

Boganov turned stiffly. "In here," he said. He led the way into a small, empty office and indicated a chair. He remained standing, and so did Jub.

"You've come to arrest me?" asked Boganov.

"That depends. Suppose I ask you a few questions first."

"You can spare yourself the breath. I'm fond of Fern. Very fond. When I came in the other night and saw you and saw how she was dressed—well, I lost my temper." His eyes flashed and his jaw jutted forward. "I get angry now, when I think of it."

"No need to be jealous," remarked Jub suavely. "The situation wasn't what it looked like."

"I saw what I saw," said Boganov stubbornly.

"What did Fern tell you?"

"I haven't seen her since. I don't intend to see her. She keeps calling, but I'm still angry. I'll wait till it wears off."

"Suit yourself," said Jub. "Ever been up to the Kent place in Connecticut?"

"I visited there last summer."

"Drive up?" asked Jub.

"I don't remember."

"Then you'd better make an effort," said Jub dryly. "I can book you on an assault charge any time I want. Not many people smack down a cop and get away with it. Did you drive up?"

"Once I drove. The other times I went by train."

"When did you drive?"

"I don't remem—" Boganov bit his lips and didn't quite finish the word. "In August," he said sullenly. "The last week in August. On a weekday."

"Where's your car?"

"I sold it ten days ago." Boganov mentioned the name of a dealer and Jub jotted down the address. It would be easy to check.

"Do you know Andrea Minx?" asked Jub.

"No."

"Then why did you try to see her Monday night?"

Boganov glared. His tight, pale mouth grew tighter and his eyebrows seemed to expand with rage. "Fern asked me to," he finally said.

"Why?"

"Has this anything to do with the Jarvis case?" demanded Boganov. "If so, I've already answered all the questions. A detective by the name of Taylor—he went into everything."

"I just explained that you'd better be cooperative. Now—about your visit to Andrea."

"I did not visit her."

"I know that, but you tried to. Why?"

Boganov hesitated a long time. Then he said, "Fern was worried about Andrea and Jarvis. Andrea had said she had no intention of marrying him, but Fern wasn't so sure. She wanted me to find out, but I never saw her."

"You were there twice."

Boganov picked up a small, steel paper cutter and rubbed the blade across his palm. "That's right."

"You brought up a carton containing dry ice."

"I? Why would I do that? Am I crazy?"

"Also, you were driving Jarvis's car."

"Who says so?"

"The garageman."

"What of it?"

"You had an accident."

"This is ridiculous. I went calling on a girl I didn't know and brought her some dry ice instead of a bouquet. I stole Jarvis's car and had an accident."

"You didn't steal it, but you had the accident."

"No!"

"You were on West End Avenue, weren't you?" asked Jub.

"I told you I tried to see Andrea."

"Did you have the car on West End Avenue?"

"I was in no accident," snapped Boganov furiously. "I brought no dry ice. I saw no one. I had nothing to do with the Jarvis case."

Jub stared hard and met Boganov's anger with a stern, fixed look. Presently Jub smiled.

"Tell me about Fern," he said quietly. "I wouldn't have expected her to go for your type."

"Fern," said Boganov, "is impulsive and she drinks too much, but there are good things in her. Her brother was killed in France and she takes it hard. She says I remind her of her brother. That makes her hate me a little, and perhaps love me. Fern is a riddle."

Jub walked over to the window. Boganov was fond of Fern. That much, at least, emerged as a hard, solid fact. For the rest, Jub felt as if he were gumming up the case. Breaking Boganov down was going to be a long-drawn-out process. Jub wasn't equipped for it. He wasn't a detective and he didn't know the technique for bearing down, and he had no right to step in without consulting Mitch Taylor.

Except that Mitch had let Boganov slip right through his hands. Or maybe Mitch had had the same experience as Jub. Boganov was like a stone wall. How do you batter down a wall?

Through its weak spot. And Boganov's weak spot was Fern. He was in love with her. He'd probably seen her every night, up until the evening he walked in and found her in a kimono and Jub answering the door. And then Boganov had got mad.

Jub turned around. "Boganov," he said, and then he stopped.

The truth hit Jub so suddenly and so unexpectedly that he stood there gaping. Then he let out a quick snort of laughter. Basically it was quite simple. Aunt Ella would have seen it immediately.

"Let me have a couple of hairs from your head," he said quietly. "I need some samples to match up."

"Are you crazy?"

"Just shake your hair and let the loose ones fall on a sheet of paper. Here. You can use this."

He ripped the top piece from a pad and held it out. Frowning, unsure of his rights, Boganov obeyed. Jub grinned and Boganov looked up suspiciously.

"What are you laughing at?" he demanded.

"I was just thinking," said Jub, "that if anyone walked in on us, he'd take me for a hair-tonic salesman trying to convince a customer. Tell me—are you bothered by dandruff?"

III

Jub found Mitch Taylor sitting at a desk in the detectives' room and going over some papers. In a far corner, somebody was tapping away on a typewriter. The sound seemed to bother Mitch. He couldn't concentrate. He looked glad of the interruption when Jub walked in.

"Hello, Jub," he called in his high, tenor voice. "What brings you?"

Jub sat down on the edge of the desk and swung one leg. "I have news for you, Mitch."

"More?" Mitch seemed less pleased. Then he asked hopefully, "You found out yet who bit that cigar?"

"No." Jub leaned forward and spoke softly. "Ready to make an arrest in the Jarvis case?"

"Who?" demanded Mitch.

"Fern can tell you. I want you to come down with me and see her."

"That dame?" exploded Mitch. "I told you before—I wouldn't go near her on a bet."

"I tell you—she knows."

"Don't fall for that malarkey," said Mitch. "She told me the same thing. She thinks it's Andrea. And why? Because she don't like Andrea. That's evidence, huh?"

"She's going to tell us something different. I have the sixty-four dollar question,* and the answer's going to break this case wide open."

Mitch looked dubious. "I don't know," he said. "The Rose Ollenbach deposition is coming in today. And I got to go uptown and arrest a guy that broke into a storeroom. I'm due there right now." He pushed a note forward on the desk. "And then I got to go and see some dame that runs a thrift shop. She says she's got something that ties in with the Jarvis case. Something hot, she says, but she wouldn't tell it over the phone. And I still haven't seen Peyser's teeth."

"All right," said Jub. "Then I'll handle this alone. It's not going to hurt me to break it all by myself, is it?"

Mitch thought it over. Jub had been all right. A little screwy sometimes, but he had a way that made you feel he knew what he was talking about. When he said he could crack a case, all of a sudden out of nothing, he meant just that.

---

* The key or essential (or most difficult) question, so named because $64 was the highest prize awarded for a winning answer to a question on the popular CBS radio quiz show *Take It or Leave It* (1941–48). By the 1950s, the phrase got inflated when the popular CBS television quiz show *The $64,000 Question* first appeared (1955–58). The show was copied in England between 1956 and 1958. CBS was involved in a notorious scandal, in which it was alleged that contestants on this and other popular game shows had been supplied with answers before the quizzes.

Mitch made up his mind suddenly. He stood up and grinned. "Come on," he said. "What are we waiting for?"

"Chiefly for you to get a squad car. I've been on my feet all morning and I need a rest. Besides, we ought to do this thing in style."

Mitch puffed up with importance. "Just leave it to me, Jub. I'll speak to the lieutenant. I'll tell him it's about a cat." And, grinning over his joke, he led the way downstairs.

Through arguments which he didn't divulge to Jub, Mitch got the squad car and settled himself comfortably behind the wheel.

"What goes?" he asked, starting the motor. "You got something on your chest, so let's have it."

"Sure," said Jub, and he told Mitch about the dry-ice clue, pointing out how it explained the cat, the chill and Andrea's burnt finger. "And what's more," he said, "a half hour ago I found out Boganov worked in an ice cream plant. He can get all the frozen carbon dioxide he wants."

Mitch frowned. "That changes things," he said. "I didn't figure Boganov. But look—didn't you maybe pull a boner? Tipping off your hand and then walking out on him? He's probably headed for the nearest railroad station right now."

"I don't think so," said Jub. "He's worried, but he's going to do something much better than run away."

"You know, huh?"

Jub shook his head. "No. But right now, let's pool what we know and see what we agree on.

"Let's call the murderer X and let's skip the motive, because we don't know it. Fern, Christie Mae, Kent, Boganov—they all have motives, one way or another, but we'll skip them. We know that somebody put a carton of dry ice in Andrea's bathroom. Since there was no dry ice left when we went upstairs, around midnight, it must have been brought pretty early in the evening, and long before Jarvis was killed. That makes it possible for Jarvis himself to have done it.

"Let's forget all the alibis and whether we believe them or not.

"We know that somebody who smoked cigars was up in Jarvis's room, and we know from the tooth marks that that person wasn't Kent, Boganov, Fern or Christie Mae. But we have no idea whether the cigar smoker was X or just a casual visitor who managed to stay clear of the investigation. We're pretty sure that, in the confusion of the crowd at the astrology lecture, X went in and out of Jarvis's room without attracting the attention of the elevator man or of anyone else.

"We haven't found the weapon, but we know it probably came from Kent's place, because it was in contact with the particular tar product which had been transported in some old paint pails."

"Yeah?" said Mitch. "Suppose Jarvis brought the weapon down and had it in his room, and this X just happened to use it because it was convenient. That breaks your connection with Kent, doesn't it?"

Jub nodded. "Yes. I hadn't thought of that. But it only strengthens the point I want to bring out. So far as we know, anybody could have done it. *Anybody.*"

"Sure," said Mitch. "And the same goes for the accident."

"The accident," said Jub, "is going to be easy. That's the first thing Fern can tell us."

"She'd better," said Mitch. "She'd better tell us something."

He pulled up in front of the Sixty-Eighth Street apartment and left the car between a pair of No Parking signs. "All right," he said. "Let's go."

Striding down the tile corridor, a step behind the cocky,

confident Taylor, Jub had a sudden doubt. He was keeping Mitch in the dark. He was betting everything on the gamble of one fact. Suppose he were wrong?

But he couldn't be. It was so simple, Jub kept telling himself. So abruptly simple. If it hadn't been for the unforeseen occurrence of an auto accident, there would have been nothing to the case. The police would have broken it by ordinary methods within twenty-four hours.

Mitch rang the bell and waited. Nothing happened. He turned to Jub and said, "She's not in. What do we do now?"

"Wait," said Jub.

"She may be out all day. I got too many things to do. You stick around here and I'll take a run up to the thrift shop and see what that dame has to say. I may as well use that car while I got it."

"Let's try the back door first," said Jub. "It might be open. You never know."

"What the hell good would that be? You want to see Fern, don't you?"

"Yes. But I'll have a place to sit down, anyhow. I'm tired."

Mitch shrugged. "Go ahead and try it."

Mitch was ringing the bell for the second time as Jub went through the fire door and crossed the rear landing. This was where Mitch had been struck in the darkness, early Monday morning. Jub glanced at the lighting fixture. Mitch must have given himself quite a sock, if he'd banged against that.

Jub put his hand on the knob of the rear door and turned it. The door was open.

He went inside and slammed it shut behind him. The kitchenette had an empty bottle and one that was partly full. Some dirty breakfast dishes were stacked in the sink. The bathroom door was closed.

Jub went past it into the living room. The bed was still messy and there was half a tumbler of whisky on the bureau. Jub stepped into the short corridor to the entrance and opened the front door.

"Come on in and look around," he said. "She's out."

Mitch entered. "I wonder who taught her to keep house," he remarked. He noticed the glass on the bureau and walked over and smelt it.

"Jub," he said suddenly, in his high, squeaky voice. "There's something wrong here."

"What?"

"I don't know. But when that dame goes on a binge, she finishes her liquor."

"Maybe somebody else didn't finish that drink."

"Then she'd have taken it herself. She wouldn't waste good stuff."

"Anybody can get saturated," said Jub. He lifted back the cover of the bed. "You can see for yourself that she slept here."

"Sure, but when? She hasn't made that bed in weeks. She just threw the cover over it whenever somebody came in."

"I'll sit down and wait," said Jub. "Go over to the thrift shop and then come back. If Fern shows up, I'll keep her till I hear from you."

Mitch didn't move. "It's cold in here," he said.

"Not particularly," said Jub.

Mitch frowned, walked over to the window and then wheeled and stepped back to the middle of the room.

"Charlie Corrigan always said," he remarked, "that when you don't know what else to do, you look. You start with the bureau drawers and the closets, and then you get down to the small things. You never know what you're going to come across."

"Hit and miss, huh?"

"Best damn investigator the department ever saw," snapped Mitch. "Taught me everything I know." He flung back a bureau drawer and remarked, "She sure liked cheap jewelry. Look at this."

He held up a handful of bright-colored necklaces. Then he slammed the drawer shut and tried the next one. Jub leaned back and wondered how long he'd have to wait for Fern. In a way, he kind of admired her. She'd certainly made a bunch of monkeys out of the police department.

But that was easy, he supposed. He'd often told himself that twenty thousand cops couldn't get a piece of information out of Aunt Ella if she wanted to hold out. The same thing probably applied to Fern. He wondered whether she'd tell the truth even now. He hadn't thought of that. If she chose to hold out—

Idly he watched Mitch approach the closet, pull open the door and then freeze. Mitch's hand dropped down to his gun.

"Come on out of there!" he barked.

Jub leaped to his feet, and Boganov stepped out of the closet.

He looked paler than ever and his thin, tight lips were like a gash across his face. His small eyes were fixed and burning.

"What the hell were you doing in there?" demanded Mitch.

Boganov didn't answer. He stood there, towering above Mitch and above Jub, and in his very height he had the advantage of them.

"Sit down!" snapped Mitch harshly. Boganov didn't move.

"I said sit down," repeated Mitch. He gave Boganov a sudden shove and Boganov staggered back, tripped over the bed and fell into it. Slowly he raised himself to a sitting posture.

"All right," said Mitch. "Tell us what you were doing in that closet."

Still Boganov stared in a daze and didn't answer. He reached in his pocket and pulled out a pack of cigarettes. Mitch snatched them out of his hand.

"Come on," he said. "Talk. We got the goods on you. You broke into the joint and that's enough to hold you on."

Boganov seemed to understand at last. "I didn't break in," he said.

"Just because the kitchen door was open?"

Boganov reached into his pocket and took out a key. "Key," he said. "She let me have one. I didn't break in."

"Why didn't you use it the other night?" asked Jub.

"I rang first. Always did." He spotted the glass on the bureau and said, "Drink. Give me a drink."

"You'll get a drink when you tell us what you were doing in that closet," said Mitch.

"I was in here," said Boganov in short, uncertain gasps. "Heard the bell ring. Heard your voices. I thought—" He stopped suddenly and his eyes wavered.

"Well?" demanded Mitch. "What did you think? What were you scared of?"

Boganov shook his head and didn't answer.

"You drove Jarvis's car Monday night," said Mitch. "You killed a man."

"No," said Boganov quickly. "I was with—" Then he stopped and made a hopeless, shrugging gesture.

Mitch stepped up and shook him. Boganov's cheeks went red. He looked at Mitch and then he looked at Jub and then he looked towards the kitchen.

"What do you want?" he asked.

"We want to know what you were doing here."

"Nothing," said Boganov. "Just waiting."

"In a closet?"

Boganov stared blankly. "Closet?" he said. "Was I in a closet?"

"Look," said Mitch. "Drop the act. Either you talk or else you come down to headquarters. You don't want to get pinched, do you?"

"No."

"Well, come on then. What were you doing here? And why hiding in the closet?"

"A coat," said Boganov shakily. "A coat for Fern."

"You don't close a door on yourself when you get a coat out of the closet."

"Getting a coat," insisted Boganov. "Then I heard you, and I hid."

"Look," said Mitch. "Drop the act. Why in hell would you want to get a coat for Fern?"

"To cover her up." Boganov licked his lips. Then he shrugged, as if the whole business were too much for him. "She ought to be covered up," he said. "Why don't you look in the bathroom?"

Without taking his eyes off Boganov, Mitch signaled to Jub. Jub turned slowly, with a sick feeling. He knew what he was going to find.

Nevertheless it was not what he expected. He opened the bathroom door slowly, and then he stood there shivering. The room was like an ice box. He knew he ought to walk to the other end of it and fling open the window, but for a moment he was paralyzed.

Fern was lying in the tub. She was stark naked. Her head had slipped down and rested wearily on her shoulder. A few wisps of whitish gas curled sluggishly along the white porcelain sides of the tub. Her flesh was pink by contrast.

She was dead, of course. Asphyxiation. The carton which had contained the dry ice was lying on its side, on the edge of the tub, where the heavy gas would flow into the tub and gradually displace the air.

Jub wondered why she hadn't got up. Then he smelt the alcohol. Drunk, he supposed. Passed out and never even knew her danger. It occurred to him that this was how Andrea was to have died. Except that she hadn't been home.

He stepped back. "Take a look, Mitch," he said.

He kept staring at Boganov while he heard Mitch stride into the bathroom and utter a long, low whistle. Then he heard Mitch's footsteps on the tile floor and heard the window bang up. Gradually he felt the warm air flow in.

Mitch didn't say anything much. He had his handcuffs out as he marched back. Boganov held up his wrists and made no protest. He knew it had to be that way, and he accepted it. But the ghost of Fern Jarvis Kent must have been convulsed with uproarious laughter.

SEVEN

I

Jub did not go directly to headquarters. It would take time for
the police to gather the last bits of evidence, and meanwhile he
had work of his own. He sat down at a telephone and kept at it
steadily. When he finally had what he needed he took a cab to
Centre Street and went into the room where the questioning
was going on.

The big-wigs were there, of course. Everybody from a
couple of lieutenants and an assistant district attorney right up
to the top. Mitch had stepped aside. The big shots kept consulting him, but they did the questioning. Andrea and Kent and
Boganov. They took the brunt of it. But Christie Mae and little
Steegler and a number of small fry were down there, too, held
for questioning.

When Jub arrived, an inspector was working on Andrea.
He was an oldish man with a lined, seamed face, like a section
of a topographical map of some battle zone. His face seemed
to be composed of neither skin nor flesh. Rather, it appeared
to have been built up out of clay. There were deep trench slits

zigzagging in an unintelligible pattern. A pair of sharp gullies ran up to the promontory of the nose which, like a high, rocky ridge, smooth and unassailable, dominated the surrounding terrain. The eyebrows were wooded thickets and the eyes were dark, stagnant pools, and everywhere the surface was torn and pitted and marked with the wounds of a thousand shell holes. When the inspector spoke, his voice had the fuzzy, vibrant quality of a gigantic loudspeaker which hurled its taunts and its directions indiscriminately across the scarred and mottled surface of the battle area.

In contrast, Andrea seemed more fragile than ever. But she was pale and composed, as if the entire future of the human race rested on the truth and dignity of the answers which she gave to this monstrous and unbelievable assault. Occasionally, when she made some damaging admission, she would tremble slightly and raise her head on its long, slender neck. Then her dark eyes would gather some inner strength and flash it forth in a look of mingled fear and disdain.

"You said the body of your cat seemed cold," said the inspector. "Just how cold?"

"I don't know. I was upset and excited. I couldn't say."

"Was it frozen?"

"How could it be?"

"Just answer the question."

There was a long pause. Then Andrea smiled, as if she had decided that even police have a sense of humor and that she might as well indulge them.

"No," she said with mock seriousness. "It was not frozen."

The inspector stepped back with an air of triumph, as if he'd made some major advance. Then he motioned to a cop who brought him a shoe box. The inspector placed it on a table and shielded the object from Andrea's view.

"You didn't like Fern Kent much, did you?"

"We were not close friends."

"Because you broke up her marriage?" demanded the inspector.

"It was broken before I even met her."

"You mean they were not living together?"

"No, but things weren't going well between them."

"How many times did you meet Lee Kent secretly?"

"I never met him secretly."

"Oh. Fern was there every time you saw him. Is that it?"

"No. But I made no secret of it."

"I see," said the inspector, with a smirk. "You just didn't bother to tell her."

"I don't know whether or not she knew that I saw Lee. I'm certain she didn't care."

"Where were you yesterday evening?"

"Friday? I was home, sleeping, from about five o'clock on."

"Can you prove that?"

"Of course not."

"When was the last time you saw Fern?"

Andrea frowned slightly, "About a week ago, I think."

"You claim you didn't see her last night?"

"I didn't see her," said Andrea stiffly.

"Then how does it happen," said the inspector, slowly, "that the elevator man at Mrs. Kent's apartment identified you as having been there late that afternoon?"

Andrea frowned again. Jub leaned forward in surprise. He assumed that the inspector was bluffing, but the inspector was deadly earnest in his attempts to pin Fern's murder on Andrea.

Jub grunted. The damn fool—what did he think, anyhow? That Andrea wanted to marry Lee and had killed Fern to get her out of the way? Even an inspector ought to have more sense than that. What evidence did he have, anyhow?

Andrea opened her mouth to answer, and then closed it. The inspector stepped closer.

"Well?" he demanded.

Andrea seemed to wilt. "I did go," she said, in a low voice.

"Why?" The word whipped out like a blow, and Andrea jerked back. "Why?"

"Simply to pay a condolence call," she murmured.

"You didn't go there to ask her to divorce Lee?"

"Of course not!" exclaimed Andrea with sudden spirit. "If you don't believe me, ask her."

"A very nice answer," said the inspector, "since Fern is dead and you killed her."

"Fern—dead?" asked Andrea. Her pale face seemed chalk white. She gave no visible sign of emotion. Her eyes left the inspector for the first time and she looked slowly around the room, with a lost, helpless gaze. When she saw Jub, her glance stayed on him for a second or two. She gave no evidence of recognition, made no mute plea for help, but the memory of that encounter stayed with Jub for a long while.

The inspector unwrapped the box slowly and took something from it. As he held up the object, Andrea uttered a little cry and raised her hand to her mouth.

"You know what this is, don't you?" said the inspector. He held up a heavy auto wrench.

Andrea nodded. "Yes. It's the murder weapon."

"How do you know?"

"It has to be."

"You think every wrench you see was used to kill somebody?"

"No, but—" She hesitated for a full second. "It looks like the one I found in my drawer last Tuesday."

"Found?" The single word snapped out like the recoil of a spring.

"Yes. Somebody must have put it there. I found it while I was looking for a handkerchief."

"Why didn't you turn it over to the police?"

"I don't know. I don't know what I was going to do."

"But you hid it in a bag of old junk, didn't you? And when the bag was called for, you watched with a sigh of relief while it went out of your house, didn't you?"

"I was afraid."

"Of what?"

Andrea didn't answer. There was a long, ominous silence.

"There was a police officer present," said the inspector, "but you never told him about it, did you?"

"Let me explain," said Andrea quickly. "I found it in my drawer, I picked it up and saw the stains. Then someone knocked at my door. I was afraid. I had to think. I put it in the thrift-shop bag so that whoever was outside wouldn't find me with it. Then someone tried to break into my room and I screamed."

"No one tried to break in," said the inspector. "That's just a story of yours, isn't it?"

"No—it's the truth!"

"How do *you* think the wrench got in your drawer?"

"They tried to frame me."

"Who?"

Andrea bit her lips. She looked down for her purse, opened it and took out a tiny blue handkerchief. She dabbed at her mouth and replaced the handkerchief.

"I don't know," she said.

The inspector dropped the wrench on the table with a bang and then thundered out with the full power of his voice. "Why did you kill Peter Jarvis?"

Andrea raised her head high and said with slow, quiet dignity, "I did not kill him, and you know it."

The inspector stepped back and exchanged some kind of signal with the assistant D. A. Then the inspector motioned to a cop who walked over to Andrea and touched her arm. He took her away.

Immediately the room burst into an uproar. Jub got up and walked over to Mitch. Mitch's eyebrows went up.

"Got it?" he asked.

Jub nodded. "Tight as a drum. When do we spring it?"

"Not yet. They're too hot on Andrea now."

"They dug up plenty."

"That's only part of it," said Mitch. "We got the deposition from the Ollenbach woman. The Minx's timing is about fifteen minutes off. Looks bad."

"What are they going to do?"

Mitch shrugged. "Everybody's going to get grilled. Then they talk it over, and then Andrea comes back. That's the grand finale." He stroked his chin. "I brought that wrench straight to the lab. They found the blood was human, they found hairs that matched up with Jarvis's, and they found the same tar and paint stuff."

"It was kept in the back of the car," said Jub. "Either Kent's car or Jarvis's. Both of them were used to transport the tar, and the stuff spilt in both baggage compartments. All the tools in there will give us spectrographs that match the tar and its traces of paint. Did you explain all that to the inspector?"

"I started to, but he picked up the wrench and looked at it. 'I don't see no tar,' he says. Can you beat it?"

Jub grunted. "How about Peyser, the hotel manager? Seen him?"

"Yeah, and he had a crooked front tooth. When I told him

about the marks on the cigar and said I wanted a cast of his teeth to match up, he admitted he'd seen Jarvis the night he was killed. Peyser claimed they talked about a new lease and that he'd lied to us because he didn't want to get into any trouble."

"Nice going," said Jub. Then a captain motioned to Mitch. He winked at Jub and walked away. Jub listened to the discussion.

It was bad. They said Andrea had concealed material evidence and that she'd obviously known Jarvis was dead before the police had even found the body. They felt pretty certain she'd killed Fern. They knew she'd been there and they figured Andrea wanted to marry Kent and had simply put Fern out of the way.

But the dry ice was a stumbling block. The elevator man at Fern's had said Andrea was not carrying a package. A minimum of fifty pounds had been brought into Fern's bathroom. Did Andrea have the strength to lift a fifty-pound carton and haul it up three flights of stairs to avoid the elevator man? She didn't look it.

They talked it over, and then the inspector who had been questioning Andrea stepped back from the group.

"Let's have the next one," he said. "You take him, Charlie."

The assistant D. A. nodded. "Sure."

Jub sat down and watched. It was still a show. It was still the first act. He didn't go on stage until the climax. The big third act was going to be all his—maybe. He glanced at Mitch. Mitch was reading over the notes that Jub had handed him. They told the story. Jub hoped the inspector and the D. A. would believe it. It seemed weak and theoretical now, in this room.

Kent walked in stiffly, nodded and sat down in the chair. The D. A. went right at him, without subtlety and without any kind of a build-up.

"You're Lee Kent, the art dealer," he began. He stroked his

thick, black mustache vigorously, as if the friction built up energy. Then he slammed out in his first attack. "You know we got you for arson, don't you?"

Kent snorted. "Of course not."

"Let me tell you how it was done," said the D. A. softly. "A new wrinkle in arson, Kent. Slick, but not foolproof. All you used was an incendiary bomb."

Kent settled back for the fight. "Where would I get an incendiary bomb?"

"From Civilian Defense headquarters, up in Connecticut. They had one on exhibition and it disappeared around the middle of July. You used to be an airplane spotter and you were in and out of the one-time Civilian Defense place. The bomb was there, together with some other war souvenirs, and you simply walked in and took it."

"That's untrue."

"Furthermore, we know where you got the whole idea. From Miss Minx. She'd read about it and she explained the scheme at breakfast, the first weekend she and Jarvis were visiting. Mrs. Kent wasn't there, but you and Jarvis and Miss Minx were.

"She explained how to fasten an incendiary to the metal furnace flue, by means of wax. When the thermostat turned on the furnace, the heat in the flue would gradually melt the wax. By and by there wouldn't be enough left to hold the bomb in balance, and it would fall off the flue and ignite from the percussion. You'd be safe in town and miles away when it finally happened. There's no trace of an incendiary, of course. It's completely consumed. And for fear that somebody might break into the cellar and find the whole set-up, you bricked up the compartment where you'd rigged the bomb."

"Ingenious," said Kent, "but out of my line. I'm neither a criminal nor a mechanic."

"Was Miss Fanny Shaftel ever in your employ?" demanded the D. A.

Kent nodded, still at ease. "Yes. She was our maid in Connecticut."

"Good. Then you'll be glad to hear what she has to say." The D. A. picked up a paper and began reading from it. "This is a sworn deposition. 'Miss Fanny Shaftel, et cetera, et cetera.' Oh, here it is.

"'Saturday morning at breakfast, some time in June and the first weekend that Miss Minx came as a visitor, I overheard her tell Mr. Kent and Mr. Jarvis about a story describing how to start a fire by attaching an incendiary bomb to the furnace flue by means of wax. After the fire, I remembered I had once seen a metal cylinder in the cellar, hidden by some firewood. I had noticed it because the kitten was playing there and got stuck behind one of the logs. I didn't know then what it was, but from a description given me by the police, I'm sure now that it was an incendiary bomb.'" The D. A. put down the sheet. "Well, what about it, Kent?"

"She's mistaken. I never had such a bomb and Miss Minx never made any such statement."

"Then how do you account for what Fanny Shaftel said? Think she made it up, out of her own limited imagination?"

"Possibly. Or possibly Miss Minx actually did explain such a device. If so, I was not present at the time."

"Your wife wanted money, didn't she?"

"Every wife does."

"A large sum. Larger than you had available."

Kent cocked his head thoughtfully. "No," he said.

"Your wife had the power to withdraw Jarvis's capital investment from your business, didn't she?"

"Yes. But she didn't use that power, didn't intend to or

threaten to or even think of it. And if you impute that she did, you're an irresponsible and slanderous liar."

"You tried to sell the house, didn't you?" asked the D. A. in honeyed tones.

"Yes."

"Why?"

"I had no use for it. It was too big for me and I didn't care to live there alone, after my wife and I had separated."

"The fact is," said the D. A., "that you tried to sell the house because you needed the money. The local real estate agent told you it was difficult to dispose of because it was so far from a railroad station, and also because the sawmill made such an infernal racket that nobody would want the house under any circumstances. So, despairing of a sale, you decided to burn down the building and collect the insurance money. Isn't that so?"

"No."

"And you continue to deny the truth of Fanny Shaftel's statement?"

"Yes."

"You think that both she and Miss Minx are liars?"

"I wouldn't care to call Miss Minx a liar, no. She may be confused. It's even barely possible that she is completely correct and I simply forgot the whole thing. I certainly put no such scheme into effect." He leaned back and frowned. "Most likely of all, however, you're making it all up."

The D. A. snapped angrily. "Just confine yourself to answering my questions. You tried to kill two people simply because they had that knowledge of the arson plan. You failed with Miss Minx and succeeded with Jarvis."

"Just confine yourself to asking me questions," drawled Kent. "Your surmises are insulting."

The D. A. stepped back in annoyance. He riffled through a few sheets of paper, rubbed up his mustache and then launched a new assault.

"Do you own a tan suit?"

"I have a light brown one. You might call it tan."

"Where is it?"

"At the cleaner's."

"What cleaner?"

"I don't remember the name. It's around the corner from my apartment."

"The Express?"

"Yes, that's the name."

"You left a suit there?"

"Certainly."

"They have no record of it."

Kent smiled. "I didn't give them my name, as I recall. I simply brought the suit in, and I probably have the receipt for it in my wallet. I usually carry those things around." He put his hand in his pocket and took out his wallet. He rummaged in it and then produced a slip.

"There it is. Express Cleaners."

"Let's have it."

Kent handed it to the D. A. who gave it to a cop with an order to go there and get the suit.

Kent put the wallet back in his pocket. "Would you mind telling me why you're so interested in that suit?"

"Sure. The man who killed Jarvis wore a tan suit. He spattered blood on it and tried to wipe it off with a towel. I want the suit."

"You can have mine, I spilt some wine on it and took it to the cleaner's. If you find any bloodstains, I suppose I'll have to admit I ought to be charged with murder. Bloodstains are, I believe, difficult if not impossible to eradicate without leaving any trace."

"All right," said the D. A. "Take him out." He seemed perfectly satisfied with the results of his questioning.

II

Emil Boganov strode sullenly into the room and sat down. He hadn't talked. Through all the preliminary questioning, he'd maintained a stubborn silence. Nobody had been able to break through the shell with which he surrounded himself.

Now he faced the group of detectives with blazing eyes and pale, tight lips. His voice came wearily, in dry, terse sentences. He gave his name and address and admitted he'd known Fern and had had an affair with her. He denied ever taking a quantity of dry ice from the plant where he worked and he challenged anyone to prove that he had.

The inspector went through the preliminaries and then got down to the real business.

"We know Fern was behind it," he said. "She wanted Andrea out of the way and she wanted her father dead."

"You're a stinking liar," said Boganov.

"You'd better give some explanations, or else confess," snapped the inspector.

"Why should I? You wouldn't believe them, anyhow."

The inspector smiled. He changed his approach suddenly and went soft.

"We're up against something tough," he said. "Maybe you can help us out."

"I can't help. I don't know anything."

"If you've got any kind of an alibi, why not give it?" cooed the inspector. "What can you lose?"

Boganov shrugged. "I have no alibi. When Fern was killed, I was home alone. That's no alibi. When Jarvis was killed, I was with Fern and now she's dead. That's no alibi, either."

"You were what?" demanded the inspector. "You were with Fern?"

"Forget it. I have nothing to say. I don't want to be bothered."

Mitch turned around and gave Jub a broad wink. Jub tightened his lips. He was getting worried.

The inspector stepped back and whispered to one of his staff. Then he cleared his throat and went ahead with his examination. "You claim you were in love with Fern," he said. "If you had even a shred of manhood, you'd want to protect her honor, wouldn't you?"

Boganov seemed to come alive for the first time. He blinked and his mouth relaxed. He took a deep breath, rose to his feet and looked around the room. And then, suddenly, his feelings flared out and he broke.

He flung himself across the table. The sharp crack of his fist sounded like a gunshot. The inspector went spinning backwards with Boganov on top of him. Instantly the room was in an uproar. A half dozen men threw themselves at Boganov. The pile seemed to whirl, lift up and then hit the floor with a crash.

One by one the detectives picked themselves up. Boganov stayed on the floor, face down. Blood from a small cut trickled from one eye. A couple of patrolmen lifted him up and carried him out.

The inspector leaned back in the chair and somebody brought him a glass of water. "The lousy son of a sea-cook," he said. "I'll get him for that! Who in hell does he think he is?" Then the inspector leaned back, closed his eyes and fainted.

Jub smiled to himself. He knew the power of the Boganov fist. He glanced at Mitch Taylor, and Mitch winked again.

A cop came in with a tan suit on his arm. "Here's Kent's suit," he said.

The inspector raised his head. "Suit?" he said. "You got it?"

The cop held up the pants and pointed to the stain just above the knee.

"Blood," he said. "Been cleaned, but the stain still shows."

The inspector took the pair of pants and caressed the stain. "Well, I'll be damned!" he said. Then he snorted. "How the hell do you know it's blood?"

The cop backed away. Mitch Taylor stepped forward.

"I got some new information, Inspector," he said. "Me and Freeman, from the lab, have been working on this all week. Before he checks up on them pants and finds out whether it's really blood, I better give you this information.

"It's like this, Inspector. The way we figure it, somebody wanted to kill Andrea, just like they killed Fern later on. Knock her out, put her in the bathtub and let the dry ice finish her. This killer, he goes up to the Minx's apartment with the dry ice, but she isn't there. The stuff is too heavy to lug up and down the stairs, so he hides the carton in the bathroom and closes the door. He doesn't notice that he's closed the cat in, but he has, and it scratches around and claws open the carton and lets the carbon dioxide come out, and that's the end of the cat.

"But the killer doesn't know that. He's outside or downstairs or around somewhere, waiting for the Minx to come home, like she always does. Only that night, she doesn't.

"Well, it's getting late and the killer's made up his mind to get Jarvis. He's keyed up to it and he can't wait. So he goes there, socks him with the wrench and leaves. He gets in his car and is on his way to have another try at the Minx. When he's looking for a place to park, what happens? He hears a scream.

He looks up and sees her at the window and he knows something has gone awful sour for him. He gets scared. He loses control of the car. Steps on the gas instead of the brake, or something like that, and hits Treeberg. After that, he's got to beat it.

"Now there's a lot of things to figure out. For instance, that cigar. I went back to the Quaker and spoke to the manager, and he smiled all over himself trying to show how obliging he was, and that's how I noticed the crooked front tooth. I told him he was in Jarvis's apartment the night of the murder and that we could prove it on account of the cigar. So he broke down and admitted it. Said he didn't mention it because he wanted to stay out of trouble, and that all he'd done was talk about a new lease."

"Huh?" said the inspector, frowning. But Mitch gave him no time to collect his thoughts.

"We got the fender of the car that hit Treeberg," he said. "It's downstairs now. We been calling garages all day, only this time we knew what section to look. What he did was to get it changed quick, and then go out and make himself a second accident, and get the second fender changed. When we checked back on the fender, what we found was the second one, and not the original one that had been in the Treeberg accident."

"Who?" said the inspector. "Who did all this?"

Mitch Taylor threw back his shoulders. In front of all these big shots, making a fool out of every one of them. He and Jub Freeman stealing the show.

"Kent," he said. "Lee Kent. The whole trouble was that when Freeman and I went down to Fern's place Monday night, she was with Boganov. She didn't know her old man was dead. All she knew was that the police were outside her door and she was going to get involved in something. So when we asked her who she was with, she gave us the one name that would make it all respectable. Lee Kent, her husband.

"After she found out what happened, she called him and told him what she'd done. She admitted that call. Kent said he'd stick by her. It was a break for him and it gave him the alibi he needed. Later on she guessed he'd done it, but she couldn't change her story any more. Not until Boganov, the guy she loved, was brought into it. That was when she was going to tell on Kent, and so he killed her. You see how it all fits, Inspector."

"Evidence?"

"The fender," said Jub. "The original fender that was in the Treeberg accident. It comes from Kent's car and was replaced in a Connecticut garage. And the special dry-ice container he'd had made, with good insulation. That's in the car, too. He bought the dry ice from a place in Yonkers.

"You brought out the motive yourself. He'd decided to burn down the house. Jarvis and Andrea knew his scheme for starting the fire, and so Kent decided to get them out of the way first. He thought he'd be safe because nobody could guess his motive unless they knew about his arson scheme. And he thought only Jarvis and Andrea knew it."

The inspector blinked. "In that case," he said, pointing to the pants, "it's got to be blood, huh?"

Jub nodded. "I'll take it over to the laboratory now. With the fender and the dry-ice container and the bloodstain on his suit, you'll have enough to charge him formally, won't you, Inspector?"

The inspector grinned. "Yeah," he said. "But I told you two hours ago that Kent had done it. Why in hell didn't you speak up then?"

Jub took the pants and went out. Mitch followed gleefully.

In the laboratory, Jub explained the process as he went along.

"This is the leuco-malachite test," he said. "It's what's called a reagent. In contact with even a trace of blood, it turns green in color and then bluish. The only trick is to keep everything clean and not have any foreign substances mixed in. Well, here goes."

With Mitch leaning over his shoulder, Jub prepared his material, scraped particles from the stained trousers and placed the minute bits on a piece of blotting paper. Then, with a glass rod, he placed a drop of the reagent on the paper and watched it soak in.

"Going to turn green first," he said. "And then, after a minute or so, kind of bluish." He stared fixedly.

"Huh?" said Mitch. "Green?"

Nothing had happened.

An hour or so later, after checking a half dozen samples and checking and rechecking the purity of his reagent, Jub shrugged his shoulders and stood up.

"No blood?" asked Mitch anxiously.

Jub shook his head. "No blood."

"You mean we're wrong?"

"Looks that way," said Jub. "The suit's been cleaned, but the blood ought to show up, regardless."

Mitch bit his lips. "And with all of them waiting for us across the street? Geez—I'll be a patrolman over in Staten Island if we don't think our way out of this one."

Jub leaned back. "Go ahead and think. I'm exhausted. Up

---

* The so-called leucomalachite green test has been in use since the early twentieth century. However, false positives are often produced by plant-based or chemical oxidants. Definitive tests for bloodstains have long been sought: As early as 1887, Sherlock Holmes, in *A Study in Scarlet* by Arthur Conan Doyle (first published in *Beeton's Christmas Annual* for 1887 and in book form by Ward, Lock & Co. in 1888), claimed to have invented an infallible test, though Sherlockian scholars have scoffed at his assertion. Today, phenolphthalein is another commonly used reagent to test for bloodstains. However, it too is merely regarded as "presumptive," and forensic science has yet to develop an infallible test that works under all circumstances.

most of the night and working all day. I haven't really slept since Thursday night."

"And by golly—you're not going to sleep again until—"

Mitch broke off suddenly. "Hey!" he said. "Look at this!" He held up the jacket of Kent's suit and pointed at the label.

Jub read it. "Adams Clothing," he said. "So what?"

"But—he doesn't buy his stuff there! He has it made to order and he told me so himself."

"Except this one."

Mitch laughed. "Don't you get it? I was up at his place and I looked in his clothes closet and there was no tan suit. Then I went to his tailor, because Amy thought I needed a new suit, and the tailor mentioned the tan suit he'd made for Kent and said what a good fit it was. And when Kent admits he has a tan suit at the cleaner's and when we get hold of it, what is it? It's this phony from a chain store!"

"You mean," said Jub, "that he destroyed his tan suit, bought this one, smeared it with wine or something and took it to the cleaner's so that he'd have a tan suit to show? Sure—he'd have to, because a lot of people would know he owned a tan suit. But if he just bought this one, Mitch, it won't fit! There hasn't been time for thorough alterations. Besides, we can show it's new and we can check the date on the bill of sale."

Mitch caressed the suit. "Looks new," he squeaked, in his high-pitched voice. "Come on—let's go."

It was hours later when Kent broke. He had no explanation of why the tan suit didn't fit him. He could not account for the disappearance of his own tan, made-to-order suit. He said it must be a mistake the cleaner had made.

As the evidence piled up, he stopped answering questions. He sat there with his head drooping and his eyes expressionless. And then, suddenly, he gave up.

"All right," he said. "I did it. Boganov was with Fern that night. I guess he can prove it, if you say so. I can't. But if Andrea hadn't happened to be out that night, you'd never have gotten me.

"I didn't want to kill anybody. I didn't want to commit arson or any other crime. Jarvis made me. He forced me into it. He wanted to break me and humiliate me and force me into bankruptcy, and I couldn't face it.

"He was working on Fern to get her consent to demanding his money back. She refused, but I didn't know how long she'd hold out. I tried to sell the house, and nobody would buy it because of that sawmill right near it. Then I thought of the arson scheme which Andrea had mentioned once. It sounded foolproof, and neither Andrea nor Jarvis would be likely to remember it. I rigged up the contraption and sealed off the section where I placed the bomb, so that nobody could possibly find it by accident.

"Then, one evening last week, I saw Jarvis. He told me he intended to get his money out of my business. He hinted that he and Andrea were going to get married and that Fern, who was fond of Andrea, would give him ten-thousand-dollars worth of consent as a wedding present. I laughed in his face. The house was due to burn down and I was counting on the insurance money.

"He read my thoughts, because I was planning what he would have done. He said I'd better not have a fire because he'd see to it that I'd never collect on my policy. He said he'd tell about the arson scheme, and he'd ordered Andrea to do the same.

"I know now that he'd told Andrea nothing of the kind, but I believed him. I was scared, and the next day I drove up to the country to dismantle the apparatus. But to my horror, I couldn't. Not without the chance of jarring that flue and knocking over the bomb. And that would have meant either burning myself alive or being arrested for arson. I was in a jam, standing there and wanting to break down a partition and not being able to. I was sick to my stomach and I thought I'd have a heart attack."

He buried his face in his hands and sobbed. After a while he looked up.

"I finally took some of my pictures," he said, "in case I had to explain that visit, and I drove home. I knew I'd have to kill both Jarvis and Andrea. There wasn't any way out. It was simply a question of how, and I forced myself to think it out.

"The fact that Boganov was in the ice cream business gave me my idea. Drug Andrea or knock her unconscious—I was prepared to do either—and then put her in the bathtub and let the carbon dioxide do the rest. That was my scheme. It wouldn't even be recognized as murder.

"Monday afternoon I bought the dry ice at a place in Yonkers, and in the evening I brought it up to Andrea's, left it outside the door and knocked. She wasn't home. I took the key from the broom closet and went in. I hid the carton in the bathroom, closed the door and went downstairs to wait.

"But I couldn't hang around and do nothing. The thought of the wax, slowly melting on a furnace flue, kept haunting me. If Andrea wasn't home, I'd kill Jarvis first and then come back and take care of her.

"I drove over to the Quaker. I had the wrench wrapped up in a paper bag. I was nervous and Jarvis noticed the fact. He kept asking what I was frightened of, and whether I had come to him for help in getting my wife back.

"I just shook my head. I couldn't speak. Jarvis said I looked queer. I laughed. I could manage just one word. 'Tired,' I said. Jarvis told me to put the package down. I did. On the table, behind him. Then I went in and washed my hands.

"I felt better when I came back. I said I'd come about

something important. I took a letter out of my pocket and put it on the table. I told him to read it carefully. He bent down to look at it, and I picked up the wrench and hit him over the head. He fell back in the chair and I hit him again. It was a pleasure.

"I took the letter and wiped my fingerprints from everything I'd touched. There was an insurance blank on the desk. I left it there. I had to wash the bloodstains from my trousers. I should have taken the towel, of course, but I didn't want to carry anything extra. I had the wrench with me, still in the paper bag. I walked down to the astrology lecture, slipped into a back row and left when the meeting broke up.

"I intended to try Andrea again. There could be no connection between the two murders. Jarvis and Andrea were the only people who knew about my arson scheme, and they'd both be dead.

"I was driving past Andrea's, slowly. I looked up. There was a light in her window and it was open. I could see her there. Then she screamed. It unnerved me, and I lost control of the car and hit somebody. Then I had to leave. I drove fast, up to Connecticut, and had my fender changed.

"When I got home, Fern called me and told me Jarvis was dead and to say I'd been with her. She explained everything over the phone. It was a lucky break and I said I'd oblige her.

"The next day I bought a tan suit, smeared some wine on it and took it to the cleaner's. And in the evening I bumped into a lamp post, on purpose, so that I could have my fender changed. I was ready.

"After Andrea's arrest and her failure to implicate me, I decided Jarvis had lied about her, that she had no recollection of her arson idea and was no danger to me in any way. The next day I went there and hid the wrench in her drawer. Since she was suspected, I felt I might as well help the case along. I still don't know how you traced the wrench to my car. Will someone tell me?"

On Monday morning Jub reported for work at the laboratory. His name had not been in the papers. The accounts had praised the police department and, in particular, a detective named Mitchell Taylor. But the real hero of the case, which was the spectroscope, received no publicity.

Jub didn't mind, for he'd met Andrea. He kept thinking of her as he put on his laboratory gown and walked over to his bench.

Callender looked up. "Morning, Jub."

"Morning, Cal. What's on for today?"

Callender indicated a sheet of paper. "A hit-and-run case out in Queens," he grumbled. "We're supposed to tell 'em what kind of a car did it and who drove the thing. What the hell do they expect, anyhow? Miracles?"

Detective Freeman answered lazily. "Sure," he said. "Miracles. Why not?"

READING GROUP GUIDE

1. Does this book feel like a classic mystery story to you? How is it different, in your mind, from, for example, a Sherlock Holmes story, a Dashiell Hammett novel like *The Maltese Falcon*, or *Murder on the Orient Express* by Agatha Christie?

2. Do the suspects seem to be drawn from life? What about the police officers/investigators? Do they seem realistic?

3. What do you think the author was aiming to achieve here that hadn't been done before?

4. How does this book compare to contemporary police procedurals you may have read by writers like Michael Connelly, Ed McBain, or Joseph Wambaugh?

5. How does this book compare to current television or film portrayals of police officers?

6. Unlike modern police procedurals, this book doesn't really

show any of the kind of crime, violence, racial unrest, etc., so often depicted today. What do you think is lost or gained by this approach?

FURTHER READING

POLICE PROCEDURALS BY LAWRENCE TREAT

H as in Hunted. New York: Duell, 1946.
Q as in Quicksand. New York: Duell, 1947.
T as in Trapped. New York: Morrow, 1947.
F as in Flight. New York: Morrow, 1948.
Big Shot. New York: Harper, 1951.
Weep for a Wanton. New York: Ace, 1956.
Lady, Drop Dead. New York and London: Abelard, 1960.

OTHER EARLY POLICE PROCEDURALS

McBain, Ed. *Cop Hater*. New York: Permabooks, 1956.
Shannon, Dell. *Case Pending*. New York: Morrow, 1960. Republished by Sourcebooks in association with the Library of Congress, 2020.
Wambaugh, Joseph. *The New Centurions*. Boston: Little, Brown, 1970.
Waugh, Hillary. *Last Seen Wearing*. New York: Doubleday, 1952.

Republished by Sourcebooks in association with the Library
of Congress, 2021.

CRITICAL STUDIES

Apostolou, John. "T as in Treat: A Short Guide to the Mystery
Fiction of Lawrence Treat." *The Armchair Detective* 27, no. 1
(Winter 1994): 74–76.

Dove, George N. *The Police Procedural.* Bowling Green, OH:
Bowling Green University Popular Press, 1982.

Panek, Leroy Lad. *The American Police Novel: A History.*
Jefferson, NC and London: McFarland, 2003.

Vicarel, Jo Ann. *A Reader's Guide to the Police Procedural.* New
York: G. K. Hall, 1995.

Waugh, Hillary. "The Police Procedural." In *The Mystery
Story,* edited by John Ball, 163–87. San Diego: University
Extension, University of California, San Diego, 1976.

ABOUT THE AUTHOR

Lawrence Treat was born Lawrence Arthur Goldstone in New York City on December 21, 1903, the son of Henry and Daisy (Stein) Goldstone.* He attended Dartmouth College, graduating with a Bachelor of Arts degree in 1924, and obtained a law degree from Columbia University in 1927. Upon graduation, Treat joined a law firm only to learn on his first day that the office was disbanding. The firm offered Treat a year's salary of severance pay, and rather than seek a new law job, he relocated to Paris to pursue his dream of becoming a writer. Like many young writers in Paris, he produced poetry but soon concluded that this would not support him. A mystery magazine found in a Paris bookstore offered him a new pathway. Deciding to utilize his legal background, Treat turned his hand to writing for the mystery market. He turned his attention to what he called "crime mystery picture puzzle books," commonplace today on supermarket shelves but then a novelty. In 1930 he experienced

---

* He legally changed his name in 1940. "Lawrence Treat," in *Gale Literature: Contemporary Authors* (Farmington Hills, MI: Gale, 2003). Gale Literature Resource Center, https://link.gale.com/apps/doc/H1000099701 /GLS?u=loc_main&sid=bookmark-GLS&xid=c0588d87.

success in one of his first forays into this genre, writing short mysteries to comprise a board game, titled *Bringing Sherlock Home*. Treat revisited these short mystery puzzles decades later with the internationally acclaimed four-part series *Crime and Puzzlement* and *You're the Detective*.

Returning to the United States, he married Margery Dallet in 1930. Treat began writing for the popular "pulp" mystery magazines and sold dozens of short stories (he would eventually pen about three hundred). His first crime novel, published in 1937 under the name Lawrence A. Goldstone, was *Run Far, Run Fast** and there is little memorable about it. In 1939, he and Margery divorced, and in 1940, he produced the first of a series of four novels about a highly intellectual academic criminologist named Carl Wayward.[†] While well received, they were, according to author Bill Delaney, "stuck in the conventional mold of the British or classic mystery and did not represent a significant contribution to the genre."[‡]

In the latter years of World War II, Treat was introduced to the realities of policing, making acquaintance with many working police officers and accompanying them on patrols. The result was a major shift in his literary output, described by Delaney as "a quantum leap forward to his writing career."[§] Treat never discussed what led to this huge change, but certainly it was a combination of factors, including his divorce from his first wife, the war, the reports of the atrocities committed during the war (mentioned by Treat in various writings), and the success

---

* Published in New York by Greystone Press.

† *B as in Banshee* (1940); the others were *D as in Dead* (1941), *H as in Hangman* (1942), and *O as in Omen* (1943), all published by Duell, Sloan & Pearce in New York.

‡ Bill Delaney (updated by Fiona Kelleghan), "Lawrence Treat," in *Critical Survey of Mystery and Detective Fiction*, ed. Carl Rollyson (Pasadena, CA and Hackensack, NJ: Salem Press, 2008 rev. ed.), 4:1736.

§ Delaney, "Lawrence Treat," 1737.

of the hard-boiled writers such as Dashiell Hammett. His legal education and participation in educational programs aimed at law enforcement professionals also led him to write more realistically than many earlier mystery writers, who often ignored the actual methods of police investigations.*

Treat struggled with an inherent problem of the new subgenre he had created. While he wanted to create realistic depictions of police work, he also wanted to retain the structure of the classic mystery: the crime, the investigation, the solution. In reality, officers work on multiple cases at once, with a virtually limitless number of suspects or "persons of interest." Criminal investigators rely heavily on informants as well as coincidence. Today, though DNA testing and other forensic science may produce seemingly magical identifications, police laboratories are underfunded and overworked, and officers may wait weeks or months for lab reports. He experimented with changing the focus of one of his procedurals to the victim†; and he tried moving his characters to a small town to limit the cast of characters.‡ Neither approach was particularly rewarding.

Treat's procedurals were far from his only output. By the end of his more than seventy-year career, he had written seventeen novels and had edited several anthologies. He taught mystery

---

* See Introduction (xi) for Treat's admonitions about the nature of the literature that a mystery writer needed to have at hand. Of course, Treat was not the first to disdain fanciful stories about detectives and police work. Dashiell Hammett complained, in a review of S. S. Van Dine's first Philo Vance novel, *The Benson Murder Case*, that "the authorities, no matter how stupid the author chose to make them, would have cleared up the mystery promptly if they had been allowed to follow the most rudimentary police routine" ("Poor Scotland Yard!" *Saturday Review of Literature* 111, no. 25 [January 15, 1927]: 510). Hammett himself, it should be noted, had worked as a private investigator.

† *H as in Hunted* (1946), for example, is ultimately "solved" by the laboratory technician Jub Freeman but the focal character is a vengeful Nazi prisoner.

‡ *Lady, Drop Dead* (1960) moved his characters Mitch Taylor and Jub Freeman out of New York; the protagonist, however, is a private detective.

writing at Columbia University, NYU, Adelphi College, Ditmas High School in Brooklyn, and public schools in Westchester County, New York, and on Martha's Vineyard. He cofounded the Mystery Writers of America, the preeminent crime writers organization, in 1945 and served variously as its president, executive vice-president, treasurer, and board member. He received two Edgar Awards, the Oscars of the mystery world, for his writing as well as a special Edgar for a television episode. Treat died on January 7, 1998.[*] He was survived by his second wife Rose Ehrenfreund Treat, whom he married in 1943.[†]

In the judgment of one scholar, while "His police procedurals…seem to belong to an older, safer, much slower-moving world," Treat "deserves great credit for having originated this fascinating form of mystery fiction."[‡]

---

[*] "Lawrence Treat, 94, Prolific Mystery Writer," *New York Times*, January 16, 1998, section B, 11.

[†] "Lawrence Treat," *Gale Literature*, 2003.

[‡] Delaney, "Lawrence Treat," 1737.